D1274080

Deadly Phine

By Darrell King   www.darrellkingproductions.com

Darrell King Productions

Library of Congress Cataloging-in-Publication data
Available upon request

Deadly Phine. Copyright © 2010 by Darrell King
Darrell King Productions
www.darrellkingproductions.com

Deadly Phine Cover Design: KanDel Media

Deadly Phine. Copyright © 2010 by Darrell King. All rights reserved. No part of this e-book may be reproduced or transmitted in any form or by any means, electronic or mechanical, including photocopy, recording, or any information storage and retrieval system, without permission in writing from the copyright owner except by a reviewer who may quote brief passages to be included in a review.

All characters, names, descriptions and traits are products of the author's imagination. Similarities to actual people – living or dead – are purely coincidental.

ISBN 13: 978-1-4660-6272-6

Deadly Phine

Darrell King   www.darrellkingproductions.com

Also Available
by Darrell King

Mack Daddy,
Legacy of a Gangsta (eBook)

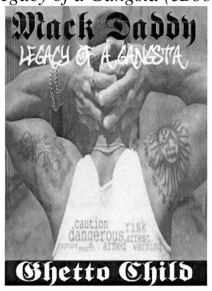

www.darrellkingproductions.com

Introduction

The worldwide fear and apprehension of AIDS with the rare but shocking cases of those infected individuals who've purposely transmitted this fearsome disease to others out of revenge or indifference have worked its way into the darkest reaches of our society's subconscious angst, influencing everything from urban legends to popular culture. A German film entitled "Via Appaia" portrayed an airline steward who has a one-night stand. The very next morning he awakens to find his lover gone and a disturbing message welcoming him to the "world of AIDS' on his mirror. Television's Law & Order *ran an episode called "Carrier" in 1998, in which a man with HIV attempted to infect scores of women.*

Chapter 1

*Every 15 seconds, someone—somewhere—dies
from complications related to AIDS.*

He had committed the ultimate act; there was no turning back now. The one and only person in the world who loved him and whom he loved was now dead ... thanks to him. It took only two minutes to smother her with the white foam-filled pillow. He was the sole witness to the jerking of the small, brittle-boned woman who was once vibrant and full of life. He heard the last breath escape her dry lips just before she gasped for air. Her eyes, although saddened with pain, had signaled that it was time for him to do what has been asked of him. And now she was finally at peace.

He had been called Ant Man by his sister, derived from his childhood love of bugs in general and his large collection of ant farms in particular. She used this moniker in reference to her younger brother so often that he eventually only responded to it, although he had been born to the name of Brian Atwood. He had known this day would come, he just hadn't known it would be like this—or this soon. With a heavy heart, he had to bear witness each and every grueling day for the last six months as he watched his only sibling waste away. Her big, beautiful, teasing cat eyes had dwindled down to look like broken-in-half green marbles in her deeply sunken eye sockets. They told the unspeakable story and relayed the suffering she was enduring. Her once-pretty olive-complexion was now dark and ashy, despite the many lotion-moisturizing sessions that he gave her two to three times each day. Her once brickhouse figure with big, thick hips and a bubble ass now gave off the appearance of a woman from a third-world country; a starving, worn down, desolate female. She had deteriorated right before his eyes and it had been painful.

Belinda was only five years older than Ant Man, but she had always appeared more so, not due to her looks, but her actions. She had inherited the role of both father and mother when their parents were suddenly killed on New Year's day ten years before in a car accident caused by a drunk driver who ran a red light. They were returning home from the twilight service held at their church.

Belinda had just turned eighteen and her brother was thirteen. She put her dream of going away to college on hold and enrolled in a local university. It was there that she met her first and only lover, Pedro Octavius Valentino. By all accounts, Pedro was gorgeous! Although three years her senior, this did not stop Belinda from falling head-over-heels in love with him. In fact, dating a junior when she herself was a freshman added even more excitement in Belinda's eyes. It wasn't until later that she would find out that everything that glitters isn't gold. But little did she know, until it was too late, that she too would fall victim to Pedro's long history of "love 'em and leave 'em" attitude. It was only after her grades had fallen, she was threatened with losing her scholarship, and had found out that she was pregnant with Pedro's baby did Belinda realize the true effect that his love had on her.

Many nights Belinda had cried to her best friend, Rita Ann Ricks, about her. The two had a special relationship dating back to elementary school. The two were so close that Belinda had even been blamed for the break up of Rita Ann and her thug lover, Maurice "Lil' Mo" Gentry. According to Lil' Mo, he got tired of the countless times that Rita Ann would run to be by Belinda's side. He even went as far as accusing them of being lovers. But it wasn't until Belinda found out that she tested HIV-positive that the two women would make life-altering changes.

"Promise me that you will look out for my little brother and continue being the big sister to him that you already are," Belinda pleaded to Rita Ann with tears in her eyes. "And promise me that you will finish school and become the lawyer that you always dreamed of becoming."

"Girl! Damn! You talking like you are already dead or close to it!" Rita Ann snarled as she fought back her own tears.

"I'm just a realist and I have to deal with reality. Although my spirit can be ever enduring, I don't know how long my body can withstand the torture. Rita, I am really worried about my baby and my brother. Before I had my baby, I thought long and hard about my death 'cause I know that I'm fadin' fast... my lil' boy Larry is only eight months old, but you know with me bein' sick with the virus an' all my son may not get to know his mother, so it will be important to me that you and Ant Man let him know how much I loved him and what a good-hearted person I was. Make sure—"

"Hold the fuck up! They did not tell you that you were dying! People live for years with HIV. There are new antidotes and procedures coming out every day. The FDA probably will have a new breakthrough drug come out tomorrow. So please, stop talking like you have one foot in the grave and the other one on a banana peel!"

"I just want to make sure that I have everything covered when my time does come," Belinda said.

Belinda's preparation took less than a month. She gave guardianship of her infant child to Pedro's parents with the stipulation that visitation would be given to both Rita Ann and to her brother, Ant Man. Belinda had been a little concerned with Mrs. Valentino one day returning to her native home of San Juan, Puerto Rico and taking her grandson with her. Belinda did not want her brother and son to be strangers to one another. Besides Mrs. Valentino and her husband Ricardo were quite the well-heeled couple and would no doubt offer little Larry a most comfortable childhood.

Rita Ann had visited Belinda every day that she could. As Belinda's illness progressed, she chose a modest hospice program over that of a sterile, impersonal medical room in which to live out her final days. Her own home would provide the necessary comforts for her until the inevitable end. Rita's work schedule was tight, but she made time to spend with her friend at the hospice care center which had been set up in the master bedroom of her southeast Washington, DC row house by caring friends and teachers, who honored her wish to die at home, rather than in an impersonal and communal hospital room. They had been best friends since elementary school, and through the years, their friendship had elevated to more of a sisterhood. They were much closer than Rita Ann and her biological sister, Trina. There were secrets between the two of them they would take to the grave. And that's what happened on December 4: Belinda Atwood took their secrets to her grave.

After Belinda's passing, Rita Ann took in 17-year old Ant Man. Although he felt as if he was left in the world alone to fend for himself, Rita Ann reminded him on a daily basis that he could be anything that he wanted to be. However, Ant Man was consumed with seeking revenge because he knew the man responsible for his sister's disease had caused her untimely death. He vowed that he would make Pedro pay for the loss of his sister.

Predictably, late on the night of December 11, the 17-year old confronted his late sister's lover on the front porch of his Manassas, Virginia home, arguing with heated intensity before their bickering gave way to a violent fist fight, which raged along the entirety of the mid-sized porch before gunshots rang out, felling Pedro Valentino to the wooden floor below, where he died shortly thereafter. The enraged gunman didn't stop there, but instead charged into the house, murdering Valentino's wife and two daughters before finally shooting the family's pet German Sheppard, who'd barked nonstop from the back yard. He then threw out his blood-spattered clothes, as well as the murder weapon, and quickly drove back across the state line into the District of Columbia, where he remained silent for at least a week before disclosing his dark secret to Rita Ann Ricks.

Rita Ann urged Ant Man to enlist in the military so that he could get away; perhaps start a new and more meaningful life. Taking her advice, he enlisted in the United States Army shortly thereafter. Ant Man knew very well that he was running away from everything, including his nephew. But there was always this voice in the back of his head telling him that he could run, but that he couldn't hide, and that eventually he'd have to return someday for his nephew.

After the horrific mass murder of their son and his family, the elder Valentinos wanted to part of the so-called "bastard child" of their late son, and promptly left for their native Puerto Rico. They were never seen nor heard from again. Rita Ann raised the curly-haired child for five years before Belinda's grandparents took custody of the cheerful, bright-eyed toddler, relocating him to Virginia's Tidewater area—specifically Hampton Roads. The young man grew up to be a fine athlete, excelling at sports such as football, basketball, and baseball. He joined the jock lore ranks of such local Tidewater sports stars as Allen Iverson and Michael Vick.

By the time he's turned thirteen, the boy was committing petty crimes throughout the neighborhood and selling drugs to boot. It was around this time that his ne'er do-well maternal uncle, Brian "Ant Man" Atwood, would explain to him the origin of his parental heritage. Though taken aback by the unpleasant reality of his parents' relationship, young Larry began using "Valentino," his late father's surname. First he used it as a nickname, but it stuck and he later legally changed his name to Lucien Octavius Valentino, a moniker that would later be spoken with hatred and dread by many.

Chapter 2

"The United States government did something that was wrong. It was an outrage to our commitment to integrity and equality for all our citizens...clearly racist." ~ President Bill Clinton's apology for the Tuskegee Syphilis Experiment to the eight remaining survivors, May16, 1997

Dusk fell on the trash littered streets of Old San Juan's most notoriously violent barrio, known as "LaPerla" or "the Pearl." It is the 16th of May, 1997, and on this day many miles across the Atlantic Ocean, far away from Puerto Rico's capital, the president of the United States had publicly apologized to eight weary-looking old men for the U.S. Government's top secret syphilis experiment. The Tuskegee Experiment, as it was known, took place from 1932 to 1972, and consisted of purposely infecting 399 rural black men with the most virulent form of syphilis, which at the time ranked as the world's most deadly sexually transmitted disease.

Seven years after the experiment ended, in October 1979, a certain Dr. Szmuness, a Polish Jew working in a secret U.S. laboratory, successfully fused together a cattle virus known scientifically as bovine leukemia and sheep visna cell cultures (HELA), and gave birth to the single most lethal STD mankind has ever known—AIDS .

An outdated rust bucket of a taxicab chug-a-lugged downhill. Dirty-looking children with snotty noses ran, barefoot, along the muddied road, throwing pebbles at the yellow checkered hooptie. The driver defiantly raised his left fist and angrily shook it, hurling insults at his juvenile tormentors as they ran, along with a dog and the occasional chicken or goat, back and forth across the road before the oncoming vehicle's approach. Finally past them, the taxi cab driver settled himself and casually lit a cigar, enjoying the Latin jazz flowing from the radio speakers.

The island's tropical beauty cannot mask the stark scenes of poverty and filth that looms large all around them as they drew toward LaPerla. As the tanned, bearded driver observed the well-dressed government official casually reading an issue of *Jet* in the backseat, he couldn't help but feel fear for the Americano's safety. Surely the young man from the Washington, DC suburbs could not know about the crime-infested underworld of LaPerla. And though his English was not strong, the driver would try his best to talk the young doctor out of vacationing in the barrio. He hoped that his stern warning would be enough to protect the bold but weary mainland traveler from bodily harm or worse. Looking up into the rearview mirror, the cabdriver smiled at this passenger as he turned the volume down on the radio slightly.

"Señor, we are getting close to the entrance of LaPerla. There are many bad men who live here in this barrio, on the streets, and along the alleys of guapo; namely the puntos, who sell the yayo and heroin. They are very mean and evil hombres who will not hesitate to kill you if you get in their way. The many tecatos who buy their drugs can also be dangerous, so they too are best to be left alone."

The thirty-one-year old Army doctor from Fort Detrick had been persuaded not to venture into the notoriously bloody neighborhood of LaPerla ever since he arrived on Puerto Rican soil. The staff at the luxurious Condado Hotel & Casino Resort specifically pointed out within the pages of their travel brochures that LaPerla was a Code Red area of old San Juan, and was to be avoided at all costs. Being a military man who had been born and raised in the rough and tumble Kentland Village community in Landover, Maryland, he had, at first, shrugged off the warnings of the locals concerning LaPerla's alleged go-hard nature. But as the rickety old car rolled down the dirt road closer toward the infamous gated barrio, he slowly began to feel a sense of uneasiness.

"Well, we have now approached the gates of LaPerla, Señor. Your fare will be $10.50, please." He got no reply from his passenger who was looking out of the taxi cab window, observing his surroundings. "Señor, rapido! Rapido! I must go now! I have other fares to pick up!" the cabdriver barked out nervously, looking around the impoverished projects as night fall descended around them.

"Slow your fuckin' roll, old man! Tonight mi amigo's cab was for free. You feelin' me?" a deep-throated menacing voice boomed outside the window from a young thug dressed in baggy jean shorts, a red baseball cap turned sideways and an oversized tee-shirt with an airbrushed picture of the Puerto Rican national flag emblazoned on the front.

The youngster's thick gold chain swung back and forth from his neck, causing the diamond-encrusted praying hands pendant to shimmer under the flickering streetlights. He stepped out of a candy apple red painted Mercedes SL 500 that thumped the reggaeton lyrics of Daddy Yankee and Hector Bambino. An alluring Puerto Rican beauty sat crossed legged in the passenger seat. The visibly shaken cabdriver fell silent as the gangsta approached his window.

"You gonna be leavin' outta here and don't lemme see you back here no more, you understand?" the young thug said gruffly in Spanish.

"Si! Si! Mi Amigo! I will leave as soon as the Americano gets out of my cab. I told him that I wanted no trouble and that I needed to get back to downtown San Juan," the driver explained, trembling as he glanced up at the tough kid, then back at the passenger sitting silently in the backseat.

"Buenos, now turn this piece of shit you call a taxi around and get the fuck up the road!"

The very presence of the twenty-something hoodlum sent the old cabdriver speeding up then winding, muddied road away from the entrance of LaPerla's gates.

Once the Army doctor had exited the taxicab, the Puerto Rican thug assisted him with his luggage, engaging in lively but brief small talk with his American peer, as they loaded the suitcases into the trunk of the Benz. Though he was treated rather well by the man, he felt uneasy still.

"Mi Amigo, hop in the whip. I won't bite you, and neither will my girl, Rosario!" the driver said jokingly as his sexy girlfriend smiled brightly at the American doctor entering the plush backseat of the car.

As the sleek red Mercedes Benz rolled through the rusted gates surrounding LaPerla, Doctor Edward Goddard looked around at the old, shoddy looking apartments stacked on top of one another among the palm trees and the multitudes of bronze-skinned residents peering at the fancy vehicle that stood out like a sore thumb against the filth and destitution of the neighborhood. The car cruised slowly along the cracked barrio streets, and the doctor, for the first time since he had flown in from the mainland U.S., realized that he was indeed more than just a little bit frightened.

As they rode along, the constant pumping reggaeton music pulsated from the speakers. The deeper they drove into LaPerla's midst, the more unpleasant the sights seemed to become. Drug dealers sold to their numerous customers along the side streets boldly in plain view beneath the bright white streetlights as though the local authorities did not even exist. Audible gunshots occasionally rang out both in the far distance and, at times, dangerously close to where they were driving down the street. And from the sounds of the shots, these were not simple peashooters, but powerful rapid fire military-issued assault weapons that were popping off. Now Dr. Goddard was as terrified as the old cabdriver had been. Slowly the tricked out Mercedes continued its trek through the mean streets of LaPerla's barrio.

As they drove deeper and deeper into the hood, the drug dealing became more evident and the number of fiends more numerous. The menacing looks of the Latin Kings street gang followed the Benz as it wound its way down the narrow cracked streets of "The Pearl."

Dr. Edward Goddard began to think back about the decision of the U.S. Government to send him to Puerto Rico as he sat in the dark backseat of the Mercedes. His little sister, TaKeisha Smith, had asked that he not make the flight to Puerto Rico because she did not want him to miss her graduation from Bladensburg High School. But the medical and military officials at the World Health Organization and

Fort Detrick insisted that he carry out the top-secret mission with which he'd been entrusted.

The young doctor was promised $100,000,000, his very own laboratory, recognition as a Professor of Epidemiology at Walter Reed Army Medical Hospital, as well as the financial support of the Center of Disease in Atlanta, GA and the National Institute of Health in Bethesda, Maryland for his efforts in the so-called "Inner City Experiment." The offer given to him by Uncle Sam was too much for him to pass up … even if it meant using his own people as guinea pigs to close the deal.

As Dr. Goddard mulled over his future career and the fortunes that were sure to come his way after his mission was completed in Puerto Rico, he realized that they had not yet reached the spot. *Where in the hell does this cat live? It seems as though we've been driving for hours through these projects,* he thought from the backseat, while upfront the driver and his lovely lady friend bobbed their heads and shook their shoulders rhythmically to the reggaeton beats filling the car's interior with a lively melody.

Minutes later as they pulled up to a part of the long narrow street that had been marked by a broad bright yellow line. The vehicle slowed to an even slower crawl before finally coming to a complete stop in the middle of the street. Soon a pair of headlights drew closer to them, accompanied by the thumping hip-hop lyrics of Big Pun and Fat Joe as the car came up the opposite side of LaPerla's two-sided street.

"What going on? Why are we stopping and who's in that truck?" demanded Dr. Goddard irritably.

Without answering the doctor at all, the driver put the Benz in park and exited from the driver's side. Without hesitation, he spoke in broken Spanish to the occupants of the Land Rover and made a quick exchange of heroin for a handful of cash from the driver that brought a sigh of irritation and disgust from his American passenger.

The young drug dealer immediately returned to the vehicle and continued to drive along the street, but made several stops along the way in which to sell his illegal substances to customers who were more than willing to buy from him. At one point, while they rode down the seemingly unending streets, the driver stopped in a particularly dark, foreboding part of the barrio where resident youths played dice in the alley and on apartment stoops. Drunks and addicts wandered about aimlessly through the side streets and past corners, while Spanish chatter could be heard coming from the surrounding buildings and the residents within. The drug dealer and his girlfriend got out of the car without disclosing to Dr. Goddard the nature of their departure, nor when they would return. The two of them simply vanished into the shadowy darkness of the crime-infested barrio.

Ain't this a bitch! I don't believe this muthafucka just did this shit to me. First he's stopping in the streets to make drug sales, and now he's gonna just up and leave me by myself in this ghetto-ass neighborhood. This can't be happening. The doctor was appalled.

No sooner had those thoughts of concern left Dr. Goddard did his worse fears began to materialize. Dozens of tough looking Puerto Rican youths arose from the stoops and alleys of the barrio and made their way toward the shiny red Benz parked along the lonely dark street. As they approached, several of the lead hoods cracked their knuckles while others could be seen brandishing switchblade knives or metal pipes. They threatened the doctor in broken Spanish, daring him to make a run for his life as the multitude marched onward like some thugged out platoon.

"Help! Somebody! Please! I'm about to be robbed. Help me! Please, somebody! Please somebody, anybody!" The doctor cried out as the hooligans neared the parked car, continually hurling threats and insults toward him as they pressed on.

Suddenly three thunderous gunshots rang out in close proximity. Three of the bandanna-wearing boys dropped to the ground, writhing horribly in agony as their blood spattered the dirty pavement below. Their friends stood frozen in fear as they looked down the still smoking barrel of the drug dealer's nine millimeter as their three partners-in-crime slowly died on the cold street in front of them.

"You lil' Chamaquitos are so stupid! You know the rule!" yelled the gun-wielding Vato. "You need to respect the fuckin' line or else you'll get your dumb ass killed. Si? This Americano here is mi amigo, you hear? And nobody but nobody is gonna do nothin' to him. Now take your dead homies and get the fuck back across the line over to your side of the barrio. Rapido! Rapido!"

Dr. Goddard was both shocked and relieved by the sudden return of the driver and his girlfriend. And though the retribution visited on the marauding youths was swift and incredibly brutal, the doctor could not have been more indebted to the drug dealer for showing up when he did. The American visitor was too overwhelmed with disbelief to thank his driver, but he didn't have to. The drug dealer knew he'd be forever grateful for having had his life spared from the street gang.

Once again, they were on the move. The slums of LaPerla eventually gave way to a radiant and lush valley in which a flowing waterfall splashed into a sparkling turquoise blue forest lagoon. Beyond that, a large eggshell-white doublewide mobile home stood defiantly among the palm groves and jungle orchids rising amidst the tangled mangrove vines of San Juan's rainforest. Dr. Goddard knew that at last they had reached their long awaited destination–the home of Lucien "Baby Don" Valentino.

Chapter 3

Nationwide, heterosexual black women are contracting HIV, the virus that causes AIDS, at a significantly higher rate than any other demographic group in the United States. Most of the HIV/AIDS cases involving African American women have come almost exclusively through heterosexual intimacy.

As the Mercedes Benz pulled into the cobblestone driveway of the enormous trailer, the doctor could hardly believe his eyes at the beauty of the surrounding property. A neatly manicured English-garden graced the four acres of fenced in land encircling the mobile home. Dr. Goddard assisted the drug dealer in removing his luggage from the trunk, all the while gazing at the huge area. He took in the lotus blossom-covered fish pools filled with Japanese Koi swimming about in lazy circles beneath the dark waters of the man-made ponds, then he noticed the banana-laden palms lining the walkway leading to the steps of Valentino's home. After five minutes, the young Puerto Rican Vato and his shapely Amiga wished the good doctor well and bid him farewell as they drove through the open gates and back up the dark jungle path toward the crowded slums of LaPerla.

Two young kids, no older than eleven or twelve, raced down the brightly lit walkway and quickly picked up Dr. Goddard's baggage and walked with them back up the long cobblestone-covered walkway. Dr. Goddard lifted the last two suitcases and carried them slowly toward the distant doorway at the end of the path. Once he'd reached the doorway, a tall, handsome, well-groomed young man in his late twenties approached him.

"C'mon in, playa. I been up for hours waitin' around here for you to arrive." The host answered graciously, extending his hand to greet the doctor.

"Don Valentino, we've met at last. I must say that it is indeed a pleasure," Dr. Goddard exclaimed to the ex-U.S. soldier as he clasped the hand of his host in a firm shake.

"Don't even mention it, dawg. Come on in and make yourself at home. I know you been driving damn near all day just to get here, so I had my peeps hook something up for you to snack on. After that you can crash out back, up in the guest room, if you want. The bed's already made and waitin' for you, cause I know you gotta be tired as hell right about now."

"Thank you very much. You must've read my mind, Don Valentino," the doctor replied as he entered into the semi-darkened living room of the trailer.

"C'mon with all o' that Don Valentino bullshit, doc. Just call me Valentino or "Loverboy," whichever one you feel most comfortable with, awiight? I'll help you take your bags to the guestroom so you can unpack, wash up and what not. I'll see you back in the dining room when you get finished."

"I appreciate your hospitality, Don … I mean Valentino," the doctor stated, while following the young man down the long hallway and into the bedroom located at the end.

Once he'd settled into the spacious well-furnished bedroom, the doctor unpacked his belongings, organized himself, took a refreshingly hot shower, dressed for bed and proceeded from the guestroom toward the dining area where a hearty seafood dinner of blackened sea bass, scallops, yellow rice and freshly tossed salad awaited him. A vintage bottle of 1922 Chablis white wine sat in between the silver trays of delicious smelling food. A mouth-watering aroma filled the entire room in which the two men sat.

"Tomorrow I will go over with you in full detail the particulars of the study along with the government approved benefits package you'll be receiving for participating in the program itself," said Doctor Goddard as he began to enjoy the succulent meal placed before him.

"Before you even flew in from the Mainland, I'd already received both an email and an official letter from Fort Detrick concerning the medical study. So don't worry about goin' over nothin'. I just wanna get started with the shots, cause the sooner I get cleared of the virus, the better I'll feel," the ex-U.S. soldier said as he poured himself and Doctor Goddard a glass of sparkling Chablis.

Suddenly, the unmistakable clatter of submachine gunfire rat-a-tat-ed just beyond the gates, broke the silence of the still night.

"Don't be alarmed, Doc. That's just my lil' ole chamaquitos out there, that's all. Ya see, Doc, I got a couple acres of reefer and a couple acres of poppy plants growing on the outskirts of the jungle, right? So every now and then some dumb ass will come sneakin' around tryin' to cuff some o' my shit. I can't have muthafuckas stealin' my shit. Know what I mean? I work too hard to keep my reefer and poppy fields growin' well and producing quality dope." Valentino spoke with pride. "Ya see, I couldn't live like this on my lil' weak-ass veteran's pension I get each month from Uncle Sam, not even down here in Puerto Rico where damn near everybody 'cept the dope pushers is broke as fuck. I sell "Boy" and weed, and plenty of it, cause I enjoy luxury and fly bitches way too much to ever walk around with short money. Besides, when you got that "monster" like I do, all that HIV medication, like AZT and shit, get damn expensive, ya know? No wonder half o' Africa is dead or dyin' o' this shit, cause most o' them is poor black folks, that's why. Well, it ain't happenin' to the "Loverboy." That's why I stay on my grind, feel me?" the debonair drug dealer concluded.

Doctor Goddard nodded in agreement. "I definitely understand."

Valentino lit a Cuban cigar and took a puff after biting off a plug from the rear of the aromatic, sun-cured stogy. He exhaled a thick white smoke ring that disappeared beneath the whirling blades of the overhead ceiling fan. He then rose up from the dinner table to pace the dining room floor.

"Ya see, Doc, I was born and raised down in Hampton Roads, Virginia. I'm no stranger to the hood. Know what I mean? So I enlisted in the Navy right after I graduated from high school in '86 to earn a career, not knowin' that I'd be overseas fightin' Iraqis during the Gulf War in the early nineties. So my early days growin' up in the projects and my military training allowed me to carve out a livin' as a pretty successful hustler down here in Puerto Rico, right next door to LaPerla where ya gotta go hard in order to get and keep respect as well as to stay alive. I don't hardly play around when it comes to makin' this money, that's why I'm called 'El Don' around here ... cause I earned that title through years of sweat, blood and tears down here in the Pearl. Trust me."

He continued: "Now I gotta lay down a few house rules for you while you hang out here with me at the crib, awiight, Doc?" Valentino didn't wait for a reply as he continued. "Awiight, check it; you're more than welcome to anything in my home ... food, dope, whatever, everything 'cept the little trailer out back in the yard about fifteen or twenty yards to the rear of this one. You'll see it during the day. It's a little blue and white single wide ... that's all. Nothin' fancy, just a little spot for my payin' customers to go shoot up or get their fuck on with a coupla my lil' hoes I got stayin' up in there. Oh yeah, I pimp bitches too. You ain't know? A nigga gots to have mo' than one hustle, Doc. On Wall Street they call it diversifyin' your portfolio."

Valentino chuckled as the doctor sat, listening intensely. "Anyway, Doc, other than havin' you hook my lil' Latinas up with some o' that AIDS cure shit, cause as much dick as I've put in them lil' trick bitches, I know for damn sho' they got that virus 'cause I don't use no raincoats. Never have…never will. Stay the fuck from around there, awiight? Cause I gots plenty fiends comin' and goin' all day and all night 'round that joint and ain't no tellin' what they might pull on you if you happen to wander around there without me there to watch your back. Besides, my girls are all young and sexy as hell, and trust me, they know how to work a nigga. Before you know it, they'll drain your ass dry of both your cum and your money. So don't sleep on them bitches, unless you wanna get burnt and fuck around and come up positive. Remember, I'm lookin' out for you, dawg ... just like you 'bout to look out for me."

Valentino smiled at the Army doctor as he slowly walked over to an open window and peered out into the humid darkness of the surrounding rainforest.

The doctor finally spoke. "You need not worry about me snooping around your property, Valentino, because as scenic as your particular oasis here in Old San Juan is, I must remind you that I'm here on an official government assignment, and believe you me, I'll have no time in which to waste Uncle Sam's money on seeking out cheap thrills," Doctor Goddard responded earnestly.

For more than 45 minutes, the two men drank heartily and touched on various topics about their military careers, places in which they'd both traveled and other subjects which related to service in the U.S. military. Dr. Goddard detailed his very unsettling trip through the heart of La Perla.

"Man, Doc, my bad … I'm sorry that you had to experience all o' that thugged out shit, but hey, that's just the way it is down here in the Pearl, baby. Half o' these cats ain't eatin' right. The economy here in Puerto Rico is so fucked right now that dudes gotta hustle just to keep their heads above water, dawg. Somethin' like two thirds of the island's whole fuckin' population is on some kinda welfare and what not, even the middle class folks bring in no more than fifteen or sixteen hundred dollars a year! Not a month, my nigga … a year! And all these years the military been down here using this island as a naval base, Washington ain't done shit to help these poor folks out one bit. No wonder muthafuckas is takin' to the streets on some hardcore gangsta-ballin' shit. Cause, dawg … Puerto Ricans is tired o' getting' shitted on just like every other hood on the mainland U.S. 'Cept I doubt if any hood on the mainland go as hard as these thirsty-ass Vatos down here in The Pearl, Doc. These cats is off the chain with that grimy gutter shit. Trust me … I know," Valentino said, taking a light drag on his cigar.

"Why doesn't the public demand that their civic leaders improve the island's overall standard of living?" Goddard asked while piling on a second helping of seafood onto his partially empty plate.

"What civic leaders? More like crooks if you ask me. Most of the politicians out here is in the drug cartels' back pockets. If you don't already know, Colombia ain't nothin' but 360 miles away. That ain't nothing but a hop, skip and jump for the big boys to drop off 'birds' on Puerto Rican soil either by air or sea. Commercial flights to and from the mainland U.S. come in and out of Puerto Rico every day. Dozens and dozens of flights come and go every hour. The cartels ain't worried bout getting' them birds passed through customs, 'cause the island is an official U.S. territory. So most o' the time packages comin' from here ain't checked again once it ends up on the mainland. So the Colombian cartels send something like a hundred and some tons o' blow over here a year. They give the Puerto Rican politicians a nice little cut of the profits and everybody's happy. So why should they change?"

Dr. Goddard shook his head dejectedly and said, "That's very unfortunate, Valentino."

"Look, enough about all of that shit. Ain't nothin' we can do bout that no way. What I wanna know 'bout is what's up with the cycles of shots I gotta take and about the government benefits I'm gonna be entitled to after I go through with this experiment."

Dr. Goddard agreed with Valentino's request and began disclosing further details of the experiment dubbed "Operation: Inner City Virus," in which Federal money would be doled out in monthly stipends to Lucien Valentino. In addition, Dr. Goddard's own personal request would be met, and Valentino would take over the position as leasing consultant of a Landover, Maryland housing project called "Brightseat Gardens Apartments." where he'd live rent free for his services.

"So, you tellin' me that as long as I take injections of Biomax Officinalis every two weeks, my HIV will never turn into full blown AIDS? Shit that's what's up! And you got me a place and everything back in the States too, huh? Cool … but why can't I stay down here in Puerto Rico while you cats do whatever it is you gotta do for me?" Valentino inquired of the doctor.

"Well, Valentino, I can answer that." Goddard answered between a mouthful of fish and rice. "You see, the government agency that's responsible for conducting this study is located in Washington, DC, so we need you to be in close proximity in order to keep tabs on your medical progress as you begin your tests."

Dr. Goddard finished up his second helping and pushed away from the table. An old Puerto Rican maid took up his empty dinner plate and took it into the kitchen after wiping down the dinner table and pouring both men a full glass of Chablis.

"I hope you enjoyed your meal and all, Doc, 'cause I'm 'bout to take my black ass to bed. I gotta lotta errands I gotta run in the mornin', like I do every mornin'. So I'll catch you later, awiight?"

When Valentino turned to leave, the doctor saw the grip of a semiautomatic handgun protruding from the rear of his jeans, which, along with the AK-47 toting militia men patrolling outside the property's gates, caused a strong sense of dread to wash over him.

The sun slowly began peaking just over the rolling green hilltops above the tropical valley, spilling through the windows of the trailer. The Army doctor proceeded into the guestroom down the hall, hoping to complete his stay in Puerto Rico in short order. The doctor emailed information to his U.S. Army superiors back at Fort Detrick right before finally allowing himself a much needed rest.

After sleeping for several hours, Goddard awoke, showered, dressed and prepared the hypodermic needles and Biomax Officinalis serum to administer to the Valentino, showing him also how to self-administer the unapproved HIV medication. The doctor tapped away on his laptop computer, detailing the particulars of his first day of Biomax-O shots. One by one, Doctor Goddard removed the various tools of his trade from the medical bags lining the floor of his room. As the doctor removed the medical devices from their containers, Valentino walked into the room.

"S'up, Doc?"

Dr. Goddard turned and smiled at his host as he entered the room. "Good morning, Valentino. Are you ready for the first day of your new life? A life free from HIV and all the pain and suffering that comes with it?"

Without an answer, Valentino pulled up a chair, seated himself upon it and began rolling up his left shirtsleeve, revealing his bare forearm. Dr. Goddard removed a fresh syringe from his medical bag and fastened it to a sizable hypodermic needle, tapping the surface of the Biomax-O-filled syringe several times before finally selecting a choice vein on Valentino's outstretched arm. He then inserted the thin, sharp point of the needle. Valentino looked on calmly as the doctor's needle sank deep into his vein, releasing the silver, mercury-like substance into his HIV-tainted bloodstream.

Within a mere matter of a few minutes after Dr. Goddard had removed the needle from Valentino's forearm, the drug dealer loudly howled out, dropping to the bedroom floor and squirmed around for several seconds groaning in pain. Several of his housekeepers stood in the doorway and lined up along the adjoining wall leading to the guestroom, looking on with concern and confusion as their employer lay tossing and turning on the shaggy carpet.

After several hellish minutes, Valentino regained his composure and raised himself from off the floor on wobbly and unsteady legs. Beads of perspiration covered his face and he appeared flushed and weak.

"Are you okay, Valentino? Are you having any trouble breathing?" Dr. Goddard asked as he helped the still woozy drug dealer over to the bed.

Suddenly, Dr. Goddard felt himself being forced backward onto the bed. Soon he was face-to-face with the barrel of a nine millimeter semiautomatic. "What the hell are you doing, Valentino!?" The terrified doctor exclaimed, shielding his face beneath his hands as the point of the gun pressed down toward him. "Look! I'm really sorry about what just happened, but I assure you that it was simply a reaction from the Biomax Offinalis coming into contact with the HIV viral antibodies within your bloodstream. Once you've taken regular injections of the Biomax-O, your natural T-cell plasma count will rise dramatically, therefore ending any further adverse reactions to the drug."

Valentino released his grasp on the doctor and lowered the pistol to his side where he slowly tucked it back down into his baggy Bermuda shorts, allowing the doctor to rise from off of the bed. "Well, why didn't you say so in the first fuckin' place? Shit! I could've peeled your cap back just now! Do you realize that shit, Doc? I thought you'd just poisoned me as sure as my name is Lucien Octavius Valentino", he replied, slowly lighting up a cigarette as he waved the servants out of the guestroom doorway and back to work. "Good lookin' out for me, Doc … You saved my life … and from that fact alone, I felt entitled to save yours. But now that we're even, you gotta watch your back around here, okay? Anything you say or do could get you hurt or killed. Seriously … so be aware of what's happenin', awiight?"

After speaking those words of caution to the doctor, Valentino silently walked out the door. The incident was never mentioned again, however, Dr. Goddard was so taken aback by the sudden show of aggression and anger by his thugged out host that he stepped up his workload in an effort to vacate Puerto Rico as soon as he could. La Perla, with its scowling thugs, constant gun battles and heavy drug trade, was only a few miles away beyond the valley to the north, and Valentino's property was constantly patrolled by tough-looking gunmen looking for trespassers to shoot down. All of this was just far too intense for Dr. Goddard, and he went about his work at a feverish pace.

During the following week, the doctor spent most of his waking hours compiling medical data and administering shots to Valentino. Dr. Goddard observed that after several consecutive days of Biomax-O injections, the T-cell count in Valentino's blood increased dramatically, yet the HIV remained even, mutating into a seemingly more lethal strain within his body. Goddard recorded his findings and immediately forwarded this amazing information back to Fort Detrick via email.

Dr. Goddard concluded within two weeks of constant study and clinical trials out back in a small tool shed, which had been cleared by Valentino's henchman to be used as a makeshift laboratory, that the Biomax Officinalis had frozen the spread of the virus within Valentino's body and the virus itself would remain in a perpetual state of suspended animation, not spreading or causing any of the unpleasant physical illnesses suffered by most HIV-positive individuals—just as long as the Biomax-O injections were continued twice every month. However, the clinical trials also revealed a massive viral load building up within Valentino's bloodstream as well, which had developed into full-blown AIDS.

The span between the incubation period and the mutation into AIDS had taken only two and a half weeks, yet Valentino's immune system functioned properly with no ill affects whatsoever. The findings showed that over time, he would be safe from any HIV/AIDS related illnesses. However, anyone coming into contact with him via unprotected sex or blood transfusion would risk infection of a highly aggressive nature, breaking down the host's immune system and causing death in a very short span of time.

Dr. Goddard named this mutated strain of HIV "HIV5X" because it proved to be five times more lethal than the common strain of the virus. The U.S. military officials were very pleased with Dr. Goddard's findings as were elite members of the World Health Organization, who helped fund Operation: Inner City Virus.

Late one evening toward the end of May, Dr. Goddard sat with Valentino on the broad rear deck of the doublewide trailer drinking margaritas and discussed his host's military experiences.

"So you actually fought in the Gulf War back in '91?" Dr. Goddard asked his host as they enjoyed the gentle late spring breeze drifting over the tropical valley that evening.

"I saw action in both 1990 and 1991 in the Gulf," Valentino replied. "I was a gunner aboard the USS New Jersey. We fired shells the size of Volkswagens on Baghdad and the surrounding areas all fuckin' day and night. The shit was crazy. I also fought briefly in Serbia when Clinton sent us over to Eastern Europe. We did a lot of police work and shit over there, as well as fightin'. That's where I got infected with HIV, 'cause them lil' hot-n'-the-ass Bosnian hoes was givin' up the drawers left and right … especially to the brothas. Know what I mean?"

Valentino leaned back in his lawn chair slightly smiling as he recalled his many sexual conquests while serving abroad in Bosnia.

"Man," he continued, "musta fucked a different broad for everyday of the week. And most of 'em were real young and tender too! Nineteen, twenty-one, twenty-two, a lot of 'em had never seen black folks before, so most of the cats from my unit was straight turnin' them young European bitches out. By the time President Clinton pulled us up outta there, niggas done had babies and all kinda shit fuckin' with them lil' hot hoes. Some cats, though, fucked around, fell into some bad pussy and tested positive for that shit. Unfortunately, I was one of o' them niggas."

Valentino sighed. "Once the military found out who was HIV positive, they flew or shipped your black ass back to the states. I ended up here in Puerto Rico where I stayed on the naval base for a month and half before I received an honorable discharge for medical reasons. After that, they washed their hands o' me pretty much, c'ept I couldn't leave the island for some strange reason or another. The military and Puerto Rican authorities never gave me or any of the other dudes who were flown down here from Bosnia any reason why we couldn't leave. About twenty-five HIV-positive soldiers were transferred here in '93; eight of them have since died of full blown AIDS, three are now dying of AIDS and those of us left are just biding our time, scattered all over Puerto Rico, living off of a measly lil' bullshit military pension. That's why I choose to live in old San Juan right here on the outskirts of La Perla. Here I ain't gotta worry 'bout no cops fuckin' with me on my grind and I get to use my old school street knowledge to get my hustle on. I got the money to pay for most of the best HIV medicine from the mainland U.S., but still I usually end up feelin' like some shit most o' the time even when I'm takin' the stuff, so I don't know what kinda game you and the rest o' them medical types is runnin', but shit, if y'all done came up with a cure for this shit, at this point, I don't give a fuck. I'm down for whatever, 'cause a nigga like me tryin' to live, know what I'm sayin?"

After several more hours spent talking about war, politics and AIDS, Dr. Goddard bid Valentino goodnight. Before retiring to bed for the night, Dr. Goddard typed in the details of the day's medical progress and conversation with Valentino into his laptop computer.

"May 25, 1997" Medical notes continued ....
Operation: Inner City Virus
Patient: Lucien Octavius Valentino
Race:Black/Hispanic
Gender:Male
Ailment:HIV/AIDS
Treatment: Biochemical Maximum Officinalis (Biomax-O)
Description:Hastens development of HIV into AIDS. Vet, prevents destruction of host's immune system. Host will be able to maintain proper physical health and live a normal human life span as long as injections of Biomax-O are continued twice a month for remainder of the patient's life. If Biomax-O injections are for any reason interrupted for over two consecutive months, patient will immediately develop, and shortly there after, die of full-blown AIDS.

While patient is receiving Biomax-O, they will enjoy normal health and vitality. Their bodies harbor the antibodies of HIV5X that makes the patient lethal to anyone coming into contact with their bodily fluids such as blood, semen or vaginal secretions causing the victim to develop AIDS within the first sixty days of contact. The patient will be rendered contagious and ill after this two-month period, after exposure and physical wasting, paralysis and finally death within the final month, after exposure to the HIV5X virus is harbored inside the body of a Biomax-O user.
Dosage:Twenty CC's at the beginning and end of each month.

Status:Currently untested beyond the scope of this highly sensitive medical/military *probe.*

AIM:Study of the damaging effects of lethal mutated strain of HIV virus on dense and poor and/or minority populations within major U.S. cities.

Target area:Washington, DC

Conclusion:To be announced.

Study status:Successful.

Sensitivity level: Top Secret.

Dr. Edward M. Goddard

U.S. Army

2400

Dr. Goddard finished up with his work at around 1:00 a.m., all the while chatting online with a U.S. Army official stationed at Fort Detrick:

Armybratzrule66: Your clinical trials seem to be quite fruitful, doc. Keep up the good work. Dude, how are you enjoying paradise?

doctorDC1919: It sucks, Mark, the subject is possibly the biggest drug dealer around these parts, he keeps a cache of guns all over the house and there's armed guards walking around all the time.

Armybratzrule66: WTF?! Are you serious? Wow that does suck . . . hopefully you won't have to stay there for long doc.

doctorDC19: True that. That's why I'm going to have to speed up this process so that I can get the fuck out of here.

Armybratzrule66: Yeah, doc, you do that so you can bring your happy ass back home, because I've taken my golf game to another level . . . and you're going to find out punk! LOL.

doctorDC19: Yeah, yeah, you said that the last time we played 18 holes down in Hilton Head and what happened then? You lost! Big time! That game set you back what? $300? At least you go to meet Michael Jordan. By the way, did you ever get his autograph?

Armybratzrule66: Yes I did get MJ's autograph on my golf bag, thank you and fuck you very much. But there's no way Im losing to you again . . . trust me.

doctorDC19: Dream big, Mark. LOL! Good night, I got a lotta work to do.

Armybratzrule66: Got it, later doc.

Telephone calls and/or conversations were officially unauthorized due to the sensitivity of this most covert of government operations, so Dr. Goddard spent many long hours discussing the progress of the study with military and medical leaders online.

By early June, Don Lucien Valentino took three separate trips to nearby Colombia, South America; twice by speedboat and once on a twin-engine plane. He traveled to the country's capitol city of Bogota in order to purchase high-grade cocaine from the infamously ruthless Medellin Cartel, from whose ranks the powerful Pablo Escobar sprang. During these trips, the doctor took time to explore and enjoy the wild, beauty of the tropical wilderness surrounding Valentino's property. Upon Valentino's return to La Perla, the two men would continue their lengthy discussions about the military, AIDS and life in general, in addition to the Biomax-O treatments and frequent blood screening.

By June 10, 1997, Lucien Valentino had successfully shipped over three hundred pounds of cocaine into both Washington, DC and Baltimore, Maryland by commercial flight. He'd hired a group of local men and women numbering somewhere between eight and nine who were fluent in English as well as Spanish to smuggle the blow into the mainland and return back shortly after the drop off on a round trip flight back to Puerto Rico. Valentino used a different individual each time in order to avoid suspicion. Most of the local custom agents checking packages at the Puerto Rican checkpoints were extremely crooked and therefore easily bribed by Valentino's cash-laden smugglers. Valentino was now used to living the flashy, fast life of a hustler and saw no reason or need to change his lifestyle once he relocated to the Washington, DC, area. He had wanted to set up a solid narcotic operation in his new residence prior to his arrival so that his success would be assured once he got there.

Along with the usual notes that Goddard complied upon his computer files daily, were a few other situations which he'd observed concerning Valentino's behavior that prompted him to record on a digital voice recorder. This was for his own personal archives, because it was fascinating to the doctor to be a part of something gso dangerous, yet so intriquing all at the same time. He had to preserve these moments to relive in the future. detailed verbally via the recording device every detail of the corrupt world of Don Lucien Octavius Valentino. The Don maintained a lively nightlife and traveled far and wide through various regions of the island in search of entertainment. Puerto Ricans knew how to have a good time, and once night fell on the tropical island, festive Latin parties featuring strong drinks, energetic reggaeton music, and lovely young Boriquas, the native women, could be found in any of the cities or small towns throughout Puerto Rico.

Valentino would shower, dress and leave his home three or four times a week returning in the wee hours of the morning, if at all. Many times when he did return he'd be accompanied by a sizable group of young, attractive Latinas who accompanied him and his henchmen over to the blue and white trailer out back where they'd always end up engaging in a wild orgy of uninhibited sex, drugs and dancing. Occasionally, a few of Valentino's female guests would remain behind for good, serving as servants and sex workers in his whorehouse. Few chose to stay by choice. Most were kept as captives against their will as the Don held the threat of violence over their heads and constantly plied them with heroin and cocaine, thus keeping them addicted and dependant on him for their basic survival.

Early in the morning on June 19, 1997, Dr. Goddard was alone in his bedroom after leaving the kitchen from an early morning breakfast of Spanish omelet, hash browns and black coffee. Three unfamiliar maids had been cleaning and cooking the meals for the past week. Theywere more attractive and much younger than most of the other solemn, poker-faced señoras who'd tended to Valentino's home when Dr. Goddard first arrived.

The pretty, young Latinas made no attempt to hide their interest in the handsome, young Army doctor from Washington, DC, even when they were casually going about their business of tidying up the place; dusting, sweeping, mopping. Dr. Goddard could always feel their gaze resting on him whenever he'd cross paths with any of them during his travels throughout the house or the surrounding gardens out in the yard. They'd quickly look away blushing red and giggling whenever he'd make direct eye contact with any of them. When he'd tried to engage them in a conversation in either English or Spanish, they'd only smile and go about their daily chores as usual. Goddard knew their fear of Valentino was great and it superseded their infatuation with him. However, on this particular morning, Valentino was not at home.

Valentino had been gone for two days on one of his many drug runs to Bogota. Dr. Goddard entered his guestroom, undressed, and enjoyed a hot shower before deciding the scope of his day's activities. He'd been particularly horny this morning and seemed to have maintained a steady hard-on since breakfast. No matter what he did to take his mind off of his heightened libido, nothing had worked. So he peeked out of his bedroom door into the silent spacious living room. Seeing or hearing no one there, he quickly walked into the living room nude, except for a bath towel wrapped around his waist. He was dripping wet from the shower. He snuck an X-rated DVD from Valentino's extensive collection, which filled the top of the entertainment center, and sprinted back into his room, only partially closing the door in his haste to view the porn film.

The lust-filled young doctor immediately went to work setting up his laptop computer and placing the disk entitled *Cum Drinking Sluts #4*. Once the title, credits and film music began playing on the computer screen, Goddard turned off the desk lamp and pulled the curtains closed at the windows. He then positioned the laptop on top of the nightstand facing the bed. Dr. Goddard, now feverish with lust, threw off his bath towel, poured a huge quantity of baby oil into the palm of his left hand and began slowly stroking his thick, heavily veined man meat, which throbbed with pleasure with each up and down stroke Goddard applied to himself. As the erotic action on the screen intensified, so did Dr. Goddard's masturbatory accompaniment.

Lost in the throes of self gratification, Dr. Goddard's guttural groans and grunts must have traveled throughout the still, early-morning atmosphere of the house. When the doctor looked over toward the doorway, he was shocked to find that the three young maids were standing in the threshold looking on with voyeuristic delight.

The three girls were all young, maybe 19 or 20, the doctor thought. The one nearest to the entrance with a curly black mane tumbling down her back and across her suntanned shoulders in silky, ebony-hued bangs seemed no older than 18. All three were bronze-skinned beauties, possessing tight, young, shapely bodies with firm, well-rounded breasts, hips and buttocks.

Dr. Goddard's shock turned into approval as the three hot-blooded Puerto Rican seductresses waltzed into the room, one after the other, and disrobing as they entered.

"Oh, my God, Marissa, he is soooo fine! And look at his dick … it's so damn thick! I wanna fuck him right now!" said the youngest of the three girls as she slowly stepped out of her nightgown, leaving it crumpled in a powder blue heap on the floor at her feet.

"Hey Papi! You don't gotta jack off," another one of the girls told the doctor, "'cause we been wantin' to fuck yo' fine ass for a while now. We wanna ride and suck that big dick o' yours right now! Please, Papi! Don't make us beg for it, please … we can't take it anymore! Please fuck us! Cause I know that you won't turn down the chance to fuck three young, horny girls like us, will you?"

The youngest-looking girl crawled onto the plush, queen-sized bed while taking Dr. Goddard's erect member into her soft hands. Goddard's breathing hastened as he locked eyes with the raven-haired beauty peering at him with wanton lust from between his hairy thighs. He moaned with bliss as the gorgeous teenager slowly stroked his thick, curved dick while fondling his heavy, shiny black testicles. She teased him by blowing gently on the large, purple-colored head of his manhood and drained a sticky rivulet of pre-cum from down the middle of the dark, swollen shaft as it trickled across her slender fingers as her equally attractive companions looked on with excitement.

"Get the fuck up outta here y'all triflin' ass bitches!" a booming voice announced, shattering the erotic dreaminess of the moment. "You don't fuck with this man. You understand? This man is on some official business that y'all lil' ignorant asses don't know shit about, feel me? You don't know what you bitches are doin'! This man ain't one o' them lil' weekend johns y'all be trickin'. This here is a muthafuckin' doctor, bitch! An Army Doctor! Y'all hoes make him sick, and we all gonna die in a couple of months. Take y'alls dumb asses back to your fuckin' hoe house in the backyard before I put my foot in y'alls asses!" Valentino yelled while finishing his rant.

"We're sorry, Papi. We won't ever do it again! P…please forgive us," the oldest girl begged Valentino, trembling before her pimp as he towered above her.

"You goddamned right you ain't ever gonna do this hot shit no more, bitch, cause from this point on, none o' y'all hoes gonna come back into my house no more unless I give you permission to! I'm only gonna have a bunch o' old broads cleaning and cooking up in here from now on. Y'all gonna just straight turn tricks and that's it! You hear what I'm sayin'?"

The three embarrassed and frightened girls gathered up their clothes, skulking sheepishly past an angrily frowning Valentino, who sharply smacked each of them as they went pass. As the three sobbing teen prostitutes ran from the trailer, Don Valentino turned to face the doctor.

"They'll be awiight … after I drop off a couple ounces o' powder to them hoes. They'll forget about this whole incident. Trust me, doc. But you … c'mon, dawg, I know you need some ass just like the next man. But I told you before that these broads was HIV positive, didn't I? I told you how slick and scandalous these hoes was, didn't I? They got to have dick. These three young bitches is my most go-hard tricks.

They'll fuck a horse if I leave 'em alone long enough. But you playin' Russian roulette with your life fuckin' round with these tricks workin' here. You of all people should know this shit! I ain't gonna be responsible for you getting' burnt by one o' these dirty pussy bitches, besides, I need you to stay healthy long enough to do what you gotta do to make me better. Then you can fuck whoever you want after that."

As Valentino departed down the hallway away from the nude, unsettled Dr. Goddard, the doctor immediately ejected the porn film that played continuously on the laptop computer screen and tossed the disk across the room before hanging his head in frustration and shame. Valentino was right. Had the doctor made the mistake of bedding any of the three HIV-positive prostitutes to whom Valentino had been administering doses of Biomax-O unbeknownst to Goddard, he would've suffered a swift and cruel death.

How could he have been so careless and stupid, he thought to himself as the strange sounds of tropical creatures entered his room from the surrounding jungle beyond. After a few minutes of self evaluation, the doctor began the preparation of his day's activities.

By the end of June, Dr. Goddard had just about fully treated Valentino and was looking forward to leaving Puerto Rico for the mainland, U.S. Over the span of weeks spent at the drug dealer's compound, the young Army doctor had seen far too much of the evil of Valentino's criminal world, and it totally sickened him.

Drug and sex-buying clients provided constant traffic at all times of the day and night, which often provoked Valentino furious temper and frightening violence. On occasions, drug users would knock on the door at early morning hours disturbing the doctor's sleep. Valentino and his henchmen, at times, brutally assaulted clientele who proved to be delinquent or who abused his whores, leaving the poor bastards broken and bloodied on the green, well-manicured lawn of Valentino's home. Afterwards, these unfortunates usually ended up on the side of a lonely road somewhere on the outskirts of La Perla or the rainforest's edge. Sometimes they survived, but for the most part they succumbed to their injuries or met their end at the hands of La Perla's roaming street gangs or the dangerous animals of the dense jungle. Either way, customers realized that interacting with Valentino could be hazardous, at best, and behaved accordingly in his presence. At any time, Valentino's temper could flare out of control, bringing danger to anyone in the line of fire.

***

On July 8, a couple from one of the small towns near the valley drove up to the compound gates hurling threats at the trailer and demanding that their daughter be released unto them immediately.

"Valentino! You will release our Maria to us at once or I will drive my truck through these gates and take her myself!" the girl's father bellowed angrily as he shook the gate furiously for several minutes.

Valentino peeped through the curtains and dialed several numbers on his cell phone and calmly gave orders in Spanish to his men patrolling the surrounding property to respond to a code red at the front gates. He ended the call, and nonchalantly walked into his spacious kitchen and seated himself as two old ladies prepared him an afternoon snack. Within ten minutes of Valentino's phone call, the couple's old blue truck was surrounded by four Land Rovers, which unloaded at least a dozen AR-15 bearing militia men who fired round after earsplitting round of white hot lead into the surprised man and his equally astonished wife.

"Oh, Mary, Mother of God, have mercy on us! Aaallleee!" screamed the terrified señora, as the gunmen leapt from the interior of the vehicles surrounding them.

The scene haunted Dr. Goddard's thoughts for several days, afterwards causing him to endure constant headaches and terrible nightmares. During the month of July, Dr. Goddard continued administering Valentino's Biomax-O shots, as well as educating the drug dealer in the knowledge of self-injection.

When Valentino was away from the compound, Goddard explored the full expanse of Valentino's home, often finding stashes of packaged narcotics or stacks of cash hidden away throughout the trailer in cabinets, behind boxes in closets, and under beds and couches. The young doctor often wished that he could contact the authorities or someone, anyone, about Valentino's lawlessness, but he could do little but observe. He was on an official top-secret military assignment and quite obviously the Army and the World Health Organization must've known better than anyone that Lucien Valentino was a notorious felon who'd largely contributed to much of La Perla's drug-related crimes.

Once during one of Goddard's unauthorized investigations of Valentino's property, he noticed a lone van parked toward the west end of the yard just outside the gate. It was running, yet Goddard couldn't see anyone sitting inside. His curiosity overcame his caution and he approached the van from the rear gate.

"Did somebody just leave their vehicle running like this?" Goddard said to himself as he approached. "Hello! … Hello! Is anybody in there?" Dr. Goddard announced himself loudly as he stood outside of the passenger's side window. He could barely see through the dark tint of the glass, so he placed his right hand on the door handle. He tugged, but it didn't so much as budge an inch. Again, Goddard attempted to pull the van's door open, but to no avail. Finally, he forced open the door with a third and final yank. What he saw caused him to recoil in horror.

A dead Puerto Rican youth lay stiff across the driver and passenger's seats. His hands and feet were bound with electrical tape as well as his mouth. A bloody bullet hole leaked gore from the center of his forehead with a large portion of his rear skull blown all across the leather seats and floor. The doctor quickly realized that the young man was not the only victim, but three more bodies were heaped across each other in the back of the van as well. It was noon and the summer sun was at its zenith in the bright blue Puerto Rican sky, bringing the temperature to nearly 100 degrees. The bodies must've been sitting in the van under the hot sun for quite some time now, because bloating had begun and the stench was unbearable.

Dark clouds of swarming flies buzzed with a loud monotonous drone as they covered the van's interior. Dr. Goddard turned and fled the scene as fast as his legs could carry him back toward the entrance of the yard. As Dr. Goddard locked the heavy gate doors behind him, he proceeded along at a rapid pace through the gorgeous Japanese-style garden leading to the double-wide trailer that Valentino called home. Once back safely inside, Goddard immediately retired to his dimly lit room where he plopped down onto the large, comfortable bed and quickly fell into a deep, though troubled, sleep that was haunted by ghastly visions of bullet-riddled corpses and bloody car seats.

The very next day, Valentino invited the doctor out onto the patio for dinner with him. The two men were entertained by a troupe of exotic dancers from a local strip club as they dined. Half way though the late evening meal, Valentino and Dr. Goddard both applauded the twelve lovely Boriquas who'd come upon the patio one after the other in five minute sessions to perform before them as they ate. Valentino paid the women handsomely and bid them farewell as his hardcore bodyguards escorted them back to the van awaiting outside the compound gates.

"Well, it's been real nice havin' you here, doc. I hope you enjoyed your lil' trip to Puerto Rico. But it's already July 14, and I know you 'bout to leave any day now, so I wish you well in your medical and military career. And I guess I'll see you when I see you, champ. My folks 'round here will take care o' you until next week when the Army flies you outta here, awiight?" Valentino said to his guest as he finished up his savory meal of lamb and black beans and rice.

"Wait a minute, Valentino … what do you mean your folks will take care of me? Where the hell will you be?" a puzzled Dr. Goddard asked with immediate concern.

"Oh, you ain't know? I got shit all set up in the states right about now. I'm ready to take you up on that offer of becoming the leasing consultant of the Brightseat Garden

Apartment complex. I just had to put some things in place before I settled in, you feel me? But to make a long story short, I'm up out this bitch at 12:35 a.m. tonight. I'm hoppin' a private redeye flight out to a small regional airport in Virginia, not far from Dulles. Besides, I gotta pick up some money from a couple o' cats from Capitol Heights. Calm your nerves, cause you know just enough Spanish and these muhfuckas 'round here know just enough English to make for smooth sailing until you bounce during the coming week."

He continued, "You gonna be wined and dined three times a day, as always. You got full access to anything in the house you'd like. You got protection from my bodyguards 24/7, and if you want some pussy, all you gotta do is say the word and my man, Hector, whose in charge o' my security team, will go out and bring back some clean hoes from around the way for you to smash off, free of charge. Then when it's time for you to roll out, my bodyguards will take you back to downtown Old San Juan where you can meet up with your superiors at the naval base. Sounds good?" the drug lord asked as he concluded his offer.

"Not really, Valentino. You see, I'm not comfortable with your lifestyle one bit, and that's when you're actually here. So I know without a shadow of a doubt that I won't be able to stand it here alone with your prostitutes, drug dealers, and thugs. No fucking way, dawg! I want out tonight, Valentino!"

"Look, nigga! What I do out here is my own fuckin' business not yours, so don't go judgin' me and shit! Your monkey ass came here to use me as a muhfuckin' lab rat. Ain't nobody ask for you or the muhfuckin' U.S. Army to come down here fuckin' with a nigga! Nigga, I do what the fuck I wanna do! And ain't shit you or nobody else g'on do about it!" Valentino shot back in anger at the doctor's words.

"Hey, man, that's your pathetic life, not mine. I came here as an enlisted member of the United States Army and one of the esteemed physicians on the World Health Organization's Medical Examiners Board. I was assigned to administer doses of an anti-AIDS vaccine, which will save your life, and more importantly, the lives of countless millions of HIV/AIDS sufferers worldwide and for generations to come. So fuck you and your dead-end dope derived 'hood rich lifestyle. I've met my end of the bargain, and now I'm gonna contact Fort Detrick and have a plane here in the next few hours. You have a few cars out back that you're not using nor do you ever use. Give me the keys and I'll drive into town my damn self."

"Awiight, doc. You got it … but I don't know how far you gonna get once you get up outta the valley, 'cause you ain't gonna last two minutes drivin' through that barrio up the hill. That's why the cabdriver dropped you off with my man Felix and his girl Rosie, 'cause them Latin Kings gang members know me and my niggas; they got love for us and big respect 'cause they know we ain't to be fucked with. But let some strange cat try to drive through La Perla like it ain't no thing. That nigga g'on get dealt with in the worst way. Believe that, my nigga! So go right ahead and go. Shit, you can drive one o' them whips out back. I got the keys hangin' on the wall in the kitchen. It don't matter though; the Army usually has pretty good death benefit packages that will cover all o' your funeral and burial expenses. And your next o' kin will be well taken care of," Valentino remarked sarcastically to the frustrated doctor.

As much as Dr. Goddard hated to admit it, he knew that his drug-dealing host was 100% correct in his grim statements. He would not last fifteen minutes on a trip through the violent slums of La Perla; vehicle or no vehicle. So, reluctantly but wisely, Goddard reconsidered his choices and took Valentino up on his offer to remain on the compound another week before leaving for the mainland.

Then, shortly before Valentino left his home for the airport, Goddard overheard him plotting, in broken Spanish to two bodyguards, Goddards's murder.

"By the end of the week, Dr. Goddard will have to leave for the states, but we gonna make sure that he doesn't leave Puerto Rico alive, you feel me? I ain't got nothin' personal against dude, matter o' fact, I kinda like him myself; s'pecially for all the nigga done did for me and my hoes and all. But he just know a lil' too much dirt on us, know what I mean? I know he's on some official military top-secret shit and all, but hey, you can never be too careful with muhfuckas, you know. Who knows, he just might turn out to be a snitch. I'd rather be safe than sorry, so drive him through the jungle and then through the barrio. Then once you drive through the front gates, I want you to put two in his skull, leave him in the car, and then shoot the driver too. Go through their pockets and remove their money, credit cards, whatever you gotta take to make it look like a robbery. Since the incident will be staged right outside of La Perla's gates, no one, including the U.S. Army, will be the wiser."

From the room, the men walked together onto the patio in order to continue with the details of their fiendish plans in the humid Puerto Rican night.

The doctor was understandably distressed over what he'd just overheard coming from the next room. He knew he had to work quickly and with a calculating and cool head. Had he not known Spanish, he would've been unaware of the terrible fate awaiting him. Goddard, by now, knew pretty much every nook and cranny within Valentino's home. He slowly began packing a few small items into one duffle bag while Valentino and his bodyguards chatted and enjoyed margaritas on the outside. After packing briefly, Dr. Goddard finished up his final medical report online for his superiors at Fort Detrick and logged off his computer, placing it along with the all important floppy disk into his duffle bag. By the time he'd completed his work, it was 1:22 a.m. and the entire mobile home was dimly lit and silent with the exception of a small AM/FM radio churning out syrupy Latin love songs from the windowsill over the sink in the kitchen. Dr. Goddard quickly made his move towards the northeastern direction of the yard where night patrolling guards usually went to sit upon the marble benches in front of the fish pond to relax and smoke for a few minutes before returning to their nightly rounds.

Manuel Rodolfo, a grumpy fellow of about 46 with a dark, olive completion, a squat, chunky build and protruding belly, was seated beneath one of the several oil lamps found throughout the garden. He enjoyed a taste of cheap rum from a metal flask as he tapped out a cigarette from a freshly opened pack of Salems he'd just pulled from his wrinkled trousers.

As the Hispanic gunman cupped his sweaty palm around the cancer stick in an attempt to light it, he was oblivious to the figure moving silently within the shadows behind him. A momentary light orange glow highlighted Rodolfo's hard looking features, with its deep lines and creases, stubbly beard, and noticeable knife scar along his right cheek a permanent reminder of his youthful career as a member of La Perla's Latin Kings street gang.

Goddard crept up behind a banana tree and cocked back on his military-issued handgun. He peeped around for a second look at the heavy-set Puerto Rican before making his final and decisive move. He felt his heart thumping loudly within his chest and tried to ignore the perspiration trickling down his forehead. He was a doctor in the U.S. Army, not a soldier. He'd seen the horrors of war, but never had been forced to take up a weapon in an offensive way against anyone—until now—and he was scared shitless. Yet his sense of self-preservation overcame his strong but brief feeling of dread, and he reacted as only a desperate man would. Without a moment's hesitation, Dr. Goddard launched his attack. Stepping out from behind the tree, the doctor rushed forward pointing the nine millimeter at the seated man's chest.

"Mi Amigo, stand up with your hands over your head where I can see them! I'm leaving here tonight and you're going to drive me back downtown to the Condado Hotel, Si? There I will meet with the men from the U.S. Army who will take me back home to the states. If you fully cooperate, you will not be harmed," Goddard said in a sharp, authoritative tone while steadying the muzzle of the nine-millimeter on the startled gunman.

Rodolfo stared at his hijacker with stern defiance and anger, even glancing quickly twice at his assault rifle lying only inches away from his grasp. Upon seeing the Puerto Rican's shifty eyes and jerky movements, Goddard drew closer, warning the man of any foolish actions on his part.

"Look here, Amigo, if you know what's good for you, you wouldn't even think about going for that AK, because you'll be dead by the time your fingers touch the fuckin' stock. And if you didn't notice already, I've got a silencer attached to this nine and I'm a pretty good shot too. So don't tempt me, fat boy. Okay? You're smarter than you look. I'm sure of it. Now act like you know before I give your ass a permanent siesta, comprende?" Dr. Goddard spoke precisely in Rodolfo's native tongue.

Slowly, the gunman arose from the bench with this hands placed firmly on top of his head. Dr. Goddard quickly snatched up the AK-47 and directed his hostage toward a Land Rover parked beneath a grove of banana trees just outside the compound's gates. Though he had the full cooperation of Valentino's bodyguard as well as possession of two weapons, the young doctor was still completely filled with anxiety and fear. The perimeter surrounding the gates were patrolled by many other well armed guards who would not hesitate to fill him with lead if anything happened to go wrong. Luckily for Dr. Goddard, most of the other gunmen were off patrolling near the edge of the jungle where most of the thieves would travel in order to plunder Valentino's bountiful drug fields. Once the two men had made it into the Land Rover, Goddard directed the driver from the backseat. Quickly the jeep took off through the dark jungle trail in route to downtown Old San Juan.

Chapter 4

The CDC says that African Americans account for more than half of the reported cases of HIV and almost half of all AIDS cases. Of all the people who live with AIDS, 42% are black.

TaKeisha Smith, Dr. Edward Goddard's half sister, grew weary of watching music videos and gossiping with her girlfriends on the phone. She'd just graduated from Bladensburg High School with honors and a 4.0 grade point average a week earlier. Her best friend, Kiara "Kee-Kee" Lowery and Kee-Kee's big sister, Yasmin, had invited her to come with them to Virginia Beach for the weekend. But very few activities seemed to take her mind off of her brother and his safety.

He hasn't called me in weeks ... no postcards, no emails, no nothing! That ain't like Eddie. I hope he's all right; probably doin' some top secret-type Army shit again, Keisha thought to herself as she undressed in front of her full length mirror. *Oh, well, lemme shower and get dressed so I can ride out to Virginia Beach with Kee-Kee and Yasmin.*

Several hours later, the three young women were in Virginia Beach enjoying the sun, surf, and flirtatious advances of the hard bodied men who shared the beach and boardwalk with them.

"TaKeisha, girl, I don't know what I'm gonna do. I got three fine ass niggas tryin' to holla and shit. What do you think I should do?" Kee-Kee questioned TaKeisha as they prepared to lay out beach towels and umbrellas upon the white sands near the incoming surf.

"You already know who I'm gonna say, right? I like J-Dub for you, girl, and that ain't never gonna change!" TaKeisha replied.

Kee-Kee smirked playfully at her best friend as she fastened the big blue and white umbrella to the rear of the outstretched towel. "I know I shouldn't have asked you ... I know that J-Dub's my baby's daddy and all. And we went together ever since middle school, but I don't know. He just acts too immature sometimes for me, you know? Plus, Kenyon Chiles and Ronnie Free been pressin' me hard to be with them. So I don't really know what way I wanna go with it."

"Well, I guess I look at J-Dub like a brother. He's been with you for so long that he just seems like family. You know? I mean that is your son's father. Why don't you give him another chance?" TaKeisha asked, lying beneath the shade of the beach umbrella.

"There you go with that ole 'baby daddy' shit again. If Jeremy wants to get back together, we gonna have to work on some things ... both of us. You know what I'm saying? He be acting like he better than everybody with that job of his and stuff; like his work is the most important thing in the world. What about me and his five-year-old son?"

"Well I'm pretty sure J-Dub will be more than willing to patch things up between you two; just take it nice and slow. He deals with a lot of day-to-day stress, you know. I don't believe he thinks he's better than you or anything like that. Like you said, I just think he's caught up in his job is all. But things could work out between you two. You'll see."

Kee-Kee placed a pair of dark sunshades over her big brown eyes and sighed as she leaned back under her umbrella preparing to read a copy of *Sister 2 Sister*. "If that fine-ass brother of yours weren't like family, I would've been jumped on his ass, girl! Now that's a real man!"

Both young women laughed heartily over the thought of Kee-Kee hooking up with Doctor Edward Goddard. Then a long silence took control as each of the youngsters became lost in their own thoughts as the gently flowing surf washed upon the beach, mixing with the cries of circling gulls overhead and laughter coming from the many beach combers splashing in the cool waters beyond.

TaKeisha wished that her friend would finally settle down with one man and work on a solid healthy relationship for once. Even Kee-Kee's older sister, Yasmin, had become upset with her promiscuity, which had resulted in four unwanted pregnancies, all ending in abortions after she had her son. As the two girls looked out upon the surf, they were suddenly approached by Yasmin who had been out for the better half of an hour shopping at the local mall just beyond the sandy fringes of the boardwalk, picking up an assortment of sultry summer dresses and haggling over shoe prices while Kiara and Kee-Kee sun worshipped.

"C'mon, y'all. Let's get up outta here and go back to the hotel. I just ordered some food and it'll be there any minute," Yasmin announced while smiling eagerly at each handsome stud that happened to make eye contact with her.

A young curly haired, broad-shouldered lifeguard took the opportunity to approach the attractive trio, striking up a brief, but lively, conversation with Yasmin, whose bold preoccupation with him was the primary reason for his courage in the first place. Before they left the beach for lunch, the lifeguard assured the girls that he'd watch over their belongings until they returned from their hotel room. As Yasmin and Kee-Kee giggled like school girls in the presence of the dark-skinned Adonis standing in their midst, TaKeisha still found herself distracted, unable to think about anything but the whereabouts and safety of her beloved older brother.

***

At 6:45 a.m., the Cessna Skyhawk SP bearing La Perla's top drug dealer appeared like a white snowball against the dark slate gray skyline above North Carolina's mist-shrouded Appalachian peaks. It cruised above a rapidly moving storm system stretching across the tar heel state and on into Virginia.

Inside the comfortable confines of the spacious Skyhawk SP, Lucien Valentino calmly looked down at his sparkling diamond-clustered Rolex and occasionally out the small window to his left to see the beauty of the morning's sun spreading its glorious golden rays across the picturesque mountain range below, eagerly anticipating the touchdown at the small craft airport outside of Dulles airport. The pilot and his female sidekick counted and recounted the $13,000 Valentino had given them for the flight with gleeful greed up front in the modest cockpit of the aircraft as a fittingly amused Valentino looked on. By the time the Cessna entered Virginia's airspace, it was 7:22 a.m. and the weather was a comfortable 63 degrees, sunny with clear blue skies overhead.

Once the small plane began its descent down toward the narrow runway, Valentino's slight smile disappeared, replaced by a stern look of seriousness and depth. The wheels of the Cessna skidded along the slick, dark gray asphalt runway that had gotten drenched by a downpour earlier that morning, long before the sun rose above the horizon. Valentino arose from his seat and stooped down low as he exited the small twin-engine plane along with the pilot and his lady friend. A dark-skinned, bald gentleman dressed in a snazzy navy blue double-breasted pinstriped suit met them immediately. Standing at least six-foot-three, wearing ultra-dark Ray Ban sunshades and sporting a neatly trimmed goatee, the unidentified man appeared very intense and menacing as he stood off to the side conversing with Valentino in a barely audible monotone voice while a small crew of baggage handlers quickly removed Valentino's luggage from the plane. Valentino bid goodbye to the pilot and his woman as the tall man whose stern demeanor remained solemn and intimidating as he escorted him over to an awaiting cream-colored limousine.

"We're on our way to Landover, Maryland. Right, Tommy? Brightseat Garden Apartments, ain't that right?" Valentino asked his well-dressed chauffeur from the plush backseat of the limo as it slowly pulled away from the airport and on towards the busy highway in the distance. Thomas Broom, a cold-hearted killer and successful drug trafficker had been an important connection for Valentino for well over a decade, helping him to make aquaintances with some of the game's most infamous heavyweights, such as New Orleans' Marion 'Snookey' Lake, L.A.'s Divante Lovett and DC's own Katrina 'Southeast Trina' Ricks.

"Oh, no doubt. But I thought you said you needed to pick up that package from them young'uns out Kentland first though?" the mean looking driver inquired as he glanced up into the rearview mirror at Valentino.

"You know how we do, Tommy. That payment gonna be picked up before we do anything else, dawg. C'mon now, you been knowin' me since 1990, ain't shit changed, baby boy."

Pleased with his friend's answer, the straight-faced Thomas Broome slipped a "Best of Rick James" CD into the stereo and merged into the overwhelming traffic flow of the Capital Beltway as the hypnotic, electric guitar laced lyrics of "Mary Jane" filled the limo with punk funk dreaminess. Thomas Broome had been a premier drug connection for Valentino for three and a half years, now linking the Puerto Rican drug lord with many of the east coast's most notorious ballers, such as DC's own Maurice Lil Mo' Gentry and New Orleans crime boss Marion "Snookey" Lake, to name but a few. Over the years Broome had helped Valentino earn an enviable income selling narcotics between Puerto Rico and the mainland U.S. and had himself become rich in the process. A hardened criminal, Thomas Broome was no stranger to violence. Early in his criminal career he had murdered over a dozen people between Prince George's County and the District of Columbia—all by the tender age of sixteen. As thugs go, the two men were definitely cut from the same cloth.

Two days later, the Prince George's County police were alerted to a small single family home in Kentland, Maryland, to discover five male residents of the modest two story house dead of gunshot wounds to the back of the head. The execution style murders seemed to have occurred with little or no signs of struggle when investigated by the police. Though few locals spoke publicly on camera about the multiple murders privately, not wanting to be labeled as snitches, there were rumors of a tall, handsome stranger in the vicinity during the time of the shootings. It was said that the man, who was accompanied by another stranger, appeared to be clean cut, well-dressed and courteous to the residents of the tight-knit Kentland neighborhood. The neighborhood women especially remembered the charming out-of-towner as being quite generous with both money and flattery, and left an indelible impression on most of the love-struck young ladies before leaving the area. Still though, even as a community so used to random acts of violence, was horrified by the brutality of the slayings that had occurred.

"I sure as hell hope they catch his bitch ass whoever he is, 'cuz it was fucked up what he did to Mooka and them. Even if they had robbed 'em and shit, they ain't had to kill 'em. Don't make no damn sense," TaKeisha said to Yasmin and Kee-Kee as they discussed the incident just after a breaking news report interrupted their daily, lunchtime episode of *All of My Children.*

"You ain't gotta worry 'bout that shit, Keisha, 'cuz you know how niggas go out in Kentland. Shit, by the time we get back home, dude gonna already be dead. Lil' Tony, Dip, Kenny, and all them niggas g'on punish slim. I'm trying to tell you!"

Yasmin chimmed in. "Anyway, fuck all that shit. I'm trying to hit that beach before the sun goes down. Besides, it's just too many fine ass men out there for me to miss out on. C'mon, girls. Let's go. Fuck a Erica Kane right about now," Yasmin exclaimed as she quickly hopped off the hotel bed en route to the door.

Smiling, TaKeisha motioned with a quick head gesture for Kee-Kee and Yasmin to go on without her. She explained that she'd catch up with them right after the soap opera ended as she badly wanted to see the conclusion of this latest and most gripping episode. All in all, the Virginia Beach getaway was a fun-filled, flirt fest for the three friends who thoroughly enjoyed their vacation and brought back a camcorder full of memorable footage for all to see.

By the end of July, Kee-Kee was once again heavily preoccupied by the weekly lure of booze-filled nightlife and shallow mid-summer flings with a wide variety of strange men. Often, this behavior led to heated arguments between Kee-Kee and Yasmin, but did little to keep the younger woman from running the streets. At the end of her rope with her sister's increasingly reckless sex life, Yasmin called upon TaKeisha, asking her to talk some sense into Kee-Kee. TaKeisha agreed to have the much-needed talk with her best friend. TaKeisha invited Kee-Kee over to her house feigning interest in accompanying her to one of her frequent hangouts, only to lay into her once she'd gotten comfortable on the soft, plush, sleigh bed in TaKeisha's room.

"You know what, Kee-Kee, you been hangin' out at all these clubs like every other day and shit. Don't you think that you are like overdoing it a little?"

"Naw, young. I ain't overdoin' nothing. I'm just havin' fun and shit. That's all. You know, enjoying the summer, that's all. Why you trippin'?"

TaKeisha paused as if to find the proper words to say before taking Kee-Kee's hands into her own. "Kee-Kee, it's all right to have fun and all. I know it's summer and yeah, shit, I should be getting my swerve on too before I go back to school this fall. But that's really not what I'm talking about."

Kee-Kee's almonds shaped eyes narrowed slightly and she shifted uncomfortably on the bed. "Well, what do you mean, TaKeisha?" Kee-Kee asked with growing irritation.

"You fuckin' around with too many niggas that you're meeting at the club and shit. That ain't cute. You got a little boy to think about. You ain't got time to be laying up with all these muthafuckas, girl. You don't even know half of these dudes you be fuckin' with!" TaKeisha spat with blunt honesty.

Kee-Kee chuckled to herself as she pulled her hands away from TaKeisha's. "Oh, I get it. You been talkin' to Yasmin's dumb ass, huh? That bitch ain't got no man so quite naturally she gonna hate. But I thought you had my back, TaKeisha. I'm 24 fuckin' years old, girl. I'm grown! And who I fuck with is my muthafuckin' business; not Yasmin's, yours, or nobody else's. You feel me? So don't come at me with none of that old bullshit Yasmin talkin' bout, awiight? Now if you trying to come party with a sista and shit, getcha self together, 'cuz I'm out da door after I find my red pumps to go with this skirt. I think you got 'em in your closet. Remember I let you borrow them last month?"

Sighing as she arose from her bed, TaKeisha reluctantly prepared herself to accompany Kee-Kee to the club for the night. Although she had been certain earlier that after their talk, Kee-Kee would have had a change of heart about going out, that was not to be. It appeared as though Kee-Kee was going out with or without her best friend. So TaKeisha figured she'd go ahead and join her instead of letting her girl go out alone. Plus, this way, she could keep an eye on her as well.

For several hours, the two youngsters club hopped, darting in and out of nightclubs throughout the District, finally completing their night of entertainment at the Classics Nightclub out in P.G. County. Though both girls drove around town in Kee-Kee's Honda Accord, Kee-Kee ended up leaving Classics with a handsome, thirty something man. Well attired, iced out and pushing a black pimped out BMW 645 CI with glistening 20 inch chrome rims, the wavy haired, square-jawed player seemed to be either a baller or some local celebrity, which totally fit the bill of Kee-Kee's type of man.

After several minutes of laughter and small talk with TaKeisha and another young man, Kee-Kee had excitedly hopped into the passenger's seat of the sleek vehicle and disappeared with her new beau down the street of Allentown Road. TaKeisha had to drive Kee-Kee's car home.

The next morning when TaKeisha phoned Kee-Kee, she didn't get a response except for the same monotonous message on her answering machine picking up over and over, prompting TaKeisha to disconnect as soon as the recorded message began to play. Finally, around 3:45 p.m. in the afternoon, TaKeisha heard a car pull up. She looked out of the window and noticed Kee-Kee exiting the same BMW in which she'd left the club in the previous night. Filled with curiosity, TaKeisha rushed downstairs from her bedroom to spy on the two lovers from the French windows of her living room foyer. From there she saw the stranger, tall, sexy and well attired in a fresh looking Sean John sweat suit and white K-Swiss sneakers, take Kee-Kee by the hand as she emerged from the inside of the beamer and stepped up onto the curb just outside of TaKeisha's townhouse.

Kee-Kee smiled broadly and giggled like a love-struck teenager as the driver, who'd eased out of the driver's side, walked around and took her in his arms and joined lips with hers in a lengthy and passionate kiss, which even made TaKeisha's own heart race. When their lips at last parted, the young, handsome baller took out a small black velvet box from his sweatpants, producing a sparkling diamond necklace, and from there, placing it carefully around Kee-Kee's slender neck. Surprised and excited, Kee-Kee threw her arms around her new man's neck, planting yet another sultry caress upon his full lips, right before he disappeared around the corner and onto Landover Road in the direction of the Capitol Beltway.

TaKeisha could hardly contain herself as she burst outside the door before Kee-Kee could even knock. "Oh, girl!" TaKeisha yelled as she flung open the door and greeted her friend. "Well, well, well … you lil' freak body you. You spent the whole night out with dude, huh?" TaKeisha said eagerly awaiting the details of Kee-Kee's latest one-night stand.

"You don't know the half of it," Kee-Kee cooed as she stepped inside TaKeisha's house. She gave a recount to TaKeisha every aspect of her night of passion with the attractive, well-paid stranger.

"Now, TaKeisha, keep this to yourself, awiight? Don't tell nobody else, not yo' mama, none of our girlfriends, and 'specially not my sister, awiight? 'Cause I don't want Yasmin all up in my muhfuckin' business, cause that bitch cause too much drama for me. Know what I'm saying?" Kee-Kee said, looking TaKeisha dead serious in the eyes.

Although the sisters were just one year apart—and in fact shared the same birthday—Yasmin and Kee-Kee always fought and disagreed when it came to men. As roommates, the sisters couldn't help but be in each other's business. Yasmin was always on Kee-Kee's case about the number of men she was going through and was the first one to read her the riot act when she turned up pregnant. But Kee-Kee figured Yasmin was just mad because she had stolen her man from her. Jeremy might have been Kee-Kee's baby daddy, but Yasmin had been the one eyeing him originally; that was until Kee-Kee swooped him up from right under her nose. Yasmin had assured her that there were no hard feelings, but Kee-Kee begged to differ.

"Girl, ain't nobody gonna tell nothing," TaKeisha promised her friend. "You know I ain't no snitch and shit."

The two young ladies proceeded upstairs to the bedroom where they spent most of the day gossiping on the phone with other girlfriends about various neighborhood going-ons, and surfing the Internet.

"I hope you didn't think that I was being nosey or anything, Kee-Kee," TaKeisha said while gently combing through Kee-Kee's soft, curly hair as she laid sprawled out across the stuffed animal covered bed while going through a collection of music CDs.

"Stop lunchin', young … I ain't worried bout you. You my peeps. I fucks with you. You know that!" Kee-Kee answered. "Right?"

"Right," TaKeisha sighed as she finished brushing Kee-Kee's hair.

* * *

After July turned into August, TaKeisha became increasingly worried about the stranger with whom Kee-Kee had developed a deep affection for over the past few weeks. She was spending days and sometimes entire weekends at the man's home, yet his name, occupation and origin remained a mystery as he cautioned Kee-Kee against disclosing the details of their relationship to anyone. In addition to worrying about Kee-Kee's very peculiar love affair, TaKeisha also continud to worry about her brother, who had not yet contacted TaKeisha.

By mid-August, Kee-Kee spent almost all of her time out with the man whom she referred to simply as "my Boo," neglecting her son by leaving him at her mother's house all the time. And whenever she and TaKeisha did get a chance to hang out together at Landover Mall or around their Kentland neighborhood, their quality time was often cut short by phone calls or pages sent to Kee-Kee by the mystery man requesting her company to which she always had the same response.

"Look, TaKeisha, girl, I hate to eat and run, but I gotta dip 'cuz me and my Boo 'bout to get into some thangs a lil' later on. Know what I mean?" Kee-Kee said, nudging TaKeisha while winking mischievously as she arose from her seat.

TaKeisha stared at her friend in both anger and disbelief as Kee-Kee gathered up her purse and car keys from the seat and headed towards the front door of the mall away from the food court. For what seemed like a long while, perhaps two or three minutes, TaKeisha simply sat in her seat staring ahead blankly in utter astonishment and slack-jawed silence as Kee-Kee slowly melted into the bustling Saturday afternoon crowd at the mall. When the initial shock wore off, TaKeisha got up from her seat and worked her way quickly, if not rudely, through the noisy, slow moving shoppers, walking hither and thither throughout the mall's aisles.

When TaKeisha caught up with Kee-Kee in the outside parking lot, she loudly told her off as Kee-Kee sat behind the wheel of her car.

"I can't fuckin' believe you, Kee-Kee! Every time this muthafucka rings your phone, you gotta jump right up and run over to him like some lil' dog on a leash! Now I know that that's your new man and all, but girl, ain't that much dick in the world to make a bitch wanna be at a nigga's beck and call all like that! You don't even seem to give a fuck about your friends or nobody else … including your own child … just this strange ass, secretive-type dude you been fuckin' with. The shit ain't right. Kee-Kee, you can't keep treating your friends like shit over some dumb ass nigga! You betta wake the fuck up, girlfriend!"

Kee-Kee hung her head down shamefully as TaKeisha's harsh words hit home. "I know. I know. You're right. But I'm in love, TaKeisha. I … I just can't stay away from him. I ain't never felt this way about no other man…not even my son's father. I don't know what to tell you … except that the nigga gotta a bitch like me feenin' like shit, girl. Please try to understand TaKeisha, okay? I'm sorry but I …I gotta go!"

TaKeisha couldn't help but feel sorry, not for herself, but for Kee-Kee as she watched her head toward the traffic of Landover Road. She'd seen Kee-Kee infatuated over guys before, but never, ever to this extent, and it was truly painful to watch.

By August's end, Yasmin had gone out of town on vacation to Aruba for two weeks. TaKeisha, when driving by Kee-Kee's house to get to her own, noticed that along with Kee-Kee's own car, her boyfriend's black Beamer was parked in the driveway each day of Yasmin's absence. Even more disturbing than that was Kee-Kee's behavior. She seemed fine when she was alone, but whenever her "friend" was at her house, she'd become very reclusive and displayed strange behavior.

When she spent the night over to TaKeisha's house, TaKeisha noticed small purple-colored blemishes and spots all over Kee-Kee's fair skin, and saw her that her friend sweated profusely in her sleep during the night, even though the bedroom as well as the rest of the house was comfortably cool from the air conditioner, which ran all day and night throughout the hot and hazy Washington summer. When asked about her condition, Kee-Kee shrugged it off as merely a food allergy or contact with poison ivy during one of her walks through the park. TaKeisha suggested that her friend see a doctor about it, but Kee-Kee refused. The matter was never brought up again.

TaKeisha soon forgot all about Kee-Kee's "allergic reaction," and was distracted soon after by a late night call from her brother.

"Hello," TaKeisha answered the phone, which had awakened her from her sleep.

"Hey, Sis."

TaKeisha sat straight up in bed after hearing the very familiar voice that she had long been waiting to hear. "Eddie, is that you?"

"Who else would it be?" Not waiting for his sister to reply, the doctor instructed his sister that he was purchasing her a roundtrip ticket to Orlando Florida, and that the two of them would then fly back to the DC area together.

On the 12 of September, Kee-Kee spent the entire day with TaKeisha before helping her pack for her trip and dropping her off at Dulles International Airport later that night. As the girls placed the last of TaKeisha's luggage on the luggage cart, they embraced warmly before TaKeisha's flight boarded for Florida.

"I'll call you tomorrow, awiight? Tell Yaz that I want to know how her vacation went too, okay?" TaKeisha told her best friend.

"I got you…you just have fun at Disney World with that fine-ass brother of yours and quit worrying about shit all the damn time. Look at me, I'm doin' lovely … ain't shit the matter with me. You just do you while you down there, awiight? So have a pleasant and safe flight out. Now get your lil' ass on that plane before you fuck around on get left."

Once more, the two girls hugged each other for a long while before TaKeisha walked away briskly towards the United Airlines flight #118 awaiting her and a long line of Florida-bound passengers slowly shuffling their way across the runway and onto the stairs. Within minutes, TaKeisha was lounging comfortably in a cushioned seat, and dining on barbecued babyback ribs, corn and smothered mashed potatoes. A good looking flight attendant brought a list of preferred beverages from which she selected an apple martini.

"Excellent choice, young lady. I will be back in a second with your drink."

Damn, he got a nice butt, TaKeisha thought to herself as she watched the flight attendant walk away down the aisle.

TaKeisha had flown several times before, but never in first class prior to this trip. Edward had prepaid for her flight in advance and wanted for her to fly down to the sunshine state in class. Yet, still, even as she enjoyed the comfort of first class seating and all the extra amenities that came along with it, no matter how hard she tried, her mind drifted back to her friend, and she struggled to shake the thought that Kee-Kee had gotten herself caught up in something very bad.

Chapter 5

Blacks who are HIV positive are more than seven times likely to die from AIDS than whites.

On September 15, 1997, Prince George's County police arrested Lucien Valentino's chauffer, Thomas Broome, as he exited the "Crossroads," a popular local Caribbean-themed nightclub. The cops had been following several leads on the Kentland murders that had occurred almost two months earlier. They were glad that the tips from resident dime droppers had finally led to an arrest in the case, yet there was still one more suspect who was still at large. Now they just had to figure out how to get to him.

"Y'all ain't gonna hold me behind bars for long, 'cuz my lawyers g'on see that I get up outta here before the weeks over with. Y'all cops need to be workin' on catchin' up with the real big baller; I ain't nobody but a small fry in the game. C'mon now, getcha weight up, P.G.!" barked Broome during his interrogation process later that night after his arrest.

Thomas Broome appeared to be belligerent and combative toward the officers during the interview, and as he was a man of formidable size, the lead detective decided it best to call reinforcements into the interview room.

"Hey, look, I don't wanna take any chances with this cocksucker. Get me two more officers in here … pronto!" the detective, a middle aged man with silver flecked thinning hair and mustache said sharply over the intercom as he briefly stepped away from the small metal table in the center of the room.

Within a three-minute span, two beefy P.G. County cops donning dark colored BDU's burst into the interrogation area and immediately set upon Thomas Broome, roughly forcing him to the cold, hard surface of the floor as he fought diligently to free himself from their locking grasp.

"Get the fuck up off me y'all punk ass pigs! I ain't Rodney King … muhfuckas! I'll fuckin' kill one o' y'all niggas!" Broome growled as he fell hard to the floor along with his jailers toppling the metal chair in which he'd sat with a loud, metallic sounding clang that reverberated throughout the small, drab-looking enclosure.

As Broome was handcuffed and taken from the immediate area to a temporary holding cell, the lead detective and his colleagues could not help but dwell on the sudden aggression displayed by Thomas Broome.

"Detective, we've got Broome locked away upstairs in a holding cell until further notice. His bond is set a fifty G's, so it's my guess that he won't be goin' anywhere for a lil' while," a burly sergeant said while standing in the doorway of the interrogation room.

"Sweet … now let's just work on this maggot's rap sheet a while longer before we question him again. Shall we? He did mention something about us going after, quote, 'the real big baller,' whoever that is. We could be onto something here. I'm thinking that maybe we can get this guy to cop a plea deal for a lighter sentence if he gives up the one we're after. Trust me, I'm an expert on getting' creeps like this Broome character to spill their guts."

Little did the unsuspecting Sergeant Jeremy Williams know just how very close to home the Kentland murder case would actually hit.

***

Ronald Free, a student athlete at Bowie State University and good friend of Sergeant Williams, had remained friends with both Kee-Kee and Yasmin after Jeremy's break-up with the younger of the two sisters. As of late, however, he had not talked much to Kee-Kee or Yasmin due to the rigorous demands of late summer football practice in preparation for the upcoming season. Further, whenever he had tried to holler at Kee-Kee, she didn't seem to have time for him anymore. When Ronald planned a lively birthday celebration at the Republic Gardens Nightclub and had made the motion to invite Kee-Kee, he was shocked that she actually showed up. Jeremy, among scores of other friends and associates, attended the party as well.

The party itself was off the hook. Keenly alive and entertaining with vivacious music, dancing, laughter and excitement were coupled at the party with a plentitude of flowing alcohol that lasted well into the wee hours of the morning. Only the news of Yasmin's mysterious, yet potentially fatal, illness brought a damper to the festivities.

"Yeah, I don't know what's wrong with my sister," Kee-Kee relayed to Ronnie and Jeremy, "but ever since she got back from her vacation, she's been sick as a dog. She's probably no more than ninety something pounds now. Doctors say she's tested negative for AIDS and it's not any form of cancer or nothing. Yet still the shit is eating Yasmin up," Kee-Kee mentioned sadly as she slowly sipped on a glass of Petrone and lime juice.

Jeremy sighed and shook his head. "Well, I'll go by P.G. Hospital to see her tomorrow evening after my shift. I'll pick up a get well card and a bouquet of long stem roses too. That should make her feel a little better. You think?" Ronnie lifted Kee-Kee's face by her chin and smiled into her eyes.

"Yeah," Kee-Kee agreed with a smile. "I think it'd make her feel real good."

After visiting with Yasmin the following day, Jeremy was so distraught over seeing how emaciated the unknown disease had made the once voluptuous Yasmin, that he at once phoned Detective Taylor Goehring, whose wife, Diane, worked at the National Institute of Health in Bethesda, Maryland as a virologist in the Infectious Diseases Department. During the days that followed, Detective Goehring's wife painstakingly researched possible sources of the aggressive, wasting illness that had befallen the unfortunate Yasmin.

Jeremy was grateful for all of Diane's efforts. On October 12, he invited Detective Goehring and his wife to Jeremy Junior's sixth birthday. After the kiddie party, the group dropped off Jeremy Jr. at his paternal grandmother's home in Landover Hills, and proceeded to Prince George's County Hospital to visit Yasmin. Once there, they all chatted and briefly laughed with a bedridden, weak and visibly deteriorating Yasmin who, despite her grim condition, kept up a cheerful attitude.

Before the visit was over, Kee-Kee, torn apart by her older sibling's worsening health, bolted from the hospital room where she broke down into tears once out in the hallway. She was at once comforted by Mrs. Goehring and two nurses who were passing along the corridors at the time.

The ride home proved to be a difficult one as Kee-Kee's mournful, non-stop crying left everyone choked up and teary-eyed as well. And after Jeremy had walked Kee-Kee to her door, Detective Goehring met him at the curb.

"Listen kid, I'm real sorry about what's happening right now to your lil' boy's aunt and Diane is doing her damnest to pinpoint the cause and description of this illness, because like the rest of the doctors and medical specialists out there, nobody's got a fuckin' clue about what it is that's killing that young lady. But believe you me, if anybody can find out, it's my wife ... just give her some more time."

Unfortunately, it seemed that Yasmin appeared to have very less and less time every day. She'd lost so much weight and had become so weak and ashen, that by October 21, she fell into a coma. Her vital signs were barely active and she was kept alive via life support machinery. To overcome her sorrows, Kee-Kee found escape through liquor, marijuana, and sex with her Boo, A.K.A. Lucien Valentino.

She could not resist the way this man made her feel. His warm body embracing her own was beyond comforting. His strong arms and powerful chest pressed against her brought tingles up and down her spine. His moist tongue caressing its way along her inner thigh en route to her sweet spot brought her shudders of delight. And his hefty nine inch, curved member rocked her body with multiple orgasms whenever he long stroked her, penetrating her long, deep and hard, working her dripping vagina walls just the way she liked it … pounding away with gusto so that she felt every single inch and breadth of his well-endowed manhood, always leaving her sweaty, breathless, and so very satisfied. Yet shortly after each and every sexual encounter with Valentino, Kee-Kee developed the same strange flu-like symptoms; night sweats, fever, coughing, fatigue and diarrhea.

What the fuck is wrong with me? thought Kee-Kee. *I never used to get sick, except when I was pregnant with Junior.*

She'd taken two pregnancy tests at home and both came back negative. By October 28, Kee-Kee had developed rashes all across her body again. She eventually followed TaKeisha's advice and finally consulted her family doctor. She was diagnosed, treated for the rashes, and released after a two-day pre-cautionary stay in the hospital. Still nothing more than a pesky skin infection was determined to be the cause.

"Detective, I'm really worried about my son's mother. She's been sick off and on and now she's come down with all these weird looking rashes all over her body," Jeremy told Goehring. "Her doctor can't seem to find out what is causing it either. The doctor says it's probably just a skin infection she picked up in a public swimming pool or bathroom. But I don't buy that. Hell, I'm no doctor, but I think it's something else."

Detective Goehring stroked his chin as he studied the sense of urgency in the young police sergeant's eyes. "Sergeant Williams, I know that this is gonna sound very unusual, but I'm gonna need a blood sample from your son's mother. Now don't ask me why, but I've got a hunch that Diane or anyone of the physicians on her floor at NIH can get to the bottom of what's going on and more than likely can prescribe an antidote for it or lead her to a proper medical specialist who can. It's worth a shot. Don't you think? Meanwhile I need for you to monitor who she's seeing. Maybe she's picking up some sort of virus from somewhere or something. I hate to ask you this, but does your son's mother take drugs?"

"No, not that I know of."

"Well, anyway, have an unmarked squad car follow he from time to time or have a private eye provide surveillance for you, alright?"

Looking on with utter confusion as to the detective's strange request, Sergeant Jeremy Williams shook his head before speaking.

"Say what? Why should I be eavesdropping on Kee-Kee? We have a child together, but she and I aren't together anymore. I'm just concerned about her health and all, not her personal life. So, I can't see why any spying type shit is necessary."

"Williams, trust me on this. I haven't been a detective on this force for fourteen years for nothin' … I think that her illness as well as her older sister's are linked some how and I'm starting to believe that it's been transmitted to them from something other than a plant or insect. I think there's a contagious person out here going around making people sick, kinda like the Typhoid Mary case back during the early 1900s. So please, for Kiara's sake, do it. Keep in mind that this could ultimately even effect your son if we don't get to the bottom of it."

Despite the extreme peculiarity of the request, Jeremy highly respected the detective's judgment in unusual circumstances such as this, and wanted to do whatever was necessary to bring relief to his ailing baby's mama. So he promptly hired a private investigator from the local yellow pages so as not to use any of his own officers for such an odd assignment.

Unfortunately, the investigator let him down. On the day after the Halloween festivities, Jeremy was enraged to find the incompetent private eye asleep and loudly snoring behind the wheel of his company car across the street from Kee-Kee's own vehicle in the driveway. The morning newspaper lay upon the dew-covered lawn untouched. She'd been gone all night long. Sergeant Williams angrily demanded the startled, still drowsy, investigator to explain his grossly inept work performance.

"Mr. Williams, she was in the house most of the night on yesterday. I swear to God!" the private eye exclaimed. "I remember seeing a couple groups of trick-or-treaters come up and ring the doorbell and she came out each time smiling and giving out candy to all the little kids. Then once the Halloween traffic slowed and died out, I noticed her moving around inside the house through the Venetian blinds for about thirty minutes or so. Then she turned off all the lights and I assumed she'd called it a night. I stayed right here just like you told me to. I stayed awake for like another whole couple of hours or so before I started getting' sleepy. By the time I dozed off, her car was still parked in the driveway and I didn't see anybody come over there to visit, pick her up or nothin'," the investigator explained excitedly in his defense, but the sergeant would have none of it.

"Dawg, that's sounds good and all. But the bottom line is she ain't here right now at this moment. And to make it so bad, you were knocked out sleep, Champ! I ain't payin' you damn near twenty dollars an hour to sit up in your ride snoozin' when I told you to keep your eye on Ms. Kiara Reeves. When she moves, you move! Wherever she goes, you go ... you know, undercover-type shit. But it's all good though, Champ. I'm g'on pay you for eight hours and eight hours only. But you ain't gotta worry about coming back up here t'morrow, 'cause your service is no longer needed as of now!"

Jeremy took out his wallet and pulled out a couple of hundred dollars, placed it into the private eye's outstretched hand, quickly signed a receipt form, received his pink copy of it, and walked away still angered and frustrated at the thought of wasting his hard earned money on a totally worthless private detective agency instead of assigning one of his rookie officers to watch Kee-Kee. The following day at work was a difficult one for Sergeant Williams, whose preoccupation with Kee-Kee's strange illness, as well as her unknown activities, made it nearly impossible to perform his duties as an officer. All of the cops under his supervision noticed his troubled demeanor and tried helping him as best as they possibly could. When their best efforts failed, a few of the Sergeant's most loyal beat cops consulted with Detective Goehring to speak to their obviously distressed leader. The detective eagerly agreed and requested that Sergeant Williams join him for a few drinks at a nearby pub frequented by cops and firefighters.

"Jeremy, I've listened to some of your officers today and they all seem awfully concerned about your well being, my friend. And well, frankly, so am I. I spoke to Captain McAllister a little while ago and he agreed to give you a week's paid vacation. So go and get yourself a much needed break, okay? Go somewhere you haven't gone in awhile ... Vegas, Honolulu, Cancun maybe, huh? Play some golf, do some hiking, camping, or hell, just spend the week doing nothing but resting or doing the whole 'daddy thing' with your little boy. Don't worry about nothing else, Jeremy, 'cause I'm gonna see to it that Kee-Kee is taken care of and watched closely by a few of my most trusted detectives in the department. So chill out and do yourself this really big favor, okay? For me?"

Jeremy drank deep from the half filled mug of his fifth round of Heineken. "Yeah, I guess you're right, detective. With my worrying about Kee-Kee on top of trying to do my job as a cop, well, I guess I am jive a lil' bit stressed out, you know?" he responded wearily, looking down at his now empty beer mug.

Detective Goehring reassured his co-worker and together they drank a final round of beer before leaving the pub for home.

From November 11 until the 19, Detective Goehring had two of his leading detectives secretly observe and record Kee-Kee's activities from dawn until dusk. He himself accompanied Kee-Kee to the hospital to visit Yasmin. For the time being, Kee-Kee had regained her strength, beauty, and vibrant energy that had for a long while seemed to have left her during her previous bout with that strange illness. Yet even with everything the detective had put forward, nothing could prevent Kiara Reeves from answering a late night phone call on the 22nd of November.

I shouldn't even answer this fuckin' phone. He know he's wrong as shit. But I do miss his phine ass though...plus I gotta get me some money, so guess what? I gotta take this booty call tonight baby!

Chapter 6

Anthony E. Whitfield, December 2004: Black man from Lacey, WA infects his own wife and four other women with HIV and exposed 17 others to the virus, which landed him in prison with a 178-year sentence. After his conviction, racist leaflets circulated throughout Olympia, Washington, asking whites not to have sex with blacks in order to avoid AIDS. Over 100 homes received these leaflets. 142 people as of 2002have been currently convicted of criminal HIV transmission here in the United States.

On November 23, as Thomas Broome was being transferred from his original holding cell to another facility in Clinton, Maryland, to await his January 8 murder trial, he viciously attacked one of the two officers who were escorting him from the Palmer Park precinct toward the police van waiting outside. After slashing the first cop badly across the face with a razor blade he'd hidden underneath his tongue, he lunged for the fallen policeman's service weapon, but was struck from behind by the second officer within seconds after Broome had wounded his partner. Broome collapsed unconscious to the floor of the lobby of the precinct beside the bloodied police officer who writhed in agony from the deep gash across the left side of his face. Soon the lobby was filled with P.G. County cops, with two officers quickly attending to the wounded man on the floor below.

By the time Sergeant Jeremy Williams arrived on the scene, a half hour later, the ambulance had taken both Officer Linwood and his assailant to the P.G. County Hospital. Jeremy was anxious to learn how the murder suspect could've freed himself from the handcuffs before assaulting Officer Linwood. After a tense two day investigation where every cop on

Sergeant Williams' watch was placed on the hot seat for the unfortunate incident, it was finally determined that Thomas Broome had somehow secured a set of handcuff keys that had been found on his person before he was taken to the hospital.

The very next day shortly before the annual Thanksgiving holiday, a dapper gentleman approached the entrance of the infamous Jessup State Penitentiary after exiting the sleek BMW 645 CI he'd parked in the visitors' lot. The tall, good looking stranger went up to the guards' booth showed his identification card, filled out the visitor's log and followed his two hulking escorts in sullen silence past the curious inmates exercising in the yard toward the telephone booths located in the lobby.

The stranger pulled up a chair and seated himself in front of the large plexi-glass window, awaiting his inmate's arrival. The correctional officer who stood off at a distance wondered to himself about why this stranger would request to speak to one of the most notoriously violent prisoners in the history of Jessup State Penitentiary.

"Ain't none o' my business, Champ, but I hope you know this cat personally, 'cause Brian Atwood is a lifer with big connections outside these prison walls, you know? He's been known to have put contracts out on Federal judges, lawyers, even cops. So if I were you, I'd be damn careful 'bout what I said to him. Know what I'm saying? They don't call this dude 'Heatseeker' for nothing. 'Cuz he'll find your monkey ass sooner or later," the C.O. quipped sarcastically as he walked up close to Valentino.

"Oh, you ain't gotta worry bout me, my dude. You see, ole boy might have a little bit o' muscle up in here and a little bit out on the streets of B-more and what not, but me … I got power everywhere. He don't … now take this and get the fuck on," Valentino answered with a sarcastic grin on his handsome face as he handed the nosey guard a rubber band wrapped wad of bills.

The prison guard quickly slipped the knot of cash into his left pants pocket and returned to his post, watching in silence as Valentino spoke through the phone to the orange jumpsuit-wearing Brian Atwood on the opposite side of the plexiglass window for the next twenty minutes.

By the time his now infamous nephew had left the Tidewater area for the Army, Brian "Ant Man" Atwood had been arrested a record seventeen times for various offenses ranging from pick pocketing to major drug trafficking charges. The hot-tempered Ant Man was never charged or convicted for the murder of Pedro Valentino and his family. However, many more slayings would come later and for these there would indeed be arrests and jail time. With his latest dastardly deed, an armed car jacking landing him in the Jessup Men's Correctional Facility for a five-year term shortly before his nephew arrived from Puerto Rico.

After his conversation ended, Atwood nodded and smiled at the stylish, bejeweled Valentino before being led back down the dark hall towards his lonely cell at the end.

As Valentino walked past the outside guards' booth and towards his Beamer, the two guards spoke among themselves about the strange visit he'd just had with the bloodthirsty Brian Atwood and how compliant the vicious murderer was during their monitored conversation. That same night, Atwood and several of his fellow thugs prepared handwritten notes—know as "kites" in prison jargon–and sent them out to the other inmates throughout their prison wing. By the time the guards got wind of the letter distribution, it was too late. For two whole days the kites had circulated all over the entire upper level of the F block and several dozen had been delivered to prisoners along the lower tier of the F block by the time the guards found out about it. And when a letter or two were recovered, the cryptic language in which it was written could not be deciphered by the correctional officers, preventing them from stopping the inevitable.

Chapter 7

The Inner London Crown Court sentenced Mohammed Dica to eight years in prison after he was found guilty on two counts of biological grievous harm for deliberately infecting two women with HIV. He actively persuaded the women to have unprotected sex with him knowing that he had HIV. He said that he was negative and single with a successful career as an attorney, when in fact he was HIV-positive, unemployed and a married man with several children.

Kee-Kee disappeared with her dashingly handsome lover for the Thanksgiving day festivities, and didn't return home until December 3. The lovers spent the holiday as well as the following week in Pennsylvania at the Pocono's Ski Resort. While there, they enjoyed all the amenities the famed romantic getaway had to offer, including skiing, horseback riding, dancing, and fine dining. At night they eagerly satisfied their burning lust for one another on a great heart-shaped satin bed before the warm golden glow of crackling flames dancing inside the accompanying fireplace as the romantic ballad of Guys' *Let's Chill* crooned from the nearby stereo speakers. Kee-Kee thought about the warnings she'd received from her loved ones, but how could she resist this man?

After sharing a bottle of aged Parisian Merlot, Lucien Valentino took his young bun-bun into his powerful arms, placing his full lips gently onto hers. Kee-Kee moaned with the heat of sexual arousal as Valentino's tongue trailed a slick path down her slender neck towards her erect nipples, bringing her dangerously close to the point of orgasm. She wanted to resist him, she really did, but she had once again gone much too far now to turn back.

As Valentino moved his tight muscular body on top of her, she literally begged for him to fulfill her wanton desire with the type of long, stiff satisfaction he'd given her so many times before. And as always, he met her womanly needs as only he could. He stroked, ever so slowly, deeply penetrating her. He filled her up and worked her vaginal walls with precise, steady thrusts, stimulating her G-spot with each rocking movement. Kee-Kee was now drunk with pleasure, and she spread her thick thighs and shapely calves far above the wide, sinewy back of her man.

"Fuck…me harder! Pl…please!" panted Kee-Kee as she clamped her nails into her lover's tight buttocks, encouraging him to pump himself into her with more force. He obliged and taking her legs into his arms, rocked her with brute force, bringing the 23-year-old woman to a blanket-soaking climax and causing her to cry out in ecstasy. Moments later, Valentino grunted loudly as his massive penis spasmed twice, spurting out stream after thick stream of dense semen deep into Kee-Kee's dripping pussy.

At the exact same time back in P.G. County, Maryland, Kee-Kee's older sister, Yasmin, woke up momentarily out of her long coma, let out a blood-curdling scream and collapsed back down onto her hospital bed. Her vital signs flat lined, bringing scores of doctors and nurses racing into her room. Instantly, the hospital staff went to work frantically trying to save the dying woman's life. Sadly, all efforts to revive her failed, and at 2:22 a.m. on December 2, 1997, Yasmin Nicole Reeves was pronounced dead. She was only 27 years old.

Upon the following autopsy report, the hospital coroner reported that Yasmin's death was due to complications from an AIDS-like virus that had aggressively attacked her immune system and caused her death in a relatively short span of time from incubation. Because of the conflict of the coroner's report with the test the doctors had run on Yasmin, this report was not released due to the uncertainty of the final diagnosis. Ultimately, before the body was released to the J.B. Jenkins Funeral Home, the cause of death was classified as acute pneumonia. Yasmin was laid to rest seven days later, on December 9. Her memorial service drew a multitude of teary-eyed mourners from all across P.G. County and the greater region, filling up the spacious sanctuary of Shiloh Baptist Church of Glenarden. Many of her closest friends attended the solemn service, including TaKeisha. She was hurting tremendously over Yasmin's passing, but was nevertheless strong for Kee-Kee, who sobbed hysterically throughout the service and even more so at her late sister's burial site in Harmony Cemetery an hour and a half later. TaKeisha wished she could have spent more quality time with Yasmin while she lived out the final weeks of her life at the hospital. TaKeisha, however ,had been overwhelmed with responsibilities at both school and work since returning home from Florida some time earlier.

As expected, Kee-Kee took her older sister's death quite hard—so hard that, along with the help of his mother, Sergeant Williams had to take over the parenting duties of Jeremy Jr. Kee-Kee had a nervous breakdown a week after Yasmin's burial. By mid-December, Kee-Kee received word from her healthcare provider that she'd tested positive for HIV and that she'd have to come in the clinic for a battery of tests to be absolutely sure.

For three weeks, Kee-Kee underwent a series of medical tests to determine her physical status. By the 29th of December, it was determined that Kee-Kee did indeed have HIV; however, her doctor was amazed as to the rapid and aggressive spread of the virus from invasion period to incubation period. The time period from invasion to infection normally would take from five to ten years. But for Kee-Kee it had only taken a few months for the invasion period to the dangerous yet inactive incubation period.

Kee-Kee was informed of this unbelievable finding and she was questioned about her sex life and past partners. Immediately and angrily, Kee-Kee fingered her latest loverboy was the culprit; yet he seemed to appear just fine. When the P.G. Health Department rounded up eight of the nine men whom Kee-Kee had named, all tested negative for the virus with the exception of a certain Simon Harker, who could not be found. It finally dawned on Kee-Kee how utterly stupid and reckless she'd been concerning her health. She had not an address for her so-called "Boo," either at home or work because the two always hooked up at local hotels. He'd also given her a bogus name to top it all off. She did, however, retain the make and model of his car: DSARYI Maryland BMW 645 CI. The P.G. County police made a search after his vehicle's information was given by the women's health clinic of Landover. Yet still, once the luxury sports vehicle was found, it was currently on the sales lot of the Passport BMW of Marlow Heights, having been recently sold by the owner. Three weeks went by with no trace of the smooth-talking, iced out player who'd swept Kee-Kee off her feet and was responsible for infecting her with this unidentified new strain of HIV, which was rapidly morphing into full blown AIDS within her body.

Bitter and angry over the biological death sentence given to her by a callous and unsympathetic boyfriend, Kee-Kee plotted revenge against every man she'd encounter from now until her condition rendered her too weak to sexually spread the virus or "gift" as she'd grown used to calling the dreadful disease.

For about three months, tens of dozens of area men of various ages and walks of life began testing positive for the deadly strain of HIV. So many Washington-area men became ill with HIV5X that the local Washington, DC media ran full coverage on the growing health scare overshadowing the Beltway region's black community, calling it a sexually transmitted pandemic.

As months passed, disturbing rumors began circulating around the region that an attractive light brown complexioned dime piece who hung out at local nightclubs picking up guys randomly, sleeping with anyone who bought her a drink or two, was the source of the disease. It was rumored that this HIV-infected hottie would leave a handwritten note either in the pants pocket or car glove compartment of her unfortunate victim explaining in frightening detail the nature of her illness and ending the letter with a chilling "Welcome to the Wonderful World of AIDS" salutation.

On April 12, 1998, Detective Goehring placed several printouts with newspaper clippings on the newly promoted

Lieutenant Jeremy Williams' tidy desk. The young, decorated police officer took the stapled printout sheets and leaned back in his cushy, blue leather recliner reading the paperwork in between long, slow sips of steaming espresso.

"This is the case of the HIV criminal exposure spree going on right now … everyone and their mama have heard about this. It's all over the news, the T.V., the radio, the paper, you name it …every police department in town is zeroing in on this case, detective. What's your point?" Jeremy shrugged.

"Yes, you're absolutely right, Jeremy, every cop out there is well aware that we have a criminal out here purposely exposing others to HIV/AIDS no doubt. Yes, every department from DC to Virginia to here in Maryland is doing everything in their power to find this woman and take her off the streets. But they don't have a clue who this mystery lady could be. But I do … believe it or not. Jeremy, the broad that's infecting all these guys…it's…I believe it's… Kiara."

A look of disbelief, shock and outrage clouded the lieutenant's smooth young features for a split moment or two before he gathered back his composure. How could Detective Goehring be so sure? Kee-Kee was still suffering, as was everyone else, from Yasmin's untimely passing, not to mention the discovery of her own HIV-positive state. Kee-Kee had moved out of her Kentland townhouse back in the middle of January. She now lived in Greenbelt with her mother. They were both helping each other cope with the pain of the loss of Yasmin.

Among the newspaper article clippings were several color photo prints of Kee-Kee entering and exiting the vehicles of several unknown men, obviously taken secretly outside of area clubs. These prints were dated from January 17, 1998 to April 3, 1998.

"Detective Goehring, these photos are certainly of my son's mother, but still, we have no evidence that she's the infected club ho' going around making all these dudes sick!" Jeremy snapped angrily, slamming the paperwork down hard upon the top of his desk.

"Jeremy, I know how difficult it must be to accept this… but if we don't act quickly to get Kiara off the streets and to a hospital, more people are gonna get sick, and in turn, they'll infect yet others as well…" Goehring's words trailed off momentarily. "I've never told anyone this but … I too am HIV-positive … I've been positive for about eight years now since the summer of 1989. I had open-heart surgery back then in July. My wife, Diane, who is negative by the way, could not donate blood to me because she's B-positive and my blood type is A-negative. I'm sure that you can understand the rest … I was the recipient of a tainted supply of blood…yessir, now that you know I've been doing my homework and I'll tell you what this type of HIV carried by Kiara is not your ordinary HIV. This particular strain is particularly deadly. It's also what killed Yasmin."

Goehring pulled out a folder. "I've got her autopsy report from the Coroner's office at P.G. County Hospital. Diane and several virologists have analyzed and studied the blood sample from Kiara that I had asked you to get for me. The experiments done with lab monkeys had terrifying results. During the NIH study, monkeys that received AIDS (HIV-2), the simian form of the immuno deficiency virus, in group A developed HIV within a period of three months. But in stark contrast, the monkeys in group B that were injected with a vaccine-laced with the cancer-causing monkey virus S.V.-40 and a mixture of Kiara's HIV-tainted hemoglobin antibodies contracted full blown AIDS within a matter of two weeks, dying from AIDS related complications a few days later. I also have the written proof of those NIH results here with me in the lab. But there's more … I took upon myself the responsibility of acquiring a court ordered permit to see Kiara's medical reports and acquired samples of her last few PAP tests from the Landover Hills Gynecological Center."

Jeremy couldn't believe what he was hearing as his friend and fellow officer continued.

"Semen samples obviously from her last sexual encounter since seeing her doctor were removed for the purpose of DNA analysis and we came up with a match for this so-called Simon Harker. This scumbag's real name is Lucien Octavius Valentino, a former naval officer who fought in both the Gulf War as well as in Bosnia. He contracted HIV along with several other U.S. soldiers while on tour in Eastern Europe and as a result was flown back across the Atlantic to Puerto Rico supposedly for HIV treatment. Now I for one know within my heart and soul, that this Valentino guy is somehow connected to our case, trust me on this. I've arranged to have a meeting this coming Sunday at my place out in Bowie. Diane's gonna prepare a wonderful meal for everyone. I've invited your good friend Ronald Free and Edward Goddard, the brother of Kiara's best friend, TaKeisha Goddard, who contacted me several times this past week eagerly requesting a sit down with department officials. Jeremy, we're on to something really big here. It'll be at 7:35 p.m. sharp. Be there."

Without a doubt, Jeremy had every intention on being there…to prove his friend wrong!

Chapter 8

Currently, South Africa has been noted as having the world's highest number of HIV/AIDS infection cases. HIV and AIDS remain a sticky subject in the country of South Africa, as well as the continent as a whole. Those living with AIDS in South Africa are shunned, have lost friends, employment, have endured beatings and have even been murdered simply for being HIV-positive.

When Sunday rolled around, everyone was assembled at 3011 Old Chapel Road in Bowie, Maryland. Ronald Free, Dr. Edward Goddard, Lt. Jeremy Williams and host Detective Taylor Goehring chatted idly, and sipped on Cabernet Sauvignon as they prepared to hear the information in which Dr. Goddard had to give them during this all important of discussions.

"The virus in which we are now dealing with is called HIV5X," Edward explained. "A most virulent strain of the common HIV virus that was developed right here in Maryland, in one of our Army labs in Fort Detrick. The genetically engineered bio-weapon was developed by the Army to be used as an instrument of war against foreign enemies. However, it had to be tested for potency before the green light was given from the World Health Organization. What better community to test such a weapon on than the poor, minority areas of the country … the program, 'Inner City Virus' was set to be used here in the greater Washington, DC metropolitan area." Dr. Goddard spoke with a harsh sense of urgency in his voice, which at times seemed to crack with emotion.

"My wife, Diane, eluded to that same fact this past week when we discussed the matter at dinner," Goehring offered. "Amazing … I find it almost impossible to believe that our government would use its citizens as guinea pigs in order to test such a deadly virus," Detective Goehring said, raising a glass goblet filled with sparkling red wine to his lips.

"I ain't surprised at all … I mean look at the Tuskegee experiment back in the forties. If the government could pull some shit off like that back in the day, what makes you think that they won't do the same type o' shit to us right now? I don't trust them muthafuckas as far as I can throw 'em," Ronnie Free exclaimed in visible frustration.

"Hey, look y'all, I know how hard this is on all of you, especially since someone we know is not only infected with this disease, but is more than likely spreading it to a whole lot of other people purposely. We gotta act fast and get Kee-Kee off the streets and into a hospital ward somewhere, then maybe we can both cure her as well as hopefully find a way to slow down this deadly virus," Jeremy interjected.

As the four men continued to jabber endlessly, Detective Goehring's wife came down the winding stairwell interrupting the ongoing discussion in order to give her husband an important phone call. After taking the phone from his spouse, Goehring jotted down some information briefly upon a well-worn notepad before hanging up the line.

One of his young detectives, whom he'd assigned to stake out Kiara Reeves' Greenbelt residence, had followed the young lady into the District where she ended up going into the Martini Lounge for a little over an hour. When she emerged from the nightclub at last, a broadly smiling, fresh-faced young man followed eagerly behind her out across the street toward their vehicles waiting in the parking lot. From there, the man drove his red Mazda Miata behind Kee-Kee's Honda back across the Beltway and on into Prince George's County where both parties parked their cars in front of a Days Inn in Hyattsville. Goehring informed the rookie detective not to act in any way until he arrived on the scene. Without hesitation, the four men raced from the house to their cars parked in Goehring's driveway. When they arrived at the hotel along

Queen's Chapel Road, Kee-Kee had just checked out of the hotel room with her latest sex victim in tow.

"Hold it right there, Kiara," Goehring said calmly. "Please let us help you. This isn't what you need to be doing, sweetheart … it's a crime. I can only imagine what you must feel like, and trust me, we're doing everything we possibly can to bring that scumbag who infected you to justice as well as offering you and your recent partners the best medical treatment that modern medicine can provide. But I cannot allow you to go on purposely spreading this virus…it ends here, Kiara … tonight," the detective said displaying his PGPD badge before her.

Kee-Kee looked over to Jeremy, who stood behind Goehring. "So I see you g'on try and lock me up, huh, Jeremy? You'd sell me out to the police? Man, fuck all y'all bamma niggas! Y'all can't feel my pain! I'm gonna fuckin' die 'cause some pretty nigga with a bad dick didn't give a shit about me. So guess what? I don't give a fuck neither!" Kee-Kee screamed back at the men assembled in front of her.

Kee-Kee's date, startled by the disturbing revelations spoken by the detective, immediately turned on his one-night stand, angrily demanding an explanation for the words which he was now hearing. During their brief but fierce argument, Kee-Kee was attacked by the now enraged young man before Detective Goehring or Jeremy could act. The sinewy youngster rushed upon Kee-Kee, reaching out with powerful hands for her throat. The two of them fell hard to the pavement with Kee-Kee screaming out in pain as she caught the brunt of the man's fist slamming up against the side of her face. Jeremy raced over and attempted to wrestle the angry attacker from further harming Kee-Kee. But just as soon as he was pulled up off of her, she charged her assailant with cat-like reflexes, withdrawing a small switchblade from the pocket of her tight-fitting denims. She quickly stabbed the man repeatedly in his chest and abdomen while he was in Jeremy's grasp. The young man fell to the pavement, fatally wounded by the gunfire of a pair of P.G. cops who'd just now arrived on the scene and feared for the safety of their Lieutenant.

The small blood stained switchblade fell from Kee-Kee's limp fingers and onto the concrete below as she lay dying from her wounds. Blood oozed from Kee-Kee's quivering lips and slid down the right side of her cheek as her head dropped down to the ground beside her now stiff outstretched arm. After a few sputtering coughs, Kee-Kee's shallow breathing ceased ... she now joined Yasmin in the eternal stillness of death. Two P.G. County officers led the still angry, struggling man away in handcuffs towards a nearby squad car as Jeremy raced over to Kee-Kee's cold form.

Detective Goehring and the others slowly moved back as Jeremy crouched over the body of his son's mother, sobbing bitterly as he held her head gently in his arms. As the lieutenant grieved over Kee-Kee's death, the men all vowed to bring the primary suspect to justice by any means necessary.

During the week after Kee-Kee's funeral, Detective Goehring visited TaKeisha Goddard to interview her about her departed friend's latest boyfriend.

"Usually I would not ask these type of obviously personal questions, especially so soon after you've lost such a dear friend, however, due to the circumstances surrounding Kiara's illness, as well as the overwhelming cases of HIV5X that resulted from her own intentional spreading of this most virulent strain of AIDS, I fear that the man who infected Kiara is still at large and exposing other unsuspecting young women to this killer virus. We've gotta stop this son of a bitch before he wipes out half of the metro area. It's that serious, TaKeisha," Goehring sighed as he leaned back in his chair.

"Kee-Kee was always into dating a lot of different men; sometimes she'd talk to two or three guys at the same time. Yasmin didn't like it and neither did I, but hey, whatcha g'on do? Kee-Kee was gonna do what Kee-Kee wanted, regardless," TaKeisha told him. "She stayed going out to the clubs every weekend and half of the time she ended up having a one-night stand with some dude who she thought was cute or had some long dollars. I knew that sooner or later she'd end up pregnant or catching something and I told her that to her face more than once."

TaKeisha held back tears as she continued. "I can't even remember all the different men that Kee-Kee slept with, but one o' them dudes caused her and Yasmin to start beefin'. I think it was like this tall, older guy. He was jive like a pretty boy type, you know ... brown skin, good hair. I ain't even g'on lie, the nigga was sexy as shit for real. I remember Kee-Kee meeting him at the Classics, I think ... yeah, that's it! I was with her that night too. She was on dude hard, more than any other nigga she'd fucked with except for maybe her baby's daddy, Jeremy, who also had created a little beef between the two sisters back in the day. Dude stayed coming over to Kee-Kee's house, but I think Yasmin didn't like the fact that Kee-Kee was fuckin' with a dude she'd fucked with earlier or some shit like that. But anyway, they almost came to blows over that guy. I guess Yasmin wasn't having Kee-Kee try to steal on her man a second time."

The 24-year-old TaKeisha Goddard also recounted to the chief detective details of the e-mail messages and phone conversations she'd had with her brother, Edward, while he was away on special military detail down in Puerto Rico. She said that Edward had recounted stories of drug dealing, decadence and murder while treating his patient for some terminal illness.

"You've been a tremendous help, not only to this case, but to the entire area," the detective said while jotting down the particulars of TaKeisha's oral statements on his ever-present notepad. "This is just he info I need before I make my way out to Jessup Corrections tomorrow. I think we may be onto something really big here."

TaKeisha's eyebrows rose with sudden piqued interest in the detective's upcoming prison trip.

"So, what's up with Jessup? Why you gotta go up there for?" She asked inquisitively.

"Well, I've been in contact recently with one of the suspects in the Kentland murders and I sincerely believe that he wants to plea bargain, which is shy he's willing to tell me what I want to know." Goehring paused briefly to check the number of an incoming call on his cell phone, which vibrated upon his belt, before finishing the conversation. "I'm almost certain that this guy is in some strange way connected to this killer HIV case. Don't ask me how . . . I just know."

TaKeisha moved up closer to the detective, looking squarely in his eyes and taking his hands into her own.

"Detective Goehring, please, please, please lemme go with you tomorrow. It would mean the world to me if you did me this one favor, please!"

Detective Goehring signed lightly while rubbing his thick thumbs across TaKeisha's dainty hands with fatherly affection.

"Now, TaKeisha," he said, "I know how bad you've felt recently and believe me I'm gonna do everything in my power to bring to justice whoever's responsible for the deaths of the Reeves sisters, but I just can't bring a citizen in on official police investigation duties. Not only is it against department policy, but it's totally unethical and potentially dangerous for you . . . Remember those assholes are behind bars for a good reason. They're hardened criminals with no regard for the well-being of their fellow man. So, I'm sorry, but . . . I simply can't honor that request, sweetheart. Please try to understand."

TaKeisha angrily pulled her hands away from Detective Goehring, while still holding a steely gaze.

"Naw! Hell naw! You try to understand that, detective! You don't know what it feels like to lose two of your very best friends to some bamma-ass nigga with a dirty dick! I've known those two girls since grade school, detective! Fuckin' grade school, and now they're both gone forever! That's not the way it should've ended, detective! Yasmin and Kee-Kee should've ended their days as hold ladies in a nursing home or somethin' with grandkids an' shit standin' beside their death beds, not in the prime of their lives! And Kee-Kee's got a lil' boy who's never gonna see his mommy again as he grows up into manhood. I gotta do this, man. I gotta go with you to that pen . . . Maybe I could help the investigation along even more than you would by yourself. I'm from the hood myself, so I ain's scared of nobody for real, 'cause most o' my folks is locked up right along with ya man, whoever he may be, right there in Jessup. So yeah, go hard niggas don't move me . . . Lemme do this . . . lemme do this for Yasmin and Kee-Keep, please. I'm beggin' you, detective! It's that important to me," she said with tears now streaming down her soft, brown cheeks and her voice cracking with emotion.

Detective Goehring was touched to the core by the young woman's outpouring of grief—this genuine plea for the opportunity to bring some sense of closure to her pain. Reluctantly, the normally by-the-book detective conceded to the wishes of his youthful ally.

"All right, all right . . .You can go, but I've got to be there no later than 12:30 p.m., so that means I'll be here at 10:45 a.m. sharp. Be ready to go at that time or else I'm leaving here, with or without you. Got it?"

TaKeisha eagerly agreed, feeling obligated to the memory of her friends to do whatever was possible to bring the killer to justice.

The following day around noon, Detective Goehring and his pretty young companion arrived at the imposing Maryland state penitentiary. They were escorted to an interrogation room by a prison guard to await the arrival of their requested prisoner. Within 15 minutes, the intimidating Thomas Broome entered the drab, gray-hued room shackled with handcuffs and leg irons. With a devious smile written on his hardened face, Broome shuffled into the room facing the detective and young lady. He sat down with a heavy thud in the cold metal chair and leaned in forward facing Goehring with a set of piercing, bloodshot eyes while he rested his muscular forearms on the cool of the table top before him.

"Hmmmm … so you da young'un whose girlfriend just died from dat shit, huh? Dat's fucked up, baby girl. Sorry 'bout ya loss and all, gotta be painful."

Goehring leaned forward and asked, "How'd you know about that?"

Broome chuckled heartily at the question and replied, "Just 'cause I'm locked up behind these walls don't mean shit. I got eyes and ears out there in the free world. If I need somebody touched, I can get 'em touched. If I wanna know somethin', I'm gonna know it … work ain't hard, slim. I got the power to do that. My nigga, Valentino, got that monsta, dawg, but it ain't no ordinary HIV. This some super AIDS-type shit that the Army done gave to my man. As long as he keeps up his shots with some type o' anti-AIDS serum, he stays healthy and normal. But for real, for real, he's got full blown AIDS runnin' all through his body. The man's a good lookin' muhfucka and he's got a vicious mack game. So, for real, most bitches can't resist the nigga. That's where ya problem is gonna come into play. Ain't no tellin' how many lil' chicken heads, Valentino done ran up in by now. Y'all cats betta get y'all game on man, cause time's runnin' out."

After a few more questions were both asked and answered, the interview was wrapped up and Detective Goehring and TaKeisha exited the interrogation room and walked along with their guard escorts toward the front gates. It was there that the duo entered the detective's unmarked squad car and cruised away down Rt. 175 to Baltimore Washington Parkway headed back to P.G. County.

Though the visit with the murder suspect was disturbing at best, neither the middle-aged detective nor the twenty-four year old college student could deny the dire significance of the inmate's revelations about his infected friend's murderous behavior. A week after the visit to Jessup Correctional Facility, Detective Goehring called together a meeting with the combined police forces of Prince George's and Montgomery Counties as well as the District in order to discuss the details involving the recent, alarming epidemic of AIDS related illnesses and deaths affecting the Washington, DC area, particularly the black community.

As the assembled lawmen fidgeted in their seats restlessly, conversing amongst themselves, Detective Goehring approached the grand podium from the rear of the stage and respectfully requested the attention of the uniformed audience as he spoke with his familiar baritone vice booming into the microphone and throughout the auditorium's speaker system.

"First of all, I'd like to thank all of you for coming out tonight for this most important of discussions; probably the singularly most important discussion any of you will have during your entire career in law enforcement. All of you know why you're here. You're here for the same reason that I'm here … to stop a killer. A serial killer unlike any that you've ever heard of before. This biological menace to society is the cause of this viral pandemic currently afflicting our region at an alarming rate."

Goehring paused for affect and then continued. "We must do everything in our power to quarantine the unfortunates who've become infected with the virus, and more importantly, to apprehend the individual who is responsible for the spread of this deadly new strain of AIDS. The local medical community as well as the National Center of Disease Control in Atlanta is offering us their assistance in the fight to isolate and prevent the further spread of this virus. The entire Washington, DC area is under quarantine, and even the White House has been alerted to the seriousness of this problem. The President himself has expressed concern for the health safety of not only the Beltway region, but the nation as a whole and the east coast in particular. I've spoken to a gentleman who has given me the identity and bio of the suspect involved in this case as well as the motive. I assure you that what I'm about to divulge to you at this time will be very disturbing, and at times, some of you, especially those officers who happen to be of African-American and/or Hispanic descent, will be outraged."

The officers listened intently to their superior.

"Believe me, in my thirty-two years as a lead detective on the Prince George's County police force, I've never dealt with a case as unbelievably outrageous as this one. This individual is Lawrence Oliver Atwood, he prefers to go by the moniker Don Lucien Octavius Valentino, a 29-year-old ex-Naval officer who fought in the Gulf Was as well as in the Bosnian Conflict, in which he was a member of the U.N. Peacekeepers. Somewhere down the line he and quite a few other soldiers contracted HIV from the local girls and/or guys. They were sent back to their native countries in a hurry. Our guy ended up in Puerto Rico where he spent a brief stay at the U.S. Naval base's infirmary before he was given an honorable medical discharge and a monthly stipend to hold him over for a while. But the lil' bit of change Valentino was earning from his measly military check wasn't enough to make ends meet for Valentino. So, he turned to drug dealing to supplement his income.

"Apparently, during this same time the U.S. Army, in conjunction with the World Health Organization, had developed a serum extracted from the sheep visna virus that would indefinitely prolong the life and physical health of patients suffering from HIV/AIDS. However, the new designer drug was in its experimental stage and had not been given approval by the FDA, or any other governmental watchdog group for that matter. So after the tests were ran on laboratory monkeys and the like, the decision was secretly made by certain U.S. Army officials as well as World Health Organization spokesmen to undergo an experiment with the serum known as Biomaximus Officinalis, or Biomax-O, which would be used on a live human subject.

"Valentino, who was currently living with HIV, was chosen. Being black and residing in Puerto Rico's most violent slum, La Perla, made him the easy choice for the doctors who had not revealed this decision of theirs to their colleagues in the Army or the W.H.O. Their plan would be to offer the Biomax-O injections to Valentino for free, providing both he and his girlfriends monthly supplies of the medication as a part of the experiment called 'Operation: Inner City Virus'. You see folks, this serum will indeed keep you healthy as a horse if you happen to have HIV or AIDS. You'll be able to live a normal human lifespan of 60 plus, 70, 80 years or more depending of course on factors such as diet, lifestyle … family genetics … you get the picture. But the patient or patients have to take injections twice a month at the beginning and end of each month for the rest of their lives. And that's just the tip of the iceberg, folks.

One of Goehrings' subordinates brought him a glass of water. Goehring took a sip and then continued. "You see, this Biomax stuff mutates the HIV antibodies once it makes contact with the host's blood, which super accelerates the transformation from HIV into full-blown AIDS. The patient then must continue his or her injections without interruption longer than a month or the host rapidly dies from the wasting and debilitating effects of full-blown AIDS. All within thirty days ladies and gentlemen! Oh, but wait … it's gets worse … much, much, worse. You see, once you have sex with someone who is shooting up Biomax-O, you are in immediate danger of being infected with what we now know as HIV5X. Your chances of infection after intercourse are more than 95%. And get this ... your chances of survival past 90 days is about 10%, yeah ... slim to none. Three months ... three fuckin' months and you're maggot food. And no guys, there's no cure for it ... unless of course you get your hands on some Biomax-O, right? Right. We don't have any idea who and what we're up against, but I really, really need your help, guys. I mean, hey, we're cops and all, but we're people first ... parents, children, siblings and friends. This is our community that is being destroyed ... devastated! It doesn't matter if it's here in P.G. or over in Montgomery or DC or in a poor neighborhood or a rich one. We are losing loved ones every day. We're losing ground and precious time. The threat is real. The body count is rising. We've got to act now, we cannot allow this animal nor the rogue doctors who created this Frankenstein's monster to go unpunished. And I vow on my life as an HIV-positive man that Valentino and those so-called doctors are going down as of now!"

Muted silence was immediately broken by a round of thunderous applause that filled the entirely of the auditorium as each and every officer present gave Detective Goehring a rousing standing ovation that lasted for a full five minutes as Goehring stood smiling before the loudly, clapping and whistling assembly while tears streaked down his cheeks. He knew deep down that the beginning of the end of Lucien Valentino's reign of terror was finally at hand.

Chapter 9

Wangari Maathai, Nobel Peace Prize Laureate, is widely reported to believe that HIV/AIDS was created by Western scientists for biological warfare and could not possibly have come from natural causes.

On the morning of April 29, 1998, at approximately 6:40 a.m., Detective Goehring and Lt. Jeremy Williams drove up into the crime-ridden grounds of the Brightseat Garden Apartments accompanied by three police vans filled with heavily armed P.G. S.W.A.T. officers. As the black-clad S.W.A.T. team quickly hopped out of the vans one by one, the detective and lieutenant both drew their service revolvers and carefully shuffled along the graffiti-covered walls of the building to the left marked 1313.

As the long line of P.G. cops wound around the corner and down into the lower reaches of the dimly lit slum tenement, they stepped across and through smelly trash strewn all throughout the cockroach-infested hallway, occasionally hopping over an unconscious drunk or two en route to the dark end of the ridiculously long hall. Finally, the lawmen reached the door marked T8.

"All right, Lieutenant, this is it. We've got to cautiously, but quickly, move in to catch Valentino and company napping . . . literally," Detective Goehring whispered before banging a heavy flashlight several times upon the door, which broke the stillness of the early morning. "Open up the door, Valentino. We know that you're in there! We have a warrant for your arrest. Now we can do this smooth and easy, or we can do it the hard way. Your choice, but you've got only five seconds to decide. I'm gonna start counting now... one ... two ... three ... four ... five! Move in!"

The phalanx of S.W.A.T. officers smashed into the door twice with a steel battering ram, completely collapsing the heavy door with a deafening crash with the third impact. Seconds after the door crashed to the floor inside the dark apartment did the ear-splitting sound of gunfire accompanied by bright orange flashes of flame erupt immediately from the pitch-black hallway.

"Take cover, men! Fall back and return fire!" barked Lt. Williams as bullets peppered the walls around the officers and harmlessly bounced off their bulletproof face shields and body armor. The gunfire continued to roar repeatedly causing the S.W.A.T. team to stay covered beneath their bulletproof protective covers as round after round of deadly lead shelled the shields surrounding the squatting cops.

"Return fire! Return fire, now! Do it!" yelled Lt. Williams right before squeezing off several powerful shots of his own in the direction of the enemy's fire.

With the efficiency of a well-trained killing machine, the S.W.A.T. team arose from their crouched position in unison and fired away with their submachine guns into the darkness before them. Blood curdling screams filled the dark hallway with a hideous racket as the A.K. 47's sung their lullaby of death with relentless fury. Lt. Williams ordered the S.W.A.T. team to cease firing.

"Hold your fire! Hold your fire! Goddammit!" Lt. Williams hollered above the din of the machine gunfire.

When the gunfire stopped at last, a S.W.A.T. officer found the switch to the hallway light and flicked it on, revealing a horrific scene of bloody carnage before them. Seven bullet-riddled bodies lay mangled along the blood soaked floor with their handguns lying close by where they all fell, fatally wounded. Five men and two women were among the shooting victims. For ten minutes the cops searched the apartment with careful attention to detail. Several thousand dollars worth of narcotics were recovered, as well as a trunk filled with semi-automatic weapons and unopened packages of ammunition with fresh, shiny clips. Detective Goehring called for the coroner to respond and had Lt. Williams and his officers seal off the crime scene with bright yellow and black plastic tape while several other S.W.A.T. officers cleared the immediate tenement building of the scores of curious onlookers who'd gathered outside the door and all around apartment 1313 to catch a glimpse of the aftermath from the terrible gun battle which shattered the peace of their sleepy community.

Meanwhile, only a few miles up Route 202 in the community of Kentland Village, TaKeisha Goddard was awakened from a deep and peaceful morning sleep by the continuously ringing telephone on her nearby nightstand. She had been dreaming … dreaming of she and Kee-Kee laughing together with carefree happiness and enjoying the attention of handsome guys, just before her pleasant night vision was shattered by the shrill, annoying pulse of the phone. She reached out groggily from under her bed sheets for the steadily ringing phone, her fingers fumbled around briefly before landing on the receiver and lifting it off the cradle and to her ear.

"Hello," she answered with a tone tinged with both drowsiness and irritation.

She was greeted by silence, a long silence, lasting nearly an entire fifteen seconds before the caller on the other end finally spoke.

"TaKeisha, you need not to be talkin' to dem polices, feel me? 'Cuz dat some hot shit you doin' right bout now … cut that ole bullshit out befo' you get yo lil' young ass dealt with!"

The line went dead, emitting nothing but a monotonous drone to which TaKeisha hung up immediately. TaKeisha spent over twenty-five minutes frantically trying to find out the identity of the caller who'd just issued a chilling threat against her person. She contacted the operator who could not help her at all. She dialed *69, but to her frustration, all of her efforts were unsuccessful. Once again the phone rang. She checked the caller I.D., but it read "unavailable." TaKeisha felt a sense of fear as she simply sat wrapped up in her satin bed sheets with her back up against the oak wall headboard of her queen-sized bed watching the phone ring several times before her answering machine automatically took over.

"Hi, this is TaKeisha. I'm not available right now, but if you'll be so kind as to leave your name, number, and the time of your call, I promise you that I will get up with you as soon as possible. Thank you. Bye." Bleeep.

"Damn, girl. You stay gone, don't you? And it's only ten minutes after seven in the morning. Guess I'm on military time. I hope you're not out doin' God knows what. Just kidding, little sis. I know you were raised better than that. Anyway, it's your big brother. Hit me up later around about two or two thirty this afternoon. I'll be at Fort Detrick. Bye."

TaKeisha breathed a long sigh of relief that it was just her brother and not the unknown previous caller.

By the time dusk fell on the Beltway region, Lt. Williams' taskforce, with the help of Detective Goehring's detailed leads, rounded up over a dozen crack dealers spread throughout Landover, Landover Hills, and Lanham, all of whom had been linked to the suspect Lucien Valentino.

At 11:47 p.m. that night, a code red, ten-ninety-nine was issued at Jessup's maximum security wing, A tier, cellblock #A26. Inmate #418814A was found lying nude, face down on the floor of his cell. Blood seeped from out of several dozen-stab wounds that were to be found all over his naked form. Blood covered the floor of the shadowy prison cell and leaked out from under the door of the enclosure and out into the hall where it puddled into an icky-looking red pool. Two correctional officers attempted to save Thomas Broome's life via first aid as they awaited help from the nearby paramedics.

"Broome, we gonna help you, baby, awiight? You just gotta hold on for me 'cuz the medical team is on the way right now. But you gotta fight, okay?" one of the guards said to Broome as he worked feverishly to stop the blood loss by cauterizing and patching the wounds of the critically injured criminal.

"Fuck all dat doctor shit you talkin', nigga. I'm bout to die … I know dat and so do you … it's awiight though. It's all part o' da game, champ," Broom said as he spat blood. "I done peeled many a niggas' cap back in my day. I knew it wouldn't be but a matter o' time befo' I fucked around and got got. Know what I'm sayin'? But befo' I die, I'm bringin' dat bitch ass nigga Valentino down, Slim. That triflin' bamma been runnin' up in bitches raw knowin' he got that shit. Plus, he done called me at least three times this past week talkin' bout some lil' young'un he tryin' to take out ... the way the nigga describe the broad I think it's the lil' bitch that P.G. County detective brought up here a lil' while ago. If you know what I know, you better tell P.G. to get that lil' young'un some protection or else she's gonna get her shit pushed back ... believe that!"

The medics arrived seconds after Thomas Broome finished his eye opening revelation right after he also disclosed that it was none other than his so-called friend, Lucien Valentino, who'd arranged for him to be attacked while in prison. Valentino obviously had the money and power to order such a hit. Broome was sent to the Shock Trauma Unit at the University of Maryland where he lingered between life and death for ten days, finally succumbing to his wounds on the 8th day of May 1998, at 10:11 a.m. Thomas Broome had been a monster during most of his life, yet he'd become something of a hero at the end of his lawless existence with a simple disclosure of knowledge that would prove to be invaluable in the HIV5X case.

***

At 9:26 p.m. on May 11, 1998, TaKeisha Goddard had just gotten out of her new Ford Mustang when she took the keys and made her way across the walkway towards her front door. The young woman had no idea that she'd been followed. She'd spent most of the day at work at Riverdale's Department of Agriculture and had stopped past a local supermarket in order to pick up a few groceries in order to prepare a surprise meal for her big brother when he arrived home later on that night.

As TaKeisha approached the door of her mother's Kentland home, the darkened interior and the empty parking spot revealed that her mother had stepped out. The girl fumbled around with the crowed key chain dangling loosely from her leather handbag before finally extracting the correct key from among the jingling, silvery bunch.

Slowly, with a momentary groan, just as TaKeisha stepped inside with an armful of grocery bags, she instinctively reached her hand out towards the wall to the light switch. The overhead ceiling lamp flickered briefly, and then illuminated the beautifully furnished area with a soft white glow. Suddenly, the room went dark and a strong pair of hands seized her aggressively from behind, clasping both her mouth as well as her torso pulling her up against a wall, nearby the door slammed shut with a noisy thud. The girl's eyes went wide with terror as her attacker emerged from the shadows while throwing her down to the floor and kneeling across her as she laid helpless beneath him.

"Don't try to fight back, bitch, cause I don't wanna kill you … at least not yet. All I wanna do is fuck the shit outta you. 'Cuz if you don't already know, I got whatcha call HIV5X … some super killa AIDS type shit. Once I get through shovin' dick up in you, it'll be a done deal, boo. You'll be dead in a coupla months and I'll be long gone. You see, you shouldn't have been runnin' your muthafuckin' mouth to them police and shit about shit you don't know nothin' about. Now, your lil' snitchin' ass about to catch AIDS and die just like your girls, Yasmin and Kee-Kee. How 'bout that?" snarled Valentino into the frightened girl's ear as he unbuckled his jeans while fighting to remove the panties from a desperately fighting TaKeisha.

Although the Landover native was an athletic, robust and feisty young lady, her best efforts at self-defense were no match for the brawn of the rapist who pinned her. As both of Valentino's hands were occupied with vehemently forcing apart TaKeisha's legs, she screamed out with bloodcurdling frenzy. Yet it did not prevent him from following through with his sexual assault of the twenty-four-year-old. The girl kicked wildly and attempted to bite her attacker as he forcefully penetrated her.

His erect, infected member pumped into her with reckless abandon, bringing himself to an overwhelming orgasm that caused Valentino to shudder with gratifying release as he quickly withdrew his dripping manhood from TaKeisha's cum-filled vagina.

"Now, take that one for the team, bitch!" Valentino quipped as he arose, readjusting himself and pulling up his pants. "You know what else? Since I done roughed you off, you ain't worth shit to nobody now. Any damn way ... I ain't never raped no bitch befo', but I tell you what ... it's been jive aiight though. But I can't let you live like this, so I'm about to put you outta your misery, aiight?"

Valentino pulled out a nickel-plated, chrome nine-millimeter that glistened silvery and metallic within the yellow light of the outside street lamp's glow that was filtering in through the blinds and sheer curtains of the bay window to the rear of the house. TaKeisha huddled, whimpering pitifully in the corner near the large leather couch among the scattered fruit, broken eggs, and assorted canned goods of the overturned grocery bags. She begged for her life through streaming tears as Valentino gently stroked her soft, supple cheek and neatly cornrowed locks. He placed a loaded clip into the handgun.

"Don't cry, baby girl. It won't hurt at all. I'm tryin' to tell you I'm gonna put two in your dome piece and it's a wrap after that. Trust me, you ain't gonna feel shit," the rapist said, snickering with evil delight.

Just before Valentino could commit murder, he heard the blaring of what seemed like a multitude of police squad cars racing down Landover Road. Also, there was a series of loud banging outside the front door. The next door neighbors no doubt had overheard the screaming and raucous commotion going on inside and came over to investigate.

"TaKeisha! Mrs. Goddard! It's Earl and Lewis ... are you all aiight?" the young men barked outside as the sirens wailed even closer.

"Help me! Oh, God! Please somebody help me!" TaKeisha cried out at the top of her lungs.

Instantly, the strapping young men crashed into the door, which not being locked, gave way to their combined weight.

"What the fuck, nigga?! Back your bitch ass up off o' TaKeisha!" snarled the neighbor, Earl Givens, who'd flicked on the living room lights.

Without responding, Valentino raised his weapon away from TaKeisha's forehead and toward the broad shouldered dark-complexioned teen with fury written on his face who rushed toward him from across the living room floor. The pistol recoiled violently after discharging two slugs into the chest and abdomen of the hard-charging teenager. Given's body lurched backward as he absorbed the shock of the two bullets that tore into his upper and tower torso. He careened backwards onto the floor and twitched with rapid jerks as his blood seeped into the carpet, staining it a sickly crimson. He was dead within seconds after he'd fallen.

"You, back the fuck up! And go outside to the parking lot, muthafucka! 'Cuz you about to come with me right about now … come on!" Valentino shouted out at Lewis Woodworth, who stood in the entrance of the doorway shell-shocked.

Lewis, with his mouth agape, was still in a state of utter disbelief behind the cold-blooded murder of his best friend. Valentino raced over to the door yanking the sinewy adolescent along by the scruff of his neck and pushed him out towards the parking lot, leaving the abused TaKeisha behind.

With the brightly flashing lights and howling sirens of the P.G. County police less than a few blocks away, Valentino hastened toward an elderly couple pulling up into the parking lot in a white Dodge Ram van. Without hesitation, Valentino forced himself into the backseat of the van, pressing the pistol to the head of the surprised old man as his wife shrieked with fright.

"Get your monkey ass up outta here old man! I need for you to take Martin Luther King Highway toward DC and don't stop 'til I tell you to! You get in the seat next to me, right her, young'un. And grandma, you needs to shut the fuck up with all that damn cryin' and shit befo' I pimp slap your old ass, aiight?" Valentino growled.

The seventy-five-year old driver obediently backed out of the parking lot and proceeded out of Kentland Village and he headed towards MLK Highway in the nick of time, eluding the police. As the van left the parking lot at a steady clip, the entire neighborhood soon was alive with dozens of squad cars with sirens blaring and lights blinking incandescently. Scores of uniformed cops exited the vehicles with their service revolvers drawn as they descended upon the Goddard's home, which was now considered a crime scene. It was there that they discovered a still weeping TaKeisha Goddard alone, soiled, and petrified while the dead body of her eighteen-year-old neighbor lay sprawled out, bloodied and stiff, but a few feet way.

The young woman was comforted by a female officer as another cop radioed in for an ambulance and coroner. The police also surrounded Valentino's car, a metallic bronze 1998 Mitsubishi Eclipse GS with tinted windows, left abandoned at the far right side of the large neighborhood parking lot. The biological murderer had long since sold his BMW and now he'd left his newly acquired vehicle. The police were oblivious as to his current whereabouts. They knew that they'd have to quickly place an all points bulletin to police departments and satellite offices throughout the county before Valentino escaped across the state lines into bordering Washington, DC or Virginia.

Chapter 10

The intentional transmission of HIV/AIDS is considered a crime in many countries. One of modern history's most shocking cases of criminal transmission involved the case of Brian Stewart, an Illinois-based medical student. Stewart deliberately injected his own young son with HIV-tainted blood so that the child's inevitable death would free him from child support, stating coldly that the boy would not survive past five years of age.

TaKeisha Goddard was whisked away by a speeding ambulance towards the Prince George's County Hospital. Once she'd arrived, the paramedics immediately rushed TaKeisha into a very active emergency room where several doctors quickly took to attending her. Several hours later, the young Ms. Goddard awakened to the comforting presence of her older brother, Edward Goddard, who sat but a few inches away from her bedside. Though she was somewhat weak from the earlier attack in conjunction to the sedatives, which had been administered to her by the medical staff, she still reached out to her brother and embraced him tightly while sobbing bitterly in his arms for quite some time.

Edward tried his best to be strong for his beloved baby sister for whom he felt grief that was at the time beyond description. He felt fully responsible for the suffering of so many which now included his own flesh and blood. He hadn't anticipated anything as nightmarish as this. The only things that mattered when he originally took on the responsibility of administering the serum Biomax-O to Valentino, were the riches and fame promised to him by the Illuminati elitists working clandestinely within the scientific hierarchy of the U.S. Army and the World Health Organization. However, that was long before he'd had a chance to actually witness the pure evil of not only the program itself, but of its chosen volunteer, who seemed to relish in bedding as many woman as he possibly could with little or no regard for the dire consequences which would befall them soon afterward. And it dawned on him that as a result of his lust for ill-gotten wealth and career goals he, along with the neo-Nazi scientists, was fully responsible for developing the dreaded elixer that had now unleashed upon the world this new nuclear warhead of viruses, the lethal HIV5X. It was not long before he broke down, crying right along with his sister.

TaKeisha underwent a battery of medical tests in order to determine whether or not she'd contracted the deadly HIV5X during the rape. She received the unpleasant results of the reexaminations; she had indeed tested positive for the swift moving mutated form of HIV. The physicians at the P.G. County Hospital felt impotent and helpless to assist the distraught young woman in the wake of such a monstrous terminal disease. Edward Goddard knew without a second thought what actions had to be taken in order to save his sister's life. Edward allowed his sister to sleep, for she was still both emotionally and physically spent from the events of the past few hours.

The following afternoon, on May 12, TaKeisha was discharged from the county hospital. As she was driven home, her brother informed her of his decision to cure her. TaKeisha listened intently as her brother divulged every single detail of the covert and illegal "Operation: Inner City Virus," as well as his role in the development and distribution of the highly controversial, untested drug known as Biomaximus Officinalis. During his disclosure of his government-funded experiment, he told of his secretive meeting with former Gulf War hero turned dope pusher, Lucien Valentino. While his sister continued to listen with slack-jawed disbelief, Edward described the violence, tyranny and fear that his hood-rich host visited upon both his enemies as well as employees, and at one particular occasion, even Edward himself.

By the time they pulled up into the driveway of a luxurious Lanham Hilton Grand Hotel, where they checked into while the police continued to treat their Kentland house as a crime scene, TaKeisha's head was spinning. When they entered the spacious hotel suite, their mother, Olivia, greeted them. Eddie again had to go through the difficult and exhaustive process of repeating his story of covert government operations, experimental drugs and a virulent new strain of AIDS known as HIV5X and the fugitive responsible for purposely spreading it amongst the local black population at will, creating the current medical state of emergency within the community.

"Keisha, I've got to start your injections ASAP. Without it you will surely die," her brother informed her. "These shots will allow you to live a fully normal life just as long as you continue to take your Biomax-O injections twice each month … at the beginning and near the end of the month for the rest of your life. I know it sounds tough, but hey, you'll live. Now your sex life will be truly challenging because within your body, the HIV5X antibodies will react like full blown AIDS, only more aggressive and fast acting. Any person coming into contact with your vaginal secretions or blood will put themselves at a ninety percent risk of contracting HIV5X. After which time, if they are not immediately treated with the serum of Biomax-O, the virus will quickly take hold within a week or so after transmission. The highly aggressive microbes will then fully annihilate the host's immune system, and at this point the victim would have full blown AIDS. He or she would then sicken, waste away and die within a very short span of time ...usually three months or less."

TaKeisha and her mother embraced while fighting to absorb everything in which they were hearing. It was almost surreal to the mother and daughter that this was actually happening. Yet TaKeisha had little choice but to receive the injection of Biomax-O which her brother had pleaded with her to accept.

As Eddie removed his medical kit, TaKeisha braced herself in order to take the shot of Biomax-O that Eddie warned her would be unpleasant at first. Eddie drew a hollow tube from his black leather bound medic kit. He then attached a narrow, long hypodermic needle onto the end of the plastic tube. A few drops of silver, mercury-like fluid squirted from the tip of the needle as Eddie quickly tapped the container before kneeling down beside his sister and taking her outstretched arm into his hand.

"TaKeisha, I love you so much. I am so sorry that this had to happen to you … I really am. But I will be damned if I ever let you die on me!"

Olivia Goddard held her daughter tight as her son slid the shiny metallic needle into his sister's vein. TaKeisha winced momentarily as the initial prick of the needle pierced her flesh. She then shrieked out in agony as the serum made contact with her blood stream. Hysterical with burning pain throughout her lithe, young body, TaKeisha had to be held down by both her mother and brother as she kicked, thrashed and twisted about wildly. Though her discomfort lasted for no longer than a minute or two, it seemed more like an eternity in hell for the young woman who afterwards drifted off to sleep following a long, hot bath. She was now also a participant, albeit unwillingly, of the illicit "Operation: Inner City Virus."

Chapter 11

There are several scientists and other members of the medical community worldwide who truly believe in the persistent theory that AIDS is a man-made disease created for the sole purposes of population control and bio-warfare research. These esteemed international doctors are in a minority who claim that the U.S. government, via the Tuskegee Syphilis Study and MKULTRA, has in the past demonstrated a willingness to experiment on unsuspecting citizens without their knowledge or consent.

On May 13, 1998, District police officers recovered the bodies of Valentino's three hostages near the 14th Street Bridge. All three corpses were removed charred and blackened beyond possible recognition from the smoking smoldering Dodge van that sat near the bottom of the bridge itself. The victims had all been shot execution-style in the back of the head, presumably by Valentino before he in turn torched the gasoline-covered vehicle.

After two days of intensive research, it was determined that the suspect, Lucien Valentino had taken a late night flight by private plane back to Puerto Rico. This was determined upon interviewing the air traffic controllers and staff at the small Virginia-based airstrip dubbed "McGee's Airport," located just outside the much larger Dulles.

"That bastard Valentino has beaten us to the punch! He's left the mainland, but with all the murders and a rape here in the DC area we've got linked to him, there is absolutely no way I'm gonna let that animal get away scot-free. I'll do everything I can to get into the ear of the FBI and the proper U.S. Military Police to hunt him down and bring him to justice," Detective Goehring announced to Lt. Williams as they sat in Williams' brightly lit office.

Lt. Williams nodded in agreement to the words of his good friend, and then took a stack of paperwork on Don Lucien Valentino from off his work-cluttered desk. The lieutenant sipped the last of the black coffee he'd been slowly drinking and placed the mug down as he arose to walk over to the window at the far end of the room. He stared out of it, looking across the street in solemn thought before speaking.

"Yeah, you're right, detective … but we better hurry up with whatever we do, 'cause this cat is a living, breathing weapon. And it's no telling how many more folks are gonna die if we or somebody, anybody don't get this fool off the fuckin' streets."

Both men sat afterward in silence, each acknowledging the seriousness of the task that stood before them. It took less than a week for Detective Goehring and Lt. Williams to acquire the proper arrest warrants necessary in order to travel with both the FBI and a contingent of military police to Puerto Rico in a concentrated attempt to apprehend Valentino. The U.S. Army's passenger plane carrying P.G. County police Detective Goehring, Lt. Williams, Dr. Edward Goddard and company, landed at the base in Old San Juan at approximately 6:45 p.m. on May 17, 1998.

Once the crew of law enforcement officers exited the plane with their equipment, they met with the local San Juan authorities for thirty-five minutes, detailing a map of La Perla's slum neighborhood and the surrounding jungle terrain in which Valentino's property would be located from the La Perla gate boundaries.

"I know exactly where Valentino lives and I know by now how to get here," Edward stated. "We don't need these local, yokel cops playin' tour guide for us, because hell, they're every bit as crooked and criminal as the drug runners themselves. Valentino practically runs the whole fuckin' department here in Old San Juan. No—hell no! There ain't no way I'm lettin' these fake ass cops lead us anywhere." Dr. Goddard exploded angrily as he pointed over towards the small group of Puerto Rican policemen whose previously calm demeanor was now replaced by sullen, hostile looks that followed him as he walked around the base venting.

Detective Goehring quickly made his way over to the fuming young physician, taking him over to the far end of the yard near a row of Army jeeps.

"Look, doc, you gotta keep it together, alright?" Goehring warned him. "I know that you're goin' through a tough time right now. We all are. Yeah, these few months have been one helluva roller coaster ride, kid. But we need you of all people to stay calm, okay? If you know how to get out to that scumbag Valentino's place, then hey, let's get up the road, my friend. I agree with you about these shady cops out here; the fuzz down here in Puerto Rico has always been notorious for corruption and illegal activities. So, don't worry, they're not involved in this case of ours. They'll only provide questions to our answers, got it? Now, c'mon, let's go bag this creep before it's too late."

Reluctantly, the young doctor silently shook his head in agreement and followed the detective back over towards the awaiting military cops. By 8:00 a.m. a convoy of Army jeeps loaded with armed military police set of toward the distant palm tree shrouded valley which lay the turbulent projects of La Perla, where scores of savage drug-dealing gunmen patrolled every single nook and cranny throughout the dirt poor housing area.

As the eight jeep military convoy reached the rusted, front gates at the neighborhood entrance, local lookouts—mostly young children no older than ten or eleven—raced back through the streets whistling loudly and yelling out the grim warning of Policía! to their armed employers, who quickly tossed the bulk of their neatly packaged narcotics behind bushes, garbage cans and down storm drains while the dealers themselves raced to take cover within the run-down tenement buildings and behind dense foliage nearby.

The roaring jeeps commandeered by solemnly staring MPs bearing camouflaged M16 rifles thundered pass the residents of La Perla, who looked on in silence as the camouflaged vehicles rolled along in route to the exit and rainforest beyond their hood.

The normally confrontational La Perla's drug dealers realized quickly that to fire upon such a heavily-armed force would spell certain death for them, so they calmly remained in their hiding spaces, holed up watching as the U.S. military proceeded down the street and through the exit untouched. The journey through the jungle proved to be more scenic for the soldier cops more than anything else. After no more than thirty minutes, the convoy came out of the rainforest and into the clearing where the golden rods of prairie grass waved and leaned in the late evening breeze giving rise to the huge mobile home unit in the foreground.

Chapter 12

Although modern science has discovered an understanding of the disease at its core, HIV continues to wreak havoc on minority communities in America's inner cities and rural areas largely due to poverty, a lack of education and little or no medical care. Risky behavior such as intravenous drug use, secretive bi-sexual activity widely known as "the down low" and inconsistent condom usage all work to hasten the spread of the virus throughout black America's poorest communities.

At long last the officers arrived on Lucien Valentino's property. The armed MPs followed by Detective Goehring, Lt. Williams, and Dr. Goddard charged through the gates encircling Valentino's unit of trailers swarming through the drug lord's flawlessly manicured Japanese rock garden in route to his double wide. The front door gave way before the violent entry of the Army police officers as they burst into Valentino's home yelling out orders in both English and Spanish. However, even they were unprepared for what they would discover within as well as throughout the premier mobile home. Dozens of dead bodies, primarily those of Hispanic women, many barely out of their teens, lay bloated and stinking in the trailers and out on the pristine lawn. The unfortunate women, who had served as Valentino's prostitutes and maids had suddenly become expendable in the wake of their employer's impending arrest.

Of the thirty-four corpses, most were found to have been shot to death. However, others had been poisoned with a lethal heavy metal known as thallium that was identified during the following autopsies. Valentino, it seemed, had once again foiled his pursuers, thus escaping arrest and causing Goehring, Williams and Goddard to react with animated profanity as the realization of yet another get away by the infected dope peddler brought their frustration to the forefront. After the U.S. Army secured the crime scene and removed the bodies for identification, the cops assembled outside the abandoned compound.

"Well, there's nothing more for us to see or do here any longer, men. Let's move 'em out," barked a husky voiced Army Sergeant as he leaned out of the passenger's side window of the lead jeep while the engine loudly hummed in unison with the other dark green vehicles. With frustration, anger and heavy hearts the trio from Landover, Maryland joined the crew of Army officers within the jeep convoy that trailed away one after the other back through the rugged, jungle pathway again toward the mean streets of La Perla.

***

When the jeeps motored out of the wild tangled undergrowth of the jungle trail, the head driver noticed two ragged looking peasants standing on top of a beat up hooptie waving their spindly arms frantically in an effort to bring the jeeps to a stop. Signaling the other drivers to stop, the sergeant stepped outside of his vehicle with weapon drawn as he commanded the Puerto Rican men to step down from the hood of the car. As the men hopped down onto the rocky, dirt road with their hands raised high above their heads in compliance to the orders of the policeman, they continuously jabbered away in broken Spanish, obviously attempting to explain something of great importance to the military cops who, because of their ignorance of Spanish, were totally oblivious, hearing nothing more than senseless rambling.

"Dr. Goddard, we need your help up here so we can figure out what in the hell these two are freakin' out about," stated a loud-mouthed M.P. as he watched two of his officers pat the men down thoroughly.

Within minutes after introducing himself to the Puerto Ricans in Spanish, Dr. Goddard was in awe upon hearing the men's story.

"Valentino ... he's no good. He has made many of our daughters, sisters and nieces drug addicts and whores. He has brought nothing but evil, addiction and death to La Perla. His money keeps the drug dealers and other bandits rich while La Perla's poor starve in the streets. Don Valentino is despised by all except the criminals who prey upon our people. Please, we beg of you, sir, please help us ... we beg of you. I cannot bear to watch my people suffer at the hands of that animal any longer."

Dr. Goddard first assured both men that their nightmare would soon be over and then he interpreted the men's tale to the awaiting soldiers who stood around listening with interest to what the men had to say. The peasants told a tale of almost nonstop violence and intimidation since Valentino entered the barrio with his rugged band of desperadoes. After twenty minutes of dime-dropping, the military police had more than enough proof of their suspect's whereabouts to move in for the capture. The convoy of jeeps sped along the dusty, shrub-covered prairie as the rusted jalopy before them raced toward La Perla.

Upon their approach, as usual roof-top lookouts whistled and yelled out frantic warnings down to the various groups of drug dealers who responded accordingly by scattering, seeking shelter behind and inside the surrounding tenement buildings. Once inside the vicinity of the slums, the military lawmen brought their vehicles to an abrupt halt upon the command of the lead officer. The two resident snitches leaped out of their rickety whip and raced over toward the first jeep.

"Señor, Señor ... he is there! There, in that gray building," the first man cried, excitedly pointing as his companion nodded in enthusiastic agreement.

The building, an aged, ugly, broken-down monstrosity of a structure in which a dozen or so harsh looking street thugs crowded about the steps of the front door staring toward the soldier cops with unmoving insolence, was in the heart of La Perla.

"Listen up, you kids, get off of the stoop and go home now!" the beefy Army sergeant bellowed through his bullhorn as he stood in the middle of the street between the drug dealers and his soldiers.

"Amigo, we cannot do that because it is you gringo bastard who is the fuckin' enemy, know what I mean?" a tank top wearing muscle bound youth snapped amidst the vocal agreements and hand slapping of his tattooed comrades.

Somewhat taken aback by the brazen defiance of the Puerto Rican youngsters, the soldiers tightened up on the grips of their rifles as their leader who appeared to be flushed red with anger again rose the bullhorn to his mouth.

"This is your final warning! You will cease and desist with your insubordination or face consequences of a most dire nature. Now get up off of the stoop and take your spick asses home ... NOW!"

The Puerto Rican gangstas stood their ground looking on with rebellious courage, daring the military police to make the first move.

"Fuck this shit! I'm goin' up in that muhfuckas!" Lt. Williams announced bluntly as he charged ahead without warning.

Lt. Williams raced towards the group of assorted thugs as they began rattling off round after round of white-hot lead. As he ran up on the blockade of human shields, seven gangstas immediately fell from the stoop as they were peppered by dozens of metal encased rounds, Lt. Williams could not see amidst the spray. The onrushing Prince George's County police lieutenant was savagely mowed down by gunfire raining down upon him from the upper windows and rooftop of the apartment building. That was all it took to send the slum unit into an uproar of chaotic turmoil.

The deafening clatter of semi-automatic gunfire echoed throughout the surrounding complex, frightening the hell out of the terrified residents who huddled together, praying tearfully as the gun battle raged outside their doors. Men fell wounded and dead on both sides as the acrid smell of gun smoke filled the late evening air. The criminals of La Perla proved to be more formidable than the U.S. Army expected, prompting one overzealous young M.P. to aim a rocket launcher at the building in which the rebellious drug dealers were holed up.

With perspiration beading his heavy brow, the tender-aged soldier drew a bead on the building that held the hated Lucien Valentino and tried hard to ignore the drumbeat-like thumping of his heart. Sweat had now trickled down his chiseled face and into his eyes which stung causing him to blink erratically, he felt the cold rubber stock against his strong jaw and tightened his grip on the bulky weapon in his grasp. The bull's eyes came within view and the twenty-two-year old gunner breathed in deeply held it ... then exhaled as he squeezed the trigger sending a projectile with the explosive power of two hundred and fifty pounds of TNT speeding into the old decrepit tenement building at sixty-seven miles per hour. As the rocket penetrated the building, it went up in a fiery, red orange mushroom cloud of flame and smoke accompanied by a resounding boom that literally shook the earth beneath the target building for over a mile and a half. The soldiers dropped instinctively to the ground as the building exploded.

For more than three hours the destroyed ruins of the tenement buildings billowed thick, pungent black plumes of smoke that hovered above La Perla. After several hours had passed, the U.S. Army, with the assistance of Old San Juan's metro police, recovered what they believed to be the broken and charred remains of Don Lucien Octavius Valentino from the smoking pile of bloody rubble that had once been an apartment building. Thirty-two bodies were brought out from the crater of the damaged tenement site, and were identified and tagged as those of various neighborhood drug dealers who'd given their lives in defense of Valentino.

Lt. Jeremy Williams, unfortunately, lost his life as well. He suffered over twenty-seven gunshot wounds to his head and upper body as he blindly charged the door in anger. In an effort to get at the man who had murdered both the mother and aunt of his young son, who now would be raised to adulthood by Williams' older sister, Rhonda Williams-Steed and her husband Terrance.

Edward Goddard testified before a grand jury in the U.S. Supreme Court, detailing before startled jurors and court officials alike the intricate workings of the abominable "Operation: Inner City Virus." Seventeen members of the World Health Organization were indicted on several felony counts of "malicious use of controlled biochemical agents" amongst the unsuspecting public. Each count carried a sentence of no less than twenty-five years to life in a federal prison, including the revoking of each individual's license to practice medicine anywhere in the world ever again. Only Dr. Goddard was allowed to continue to distribute the Biomaximus Officainalis in order to treat his young sister's illness.

TaKeisha Goddard would go on to graduate from Bowie State University, and on July 11, 2002, she'd marry her college sweetheart, DeShawn Warner. The handsome couple would then produce three healthy boys, Markus, Mario, and Jason. DeShawn also would be treated with Biomax-O by his brother-in-law. However, amazingly, the children of DeShawn and TaKeisha Warner would test negative for the lethal HIV5X.

Detective Goehring and his wife Diane would set up a charity fund for the treatment of HIV/AIDS in the honor of the fallen Lt. Jeremy Williams. Goehring continues to be a major force in the prevention of crime in Prince George's County, Maryland, as well as the poster boy for community AIDS awareness. However, the staunch P.G. County detective received a most disturbing email on November 30, 2002. It read:

Dear Taylor Goehring:
You have caused significant difficulty in the development and perfection of one of the most promising experiments ever known to man with the sole exception being the racial cleansing experiments performed by Der Führer Adolf Hitler during the early days of World War II. There are those who are nothing more than cattle on this earth to be used as subjects for science's sake. You have not destroyed all of us and as a result, we shall continue our Biomax-O experiments elsewhere. Many of the infected would love nothing more than life via our

special biochemical injections. The communities consisting primarily of gay men, minorities and poor whites (who are also expendable), are found throughout the Western hemisphere in great abundance will be choice target areas for our operations to set up and begin our objectives. You cannot stop us, detective, for this is much, much bigger than you and your small community. So I thank you and bid you farewell.

Sincerely,
Sentinels of the Illuminati

Detective Goehring sighed deeply as he stared solemnly at the glowing computer screen.

"Damn … when will this nightmare ever end?" he groaned, shaking his head wearily. Deep inside, the battle-weary detective knew the bitter truth; the nightmare had just begun.

Deadly Phine : Part II

"The AIDS Man Cometh"

Chapter 13

Rosaria Gonzalez took a deep drag off of a partially finished joint before crushing the roach underfoot. Lariat, California, a bustling mid-sized town of 878,000, was especially busy and active after dark, offering even the most discriminating night owls an eclectic variety of nocturnal fun. The sassy Latina exhaled a plume of marijuana smoke and sashayed with a saucy confidence across the crowded street. She smiled as she passed several young men who whistled and called sexually explicit comments her way as she bounced along. She was hot and bothered and the building moisture between her shapely thighs beckoned to be quenched with an urgency bordering on obsession. She quickened her pace as she recognized the familiar outline of the dark sport utility vehicle ahead.

Dorian Stoppard, a local real estate broker, had lost affection for Jillian, his wife of five years, and as a result showed her little attention. It was an agonizing time for the 25-year old computer programmer from Las Vegas, and eventually led her into the arms of her equally unhappily married supervisor, Seth Corman III. The adulterous lovers had been in the midst of a passionately lustful affair for the better half of six months now, and had discovered a fetish for swinging. The sexual kink which would lead them into the clutches of Lucien Valentino.

Strutting along with sexy allure, clad in her form-fitting hot pink cat suit, Rosaria licked her thick, pouty lips seductively. She looked forward to indulging with her well-hung beau and these two young good-looking fuck partners. It was always exciting having sex with perfect strangers. In fact, she had dubbed it "Extreme Fucking."

Toward the end of the Hunter Boulevard, far from the hubbub of the Cobblestone District, the pine green Ford Denali sat stoically. Though the huge truck seemed inert, the fogged up windows spoke volumes of the goings-on between the two occupants. Rosaria applied an extra coat of cherry red lipstick from a small vanity pack before stuffing it back down into a pink purse that swung loosely from her tanned shoulder. She smiled mischievously as she drew near the Denali. The lovers inside were already at it with lascivious hunger, and their impassioned moans and groans left little to the imagination. The Latin vixen stepped up to the passenger's side of the vehicle, placing her perfectly manicured hand on the back door handle. It gently opened; they'd been expecting her for quite some time now.

As she stepped into the sexually steamy SUV cabin and shut the door behind her, she was overcome with carnal heat by the sight and sounds of the naked couple grinding together in a sweat-drenched union of flesh-on-flesh delight up in the spacious front seat. She was relatively new to this realm of eroticism and thus overly excited, wherein her man Valentino, who'd experienced nearly every type of sexual fetish there was, approached these freak shows with a sense of normalcy that she found fascinating. Slowly, she began to peel off her tight-fitting outerwear, sliding the leather material down past her sizable young breasts and WASP-like waist. She wiggled free from the form-fitting cat suit, and it slid down past her wide hips and bootilicious bubble butt, falling into a pink pile at her feet on the floor of the truck.

The intense lovemaking of the youthful pair in front of her grew with each tongue twisting kiss and each strong hip thrust into a fiery furnace of unbridled lust. Rosaria could take no more. She impulsively crawled halfway over the leather seat separating her from her coupling comrades, taking Jillian's soft white hand into her own, coaxing both her and her beau to join her in the roomier backseat. Like willing sex slaves, the sweaty lovers climbed over the seats until they both joined Rosaria in a sultry threesome. Jillian's breasts were perky and firm with erect pink nipples. Rosaria's full red lips parted to suckle upon them, bringing a sudden shudder of pleasure from the pretty, green-eyed brunette panting beside her. Her moans of passion made Jillian all the more horny as she slid the index and middle fingers of her free hand in and out of Rosaria's dripping cunt. The entire cabin of the Denali was a virtual symphony of gasps, groans and heavy breathing in conjunction with the distinct smack of flesh-on-flesh. Jillian's eyes closed as she achieved orgasm with Seth penetrating her forcefully from the rear while Rosaria kneaded her tits and met her open mouth with a tongue-probing caress. "Oh, fuck yeah," Rosaria groaned.

During those lust-filled first fifteen minutes, the combination of Seth's stiff dick and Rosaria's wicked tongue and burrowing fingers had brought Jillian at least five mind-blowing orgasms. Rosaria was thoroughly enjoying her role in this mini-spectacle of wanton debauchery for more reasons than one, tasting the sweet nectar of Jillian's femininity while simultaneously taking in the rigid satisfaction of Seth's lengthy manhood as he pounded her from behind.

Rosaria couldn't help, however, but to think about the hellish existence that the pair would go through after this night of unrivaled ecstasy ended. The first signs of skin lesions, night sweats and rapid weight loss would come quickly, and they'd be a grim reminder of their night of lewd behavior.

Seth's thrusts became stronger, more vigorous as he drew closer to the point of no return. He threw his head back grunting with bestial joy as he shot his load deep into Rosaria's tight, moist love tunnel. Slowly, his sweaty, pale, nude form slid against the cool leather of the back seat, his chest rising and falling with obvious exhaustion. Jillian caressed the outline of his strong jaw that bore the faint silhouette fo a five-o'clock shadow. He wore it that way because she found it sexy. Both lovers were sexually spent and simply laid in one another's arms, basking in the solitude of the moment.

Rosaria sat beside the two love birds, smiling as she gazed upon them while they cuddled lovingly. Slowly, she began to slip into her satin panties, which lay crumpled on the floor of the vehicle. Valentino would soon request her presence and if she was not present when he expected her, it could get ugly. She must always remember that she was an escort and her man Valentino a manager of adult fantasies . . . pimps and hos were terms he chose to abandon in describing his occupation. His vocabulary was more refined than that.

With her hot pink cat suit back on, Rosaria slipped on her pink stiletto-heeled pumps and stepped out from the SUV $800 richer. She briskly made her way back across the dark, winding street toward the brightly lit cobblestone street, on through the boisterous crowd and into the parking garage on the opposite side. She flashed a quick smile, but breezed past the Ethiopian attendant, whose attempt at flirtatious small talk fell on deaf ears. She disappeared down the ramp's walkway toward her awaiting vehicle. Five minutes later, Rosaria's champagne colored '91 Ford Taurus climbed the steep ramp, pausing briefly at the parking booth where she paid her fee before cruising beneath the raised gate and onward onto Pelco Way.

It was 12:57 a.m. already and Valentino had said that she was to meet him no later than 1:00 a.m. She did not want to disappoint him. She did 55 mph all the way down Pelco Way, even running two red lights and a stop sign in her haste to make the arrival deadline. Besides, she needed a fix. She'd savored the last $50 bag of blow in the glove compartment and the delightful giddy rush had washed over her, but was now declining slowly. It was time for yet another shot of Biomax-O as well. Twice a month seemed like a bit much to the Hispanic sex kitten, but she knew she had no choice now but to submit to the injections. It was either that or death.

Up ahead, she could see the well-dressed form of her man waiting outside of Fontaine's Pool Hall. He leaned up against the lamppost near the front of the building. The pool hall, a favorite local haunt of Valentino's, had just closed ten minutes earlier . . . she was late. Even though it was a late August night, the rains from Mexico earlier in the week had rendered the southern California temperature unseasonably cool, particularly after dark, and so the distinguished white SLAVER? was dressed in the light Sean Jean sweater on the cool, crisp night.

Rosaria pulled up to the curb and exited the car, racing over to the curly haired, handsome man calmly standing out front. Puffing on a cigarette, she threw her darkly tanned arms around him and kissed his face profusely while apologizing for her tardiness. He looked upon her with deep set, piercing eyes and a gaze that seemed to sear her very soul with its intensity. He did not return her affectionate caresses, nor did he take her into his strong arms as she'd wished. Yet, he was not angry; it was just the way he was . . . the tall, dark silent type.

Without being told, Rosaria relinquished both the car keys and the night's earnings, which she placed gingerly into his open palm, a crumpled pile of green from her purse that dangled off her shoulder. The two entered the car slowly and drove away, down the dimly lit street, leaving the brightly flickering neon sign of the pool hall. Velvety smooth R&B ballads from the likes of R. Kelly, Usher and Mary J. Blige lulled Rosaria closer to the man she adored as he navigated his way through the highways and byways of the busy San Diego suburb. While his young Hispanic lover nestled snugly against him as he drove along, he was lost in thought--thoughts that consisted of stacked paper.

"Girl, you lucky you'se a good earner, or else I'd dump you' lil' spick ass on the side of the road fa sho'. You know that, right?" he said, chuckling softly before tossing his finished cigarette out of the open window, into the crisp darkness.

Rosaria's Mexican sassiness flared briefly as she smacked Valentino playfully on his shoulder, to which he laughed a bit harder, using his free arm to fend off his girlfriend's joking assault.

"Naw, I'm just fuckin' witcha . . . baby, you did good tonight. Real good, Mami."

He leaned over and kissed her gently on her forehead.

"Muchas gracias, Papi."

He smiled broadly as he refocused his attention on the lonely highway ahead, bobbing his head to the rhythm of the slow jams coming from the speakers. "You should have seen me back at the hall, Rosy. I was breakin' them cats left and right for their scrilla. At the end o' the night I walked away with over a grand—easy money, like robbin' niggas without a gun," he said with burgeoning pride swelling within his chest. "Ain't shit better than a fist full o' dollars . . . not even pussy."

He turned off onto Rock Hudson Parkway, lip-synching to Prince's hauntingly seductive "Scandalous" as he hooked the wide right. Slowly, Devine leaned over toward Rosaria, sending a shock through her as he brushed her thick, raven black hair back from her ear.

"Did you enjoy yourself earlier tonight? Did you cum hard and often?"

She fidgeted uneasily in her seat. Even though she had enjoyed the experience, as she always did, it still made her uncomfortable to tell him the details of her trysts. Somehow talking about it made her feel more like his whore and less like his girl, and that hurt.

"It was . . . well, it was okay, Papi, but I would've liked it more if you were there with me. Comprendè?"

The debonair pimp winked an eye at his blushing girl, who stared up at him with big, hazel eyes, searching his own for some trace of compassion.

"Well," Valentino said, "I do know one thing—you got their money and they've got your virus. But don't never feel bad 'bout that, baby, 'cause they're both cheaters, right? Shit, I'm quite certain that Jillian Stoppard's husband would sing your praises for givin' that cheatin' ho the kiss o' death. Don't ya think? That's some real shit for your ass. Hopefully he don't fuck her from this point on or else he's gonna be a dead man walkin'."

"Yeah, yeah I know, Papi. I know," she answered softly. A tear welled up in her eye and trickled down her cheek as she placed her head against the comfort of Valentino's cardigan sweater.

"Rosy . . . Rosy, I know you ain't cryin', are you? I dunno what for 'cause as long as you're with me you gonna live a long, long time, ya hear me? A long time . . . ya see, those Biomax-O shots that we take—they keeps us alive and healthy, right? Fuck everybody else, Rosy. Fuck 'em! Ya see the Army didn't give a shit 'bout me. All I was to them . . . I guess I was a pawn in their great big, ole' chessboard. So they used me and then cast me aside. So at this point I'm gonna use Tupac's motto: 'Fuck the world.'"

Rosaria said nothing in response. She fully realized the deadly circumstances that lay in wait for anyone unfortunately enough to lie down with her. Anyone not properly inoculated against the ravages of the fiercely aggressive HIV5X through the medium of Biomaxumus Officianalus would be a suicide waiting to happen.

Valentino sung the remainder of Prince's classic with a seductive hint of raunchiness worthy of his Royal Badness himself. Rosaria loved to hear him sing to her. His silky sweet voice reminded her of the old Marvin Gaye records she listened to as a child. As an adult, Valentino's crooning always made her hot.

As they arrived in Middletown, the illuminated 7-11 sign was a welcome sight, as was the lonely Howard Johnson's hotel, just off the entrance of Interstate 99. Rosaria moved closer to her man, resting her head up against his warm, hard body, basking in the sweet bliss of love.

Slowly, the Ford Taurus creeped up against the curb just under a streetlight. Rosaria stirred slightly, opening one of her big eyes to take in the surrounding scenery. She didn't care where they were as long as she was with Valentino, she thought, yet she did feel slightly drowsy from the six mixed drinks she'd had earlier at the Tiki Hut. Luckily, she'd eaten a beef and bean burrito before her date, which had soaked up some of the alcohol. If she hadn't, shed be in real trouble now, but still, she thought, she was tipsy.

She needed a few lines of blow to take the edge off. She knew Valentino could give it to her, but she'd have to e patient. Her handsome lover could be unpredictable and moody. Begging him for a fix could send him into one of his dark fits. She loved how he fed her three or four lines of coke, all the while fucking her in the ass as she sniffed the powdery white happiness up her nose.

She placed a diamond ring-encircled hand up to her pouty red lips to suppress a liquor-induced belch. She smiled with mild embarrassment and sat up, opening the passenger's side window to take in a breath of the cool night air coming off the

Pacific. She realized that soon she'd have to spread her shapely legs once again in order to secure the money that kept Valentino happy with her.

Instinctively, she pulled down the sun visor and peeked into the small, square, mirrored window. She teased her dark hair carefully, and licked her lips after applying yet another layer of candy apple red lipstick.

Just then, a late-model Trans Am eased up beside the car on the driver's side. A black and metallic copper-toned beauty, likely an '81 or '82, the car purred like a kitten as the giggling girls in the back seat chatted non-stop amongst themselves. There was a brief discussion of price between the Trans Am's driver and Valentino, and then the driver, a portly man, left mumbling angrily to himself, speeding off into the dark distance.

The going price for Rosaria was apparently a little steep for the middle-aged lech to afford, and he failed to secure the Latin beauty for the lower rate he'd been hoping for. It didn't matter to Valentino, as he'd made plenty form the illicit services of his pretty companion during the past few weeks. One cheap sale denied would not cost him much. Besides, he thought, he was drowsy and really only wanted his warm bed as he drove away toward their modest hideaway a few miles up the highway.

Chapter 14

Wilhelm Von Strecker, M.D., stared intently at a glass vial filled with tainted blood marked BVV/SVV hemoblobin #2. It contained a carefully mixed byproduct of Bovine Visna virus and Sheep Visna virus, which would be used to mass-produce the lethal HIV5X. Strecker peered at a sample of the mixture under a lab microscope. There, as expected, the man-made mixture joined with the healthy human blood and began rapidly mutating. It infected the healthy blood with its own tainted antibodies, adding HIV5X proteins into the hemoglobin's cellular makeup and soon transformed the bright red blood spot on the clear petri dish to a deep indigo. Streckler voiced his anger just as two fellow members of the Sentinels of the Illuminati entered the brightly lit laboratory.

"You've been working at perfecting that one serum for the last three days, Wil. What's the problem now?" Rueben Mintz, a senior member of hate group, asked.

Wilhelm frowned with the frustration wrought from untold hours of tedious research. Seth Johnson, the lone member of the World Health Organization who was present at the time, stroked his heavy gray beard while observing the vials of the HIV5X lining the countertop next to a small flowchart of human blood types.

"That's enough of the virus to wipe out more than half of the undesirables in San Diego alone . . . Excellent." Seth smiled slow and evil as he walked past the bottles of lab-created death. "Adolf Hitler would have been pleased...yes, very, very pleased, der Fuhrer would've been."

"Where's Meredith?" asked Wilhelm.

At this point he'd need a veteran molecular biologist to assist him with the more advanced stages of the experiment.

"I'm already on it, Wil," Meredith called while double testing a sample of HIV5X-tainted hemoglobin.

"Don't worry, Wil, we'll get both the perfect disease for the masses of undesirables, as well as the perfect cure for the all-important carriers."

"Have you already tested the new serum on any human or animal hosts?

"I used rodent and primate test subjects in '99. I finally got a chance to use the new serum on a human subject six months ago. It was the same heroin scumbag who was willing to be my guinea pig for drug money. He developed HIV after two injections. He's now ill with full-blown AIDS and will surely be a goner by November. However, it's the same old HIV5X that we've been recycling since 1987. So, I'm still hard at work trying to perfect the strain to churn out a virus that has a greater kill rate than what we're used to . . . HIV10X, if you will."

Wilhelm and Meredith stared at each other, briefly considering the course in which they'd go in search of upgrading the current AIDS culture. Meredith Nader was never one to quite find satisfaction with the first few results of clinical trials anyway, and this was just another stark example of her perfectionist behavior.

"You know what? What type of data did you get from the blood samples you took from the chimps you tested a few months ago?" she asked with curiosity.

"Chimps? What chimps? Do you mean the ones from the western part of Central Africa?" Wilhelm asked.

"Yes, Wil," Meredith continued, "the P.T. troglodyte chimps, remember?"

The slim German grinned at his own forgetfulness. He'd recently been binge drinking, as well as working well into the early morning hours, and it had started to show.

He opened up a small silver flash drive and placed it quickly into the hard drive of his desktop computer. Meredith looked on, anxiously awaiting an answer. He glanced at his computer screen and began tapping away at the keyboard or a few short minutes.

"There . . . I've forwarded my findings on that experiment to you in its entirety. I found a type of Simian immuno-deficiency virus that was very similar to HIV-1, found primarily in humans. I identified this one strain in June from a few samples which I'd cryogenetically preserved."

Wilhelm smiled as he relayed his scientific findings to his fellow researcher, while steadily moving his slender, pale fingers upon the keys below. Wilhelm was sure that with his latest find the already virulent HIV5X could be rendered even more deadly.

"What do you think?" Wilhelm asked as he leaned back in his swivel chair, watching Meredith reader her email.

"I think that you're a freakin' genius! Way to go, Wil!" Meredith manipulated the mouse across the pad, scrolling down the pages of scientific formulas and typed summaries, positively beaming with delight. "Now all we have to do is finish up successfully and we'll be millionaires!"

"Sure," Wilhelm said, "if we ever get the fucking microbes to act right then we're in business, however it's been a crapshoot so far."

"Well, then we just have to try harder, Wil! The Sentinels are entrusting us with this population control venture. Do you know what that means?! We not only become overnight tycoons, but we'll go down in history as perhaps the greatest scientists since the Nazi party's, Josef Mengale, the angel of death himself. We are gods, Wil...gods! We hold the very secrets of life and death within our grasp. We have both the microbes to wipe out half of the earth's population, and the cure to prevent the disease from killing its host!

"This work," she continued, flushed red as she spoke with passion, " must be completed. There is no other way. With international threats such as red China and India growing economically stronger, not to mention populating the planet by vast numbers year in and year out, we must develop a source of population control to reduce this threat as much as possible."

Rueben spoke up from across the room, saying, "I think what we have goin' with the HIV5X is working well for now."

"You might be satisfied with it, Reuben," Meredith answered, "but I'm not. I'm not and neither are the elders of the Illuminati. Right now HIV5X kills within a span of two to three months, and that's way too much time to let pass. Besides, our test subjects must take Biomax-O injections for the rest of their lives. It's too expensive and takes too long to kill the host. What I'm working on is a much more improved virus, one which will be more cost effective in that our selected carriers will only have to be subjected to a Biomax-O shot twice in a calendar year. And the tainted body fluids of that carrier would kill any sex partner of theirs within a thirty-day period. Now that's what I'm shooting for!"

It was obvious that this work meant everything to Meredith, and Wilhelm respectfully kept any further comments to himself. As members of the Sentinels of the Illuminati, their one and only job was to develop a biological agent which would wipe out so-called "free-eaters" from society to make way for the privileged, wealthy, and mostly Anglo-Saxon citizenship of the world, and nothing more.

Meredith secretly desired the slim, good-looking German—his square jaw line, strong white teeth and perfectly combed blonde hair, his neatly trimmed mustache and beard. Most of all, though, it was his piercing, gorgeous, deep-set blue eyes, which made her weak in the knees whenever he stared at her. She had loved their one sultry tryst together and, despite the fact that he was married with three kids, she wanted to fuck him just one more time. He was oh-so-good in bed, Meredith thought, but also married—and his wife was a total bitch. Meredith could not, however, pull him away from him.

They had only made love that one time—it hardly constituted any semblance of a full-fledged love affair—but she wanted more from him just the same. Meredith knew that they would never be anything more than fellow scientists and that realization alone sucked.

Wilhelm, meanwhile, was obviously not happy at home, casually mentioning now and again his sexually frigid wife and three college students to support. His work at the lab kept him sane most days, and he was now drinking more heavily than usual, which made him at times distant and aloof, even with his closest coworkers. However, it was the hatred of America's minorities and gays that drew them together in a bond that seemed unearthly. The thrill of scientific discovery, coupled with the fruition of the group's malicious goals made them an inseparable pair, in both the laboratory and the board room, a connection Meredith hoped would lead them again to her bed.

"Our friend Dr. Harrington of the World Health Organization," Meredith explained, "who has pretty much financed the Operation Inner City Virus venture from day one, has graciously allotted us a stipend of an additional three million dollars for the continuation of our program. He's going to forward it to our account by noon tomorrow, right after we speak via video conference."

Pausing, she lit up a cigarette from a pack of Virginia Slims. Cigarettes always seemed to relax her after a stressful day. The tedious push to obtain the perfect storm of virus had indeed taken its toll on her during the past few weeks.

"Wil," she said, breathing in the smoke, filling her lungs deeply with its cool, menthol essence before exhaling a cloud of grayish white mist into the atmosphere. It quickly dissipated by the overhead ceiling fans. Her follow scientists scolded her as they always did about smoking in the lab. Wilhelm especially found her occasional habit of lighting up in their work area both inconsiderate and disgusting, and gave her an earful more than anyone else in a white smock. However, Meredith was always the rebel, and would carefully finish her cigarette while gracing her irritable peers with a middle finger salute and a smirk, saying, "Fuck off." She took several slow drags before squashing it down into a small teacup sitting beside her flat screen computer and going right back to her e-mail messages with an arrogant display of nonchalance. She would need only one more week and the latest version of Biomaximus Officinalis would be finalized. It would then yield the ultra-lethal virus she'd already pre-named HIV10X.

***

While the majority of the nation's populace attempted to cope with the painful aftermath of the devastating 9-11 terror attacks, a mere two months later Rosaria roamed the midnight streets of Lariat desperately seeking cash to support her cocaine addiction, which had now taken her over almost completely. She flitted about the gas lamp-illuminated sidewalks of Mego Avenue soliciting the various men who came there in search of cheap thrills, yet she made few sales on this night, much like the other nights she'd flaunted herself upon the seedy ho stroll. She no longer appealed to sex-seeking customers as she had before. Gone were the beautiful legs that had brought wolf whistles and cat calls; now, knobby-kneed stilts had replaced them. Her hair was disheveled and dull looking, her eyes glassy and jaundice-like in their sunken sockets. She looked deathly pale and ungainly as the miniskirt she wore literally hung from her emaciated frame as if it was attached to a hanger. Her breath stank and she constantly wiped a skeletal hand across her running nose, smearing snot against the back of it.

Shivering from the chill of the night air, she wrapped her spindly arms around her narrow body as she was rebuffed by one repulsed john after another. She was even avoided by the other streetwalkers sharing the stroll with her. Prostitutes who'd once shared drinks and laughter with her now crossed over to the opposite side of the avenue whenever she drew near. She felt feverish and weak as the urge for coke surged through her insides like a firestorm.

She sniffled and coughed, dry and hacking. Still, she walked the stroll, peeking into car windows or approaching men on foot, only to be denied each time. The coke jones was kicking her ass something awful now, she thought. She felt herself giving in to a swoon as the night sky above her gave way to a swirling mass of vertigo-induced illusion. The street came up fast to meet her as she stumbled into a cluster of garbage cans beside a desolate and dark alley. Fortunately for her, she collapsed onto a heap of stuffed trash bags, which softened a potentially bone-breaking fall to the cold, hard pavement below.

She suddenly felt nauseous, but fought back the urge to puke. Her breathing was labored and raspy like that of air escaping a clogged vent. Rats, hairy and plump, scuttled around her within the filth where she laid, semiconscious and oblivious to their presence.

She reached about clawing at the plastic of the rubbish-filled bags to steady herself enough to stand or, at the very least, sit. She drew enough willpower to raise herself up from the smelly trash and stagger about, not unlike a newborn fawn on unsteady legs.

She quickly began focusing on the garbage-littered pavement at her feet for any evidence of cocaine or crack vials. She'd found drugs like this many times before, lying amidst the trash. Just last week she'd shared a full-stuffed crack pipe with a homeless woman who'd found it abandoned in the alley, along with various other refuse. The woman had allowed Rosaria to smoke with her because the Latina possessed a cigarette lighter.

Rosaria bent down low, going through the trash meticulously, picking at empty milk cartons and soda pop bottles until at last she came across a small bag of blow— probably a $50-bag, she thought—with a little more than half the original amount of cocaine left.

Her gaunt face lit up with joy and she danced a jig of delight. She reached her bony fingers down into the handbag at her side to withdraw a small, circular vanity mirror on which to divide the powder into two short, thin lines to snort. First, though, she would have to conceal herself from the other dope fiends who roamed the night streets looking to cop a quick buzz, so she ducked into the nearest alleyway. There, in the pitch darkness, she used her little lighter to prepare her lines. The first line disappeared down her nose almost instantaneously, bringing about that familiar tingling rush, followed by an intense tidal wave of pleasure, energy and a sense of general well being. Mucus drained down her already runny nose from the potent coke. She snorted it back down her throat and leaned in toward the flame-illuminated mirror in order to polish off the second line. Rats ran all around her, she saw, up ahead at the opening of the alley. The shadowy forms of the numerous ladies of the night passed by with the occasional john in tow for a back alley blow job or other lewd act. Yet, she couldn't have cared less. As long as she had the means to feed her monstrous addiction, she was loving life.

The sounds of laughter, profanity and honking car horns made for an eclectic street symphony just outside of Rosaria's filthy, makeshift dope den. Now wired and feeling frisky from the cocaine-driven euphoria, she exited the dark alley and began her hunt for potential customers anew, finally landing an old, grizzled, overweight trucker who hired her for a $50 blow job. It wasn't much, but at least she'd be able to cop another coke fix before sunrise.

**

December 28, 2001

Coventry Laboratories, 6886 East Street, Lariat, California

The morning sun peeked out above the palm tree-lined horizon of Lariat's coastline. Valentino was leaving the township of Beach Lake, where he managed two very busy brothels by the ocean. He'd stayed up nearly all night supervising the Madames he'd placed in charge of the seedy cathouses, and now after over ten-and-a-half hours, he was tired and hungry for some breakfast, but he was $3,000 richer.

He took to the Rock Hudson Parkway at approximately 8:25 a.m. in a polished Saturn Aura Greenline. He had used up the last of his Biomax-O and was now in need of a refill ASAP. He pulled into the parking lot of the Coventry Laboratory twenty minutes later. He'd already phoned Dr. Wilhelm Von Strecker while commuting on the freeway, so they were expecting him.

Coventry Laboratories needed him; their very careers depended upon his active participation in their program. As a result, regardless of what they personally thought about the flashy, arrogant, drug-dealing pimp, they'd continue to reat him with the utmost respect and honor. Lucien Valentino knew this and gladly took full advantage of their hospitality. Arriving at the lab, he gathered a few pieces of important documentation, placing the papers into a leather-bound briefcase before smoothly exiting the car.

"Aiight, I'm 'bout to handle some business right quick, but I'm gonna be up and around yo' area in about two hours, so have that money ready fa me, aiight?" he said into his cell as he pressed the car alarm on his way through the great double-glass doors of the government-funded facility.

He was becoming somewhat lethargic, as well as feverish, a sure sign that he'd gone at least a week too long without a Biomax-O injection. He ended his call and walked past a huge cedar wood desk in the grand lobby, flashing his official Coventry Laboratory pass to a stone-faced security guard manning the post and he breezed down the long, white-tiled hallway. One of the cleaning women smiled coyly at him as he walked by. The young Mexican woman had taken a liking to him, however, he paid her only scant attention. Most often when he arrived at the lab it was all about the shots and his T-cell count readings—and nothing more.

As he moved down the hallway toward the research room he literally bumped into a scientist coming around a corner. It was Dennis Brooks, a brilliant microbiologist and one of the few black scientists actively involved in the Operation Inner City program.

"Valentino?! What's up, man?"

"Ain't shit. 'Bout ta rev up on these fuckin' shots and shit, know what I'm sayin'?"

"No doubt," Dennis said. "No doubt. Check it, lemme holla atcha right quick before you go up in the lab, aiight?"

Valentino reluctantly agreed while letting the scientist know he'd have to keep it brief.

"Aiight, but we gotta make it fast 'cause I ain't had a fix o' that Biomax-O in a minute, dawg, and I'm just now startin' to feel like a pile o' shit. We got to make it snappy."

"Do you know anything about a Jillian Stoppard, or a guy named Seth Corman III?" Dennis asked.

Valentino wrinkled his brow in deep thought, then he suddenly remembered their names.

"Yeah, I know 'em. They're sex clients of mine. Why? Wassup?"

"They're both dying of AIDS as we speak," Dennis replied.

The pimp folded his arms across his chest while stepping backwards a pace or two.

"And?" he said. "Isn't that what's supposed to happen, Dennis?"

"Absolutely . . . just not to people like Mrs. Stoppard and Mr. Corman, that's all."

"What the fuck are you talkin' 'bout? I'm being paid and supplied with Biomax-O to go out here and spread this monsta' to as many muthafuckas as possible, so I dunno what kinda shit you smokin', Cuz."

"Yes," Dennis said. "You're partially right, Valentino. You are being paid to infect people on a large scale, but that would be your usual suspects. i.e. ghetto-ass black folks, poor white trash, Jews whenever possible, of course, and any other minority below an upper-middle class income bracket. Get it? You don't fuck around with the privileged. Ever! Jillian Stoppard was an impressive computer programmer and systems interface specialist for Microsoft. And her husband, who's still very healthy by the way, makes six figures a year brokering real estate deals for some of southern California's wealthiest citizens. Oh, yeah, and Mr. Corman? He just happens to have been Jillian's boss."

"Nigga, fuck them people!" Valentino said. "I don't' give a shit 'bout none o' them muthafuckas . . . you might, but I don't."

Valentino took a silk handkerchief from his linen trousers and wiped his sweaty forehead.

"You'd better, Valentino . . . Just remember, that it's because of this scientific community in general and the Sentinels of the Illuminati in particular that you're being supplied with the very serum that's keeping you alive, Mr. Valentino. Without Biomax-O you're going to be more than a little bit under the weather . . . you're going to die an agonizingly painful death. Now there's no need for that, is there, Mr. Valentino? Just do your job and we'll do ours. Is that clear?"

A surge of anger washed over the pimp as he gritted his teeth, seething in silence.

"Whatever, my man . . . you got it. It's yo' world."

"Good man," Dennis replied. "Now all I need is for you to pass that along to all your skanky streetwalkers out there and all will be well, okay?"

The scientist stopped to check the call on his cell phone, buzzing loudly against his left hip.

"I've to get going, but it's been a pleasure speaking with you today, sir, and please enjoy the rest of your day," Dennis said while giving Valentino a firm handshake and broad smile. Then he disappeared up the hall and onto an elevator.

Valentino mumbled a few profane words as he turned to leave in a huff down the hall at the opposite end. Slowly he walked past several scientists in white jackets, clustered together and engaged in deep bioterrorism talk. He stopped near a rectangular window overlooking a courtyard below and pondered briefly what Dennis had just said. He looked down quickly at his cell phone at his side again, this time scrolling through the menu to find Rosaria's number. He dialed, but it was disconnected, which drew beads of perspiration to his warm forehead.

As much as he hated to admit it, he was at the mercy of the Sentinels...He needed Biomax-O and, of course, he was used to the money they allotted him—it gave him a little extra change to blow on weekend fun—but in the end, it was the Biomax-O that he couldn't live without.

Maybe he should pay for Rosaria to go back to her native Mexico, and then she'd be out of everyone's hair, or maybe he'd kidnap one of the scientists and flee the country himself, forcing that individual to provide him with the formula for Biomax-O, thus assuring his survival in some faraway land. But no, both ideas were foolish. He really had no intention of living a life on the run anyway. Rosaria was a good earner and had only recently run away from him, due to his mistreatment of her, most likely. But he had every intention of finding her and bringing her back. Without the Biomax-O it would be impossible for her to stay away for too long.

Slowly, he backed away from the window with thoughts of finding his Mexican whore before she infected any more white folks, particularly those with financial worth. By now the virus had probably reduced her to skin and bones, yet there was no telling how many customers she'd slept with before her last Biomax-O shot wore off, changing her look. The more he thought about it, he realized that dozens more would become ill as a result. He had to get to her pronto. His own welfare depended on it.

Meredith Nader met Valentino at the entrance of the laboratory's front door, greeted and guided him into the room to his usual spot on a narrow leather-bound couch. He underwent a battery of tests just before he was given his injection, as well as a full month's supply of Biomax-O.

The scientist finished up her care of Valentino and then saw the now energetic pimp to the door before returning to glance at a cage of white rats beside a cryogenic specimen tank. After jotting down a few notes on a worn-looking pad, she went over to Wilhelm, who'd been compiling his own HIV10X data on the opposite side of the lab.

"How's the research coming along?" she asked.

"Of the ten rodents, only four remained alive after having been exposed to the 10X-strain virus. It only took placebo-fed rats a week to sicken and die, while the Biomax-O-fed rats continued to thrive after copulation. So, I'd consider that to be the breakthrough we've been looking for! We still need to perform a few more clinical trials just to be on the safe side," he said, still alternating peering down the lens of the microscope and tapping away on his computer keyboard.

"No, we don't have to do any more clinical trials, Wil!" Meredith exclaimed. "I've spent the better half of a year testing and retesting the strain. Trust me, this time, it's legit!"

"There's too much riding on the proper development of the HIV10X virus, Meredith," Wilhelm argued. "We just can't go on 'feel good' impulses. As a professional, you know this. We have to present the Illuminati elders with cold, hard facts and—more importantly—a tried and true product of population control."

"You know what, Wil?" Meredith said. "To be so good looking, you're a total asshole! Fuck you!"

For what seemed like an eternity, the two bioterrorists simply stared at one another—he with a blank look of cool nonchalance, and she with the stern look of a woman scorned.

"Okay, look, let's have just one more trial...just one more and I promise I'll approve it and pitch it to our friends at the World Health Organization, who would gladly pay us handsomely, via the Sentinels of the Illuminati, for immediate results."

"Was it my whining that changed your mind," Meredith asked, "or was it the fact that I have a really nice rack? I am giving up a whole lotta cleavage today, don't you agree?"

Wilhelm smiled broadly and then went right back to his work as before. Meredith meanwhile leaned over, placed a gentle kiss on the German's forehead and went back across the room to her workspace. She was content to know just how much power she held over Wilhelm with her earthly sexuality. He was putty in her hands to mold as she saw fit.

He, on the other hand, saw Meredith as an interesting, if irrational, personality. She was a truly brilliant biologist who'd helped develop the infamous HIV5X, and had the scientific skills to produce an even better bioweapon capable of ridding the U.S.—and eventually the world—of the minorities who he and the Sentinels hated so much. However, on the other hand, she proved often times through her over-sexed and emotional instability to be a liability that might, someday, require disposal.

After a lengthy series of clinical tests he'd try upon the Biomaximus Officinalus #2 Meredith had developed, he approved usage of the serum, which would render a user's blood and other body fluids ripe with the pathogens to form HIV10X. And Wilhelm himself would collect whatever pricey payout, as well as any accolades forthcoming from Dr. Harrington and the elders of the Sentinels of the Illuminati, not Meredith, whom he deemed unworthy of such high praise and rewards.

Just then, he received an email alert from Meredith that read: Thank you for believing in me! I knew that you of all the people I know can be called 'friend.'

He smiled slightly and quickly typed out a reply: Meredith, my dear, you know I've always believed in you. You can always trust me to do right by you and your scientific work.

Your best friend,
Wilhelm

Upon receiving his email, she looked up from her computer screen and

blew a kiss from across the room. He, in turn, reached up to catch the imaginary smooth in midair, placing it affectionately against his heart while whispering "thank you" to his infatuated coworker.

***

Valentino brushed past a group of prostitutes in skimpy skirts who quickly moved aside as he approached the rail-thin Latina standing up against a brick wall near the curb on Mego Avenue. The bony prostitute screamed out as the pimp stepped up to her, looming large and menacing. She reached into her purse with skeletal fingers, searching for the can of mace she kept for protection. But in her haste to remove it, she fumbled and it fell to the concrete below.

"Please, Papi, don't hurt me! Please, Papi, help me 'cause I'm so sick. Help me!"

She pitifully held out her skinny arms toward him, sobbing sorrowfully.

"Girl, I ain't gonna hurt you. I'm comin' out here to take you home and get you well again and cleaned up."

A heavy-set, fifty-something streetwalker snarled, walking up to the pair from out of the cluster of prostitutes huddled together, watching the drama.

""That scrawny bitch stole my money last night for dope and she aint' goin' nowhere 'til I get it back," she told Valentino.

With cat-like reflexes, Valentino smacked the whore forcefully with the back of his left hand, sending her reeling against the brick wall. She slumped against it, placing a hand gingerly against her reddened cheek as a trail of blood seeped from her left nostril. Before she could rise to her feet, Valentino's thick, ring-covered fingers gripped her throat with unyielding violence.

The prostitute fought wildly to free herself from Valentino's death grip, but to no avail. Her eyes turned bloodshot and her very life gurgled within her diaphragm. Her arms and legs flailed helplessly as the pimp pinning her to the pavement choked her mercilessly.

"Please, for the love of papa Dios, stop, Papi! She's not worth it!" Rosaria yelled.

Hearing those words caused him to relax and then, finally, release his hands from around the woman's neck. The prostitute fell over, gasping desperately for air as several of her friends rushed to her aid. She spattered and dry-heaved on the ground.

Valentino took out a small pistol and fired two shots in the sky above, causing the crowd of curious streetwalkers to scatter like roaches, opening up a path for he and Rosaria to proceed toward his vehicle. Once they climbed in, he allowed her to snort a thin line of coke while he quickly injected her with a syringe filled to the top with the new and improved Biomax-O #2. She winced from the prick of the sharp needle piercing her ashen skin. Then she yelped out a loud and high-pitched cry, a reaction to the burning sensation of the silver-colored Biomax-O coming into contact with her bloodstream.

However, the heavenly rush of the blow rapidly eased all sense of displeasure, leaving her loopy with doped-up happiness.

She rode the crest of that coke high all the way to Valentino's luxury townhouse in upscale Fujita City. In her weakened condition, she would not have survived out on the streets for much longer. Valentino had indeed saved her life.

Rosaria was locked up in the lovely beach front home during her lengthy convalescence, on strict orders by the drug-dealing pimp. Valentino kept armed thugs on the premises at all times to both protect him against possible attacks and to prevent Rosaria from attempting another escape. Three hellish months of Biomax-O shots, force-feeding and cold turkey symptoms due to cocaine deprivation had all but killed her.

Her radiant beauty, as well as her voluptuous shape had slowly returned, although she still yearned to get away from the man she'd once loved. Pack after pack of unopened condoms lined the coffee table in the cozy living room area. For a minute or two, she hated that she'd gone back to her old shapely self, because she realized that sooner or later she'd be forced, once again, to fuck a steady stream of strange men for pay, or risk the same type of abuse that had forced her to escape in the first place.

The home was even more lavishly furnished than before, and the fridge was constantly filled with frozen T.V. dinners and seemingly unending bottles of beer and wine. However much freedom she had to roam about the house and its exterior surroundings, Rosaria was still a prisoner. The grim-faced and silent gunmen watched her like a hawk, monitoring her every move from the far corners of the spacious living room or upon the sand dune-packed beach front beyond the front door.

Just as she'd expected, by the end of March 2002, she'd returned full time to prostitution, servicing no less than eight johns a day. She'd even begun to fiend for cocaine once more; however, she fought that temptation with a tenacity unseen in her before. Yet still, the threat of losing the all-important Biomax-O injections kept her in line and spreading those gorgeous legs once again for Valentino's big-spending clientele.

***

Coventry Laboratories

Wilhelm Von Strecker sat speaking with Lucien Valentino in the sun-drenched courtyard of Lariat's infamous medical lab. It had rained for most of the week all across southern California, the remnants of a storm front that had come down from the San Francisco area. However, on this particular morning, a Friday, at the springtime sun spread its golden rays far and wide across the land, creating a perfect day to get outside and soak it all up.

Wilhelm, though deeply racist, admired the handsome African American criminal who served as the star player in their population control program. He was extremely intelligent, self-sufficient and fiercely defiant at times—traits Wilhelm attributed to his hero, Adolf Hitler. Tall, robust and often wearing an ugly scowl on his otherwise attractive face, he unnerved many of the other Sentinels of the Illuminati scientists, who refused to work with him and usually avoided his presence at all costs.

"Mr. Valentino, it is always a pleasure to be graced with your presence," Wilhelm said before raising a cup of black coffee to his thin lips.

The street hustler took a deep drag from a thick Cuban cigar, exhaled and leaned back casually against the back of the wicker folding chair, across the table from the German.

Wilhelm felt something he rarely felt: intimidation...and fear. Few individuals instilled such feelings within him. For it was quite apparent that this man was no ordinary, lazy, shiftless nigger, but an adversary to be reckoned with if the situation at hand ever turned sour for whatever reason. The eyes of his patient spoke volumes of the utter savagery, calculated and precise, in which he was capable of unleashing . . . simply by staring into those eyes could he tell.

"We've perfected the Biomax-O formula," Wilhelm said between sips of joe, attempting to make eye contact without flinching or seeming weak in any way. "You'll only have to take your shots twice a year now, instead of twice each month. Isn't that great?"

Valentino again took several short puffs from the thick stogie hanging loosely out of the corner of his mouth. Wilhelm took another sip of coffee in an effort to hide his uneasiness with Valentino's silent stare, which grew creepier by the minute. After all, the man was a murderer. Dr. Goddard had documented hours of study on the daily activities of the drug lord during his assignment in Puerto Rico, which had revealed Lucien Valentino to be a ruthless and cold-hearted thug who often left a trail of bullet-riddled bodies throughout the slums of Old San Juan. It was indeed this same information that caused the majority of the Illuminati scientists to shun him.

Finishing up the last of his coffee, the German scientist finally broke the silence, saying, "All right, Mr. Valentino, let's begin your injections so that your body might build up a tolerance to this new and improved Biomax-O serum. If you don't mind, I'd like us to get started right away."

Both the doctor and his patient arose from their seats amidst the colorful, fragrant botanicals of the lush courtyard, making a brisk beeline toward a thick plexi-glass revolving door that allowed them entrance to the great hall of the facility. They walked down the hall to an elevator and boarded one of the four cars. They traveled eight floors up and emerged to enter a modest-sized room, dimly lit by many buzzing and whirring gadgets, whose lights glowed a bright, neon green throughout the room.

"You remember Meredith, don't you?" Wilhelm asked, walking over to a hospital bed where the female scientist stood preparing to open up a pack of syringes.

Meredith attached a shiny, thin needle to the syringe above a sink near the bed, greeting the drug dealer without so much as looking up from her work.

"Mr. Valentino, how the hell are you?" She said it with an air of cool indifference. Wilhelm wished that he could be as calm in the criminal's presence as his nonchalant coworker was.

"Meredith and I have perfected this drug," Wilhelm said, "so that the death rate from your sexual encounters will increase significantly, Mr. Valentino. Isn't that correct, Meredith?"

"Fuck all that neo-Nazi talk, Jack," Valentino interrupted. "What I wanna know is how much am I gonna get paid extra for this shit?"

"I'm sorry?" Wilhelm asked.

"You heard me, man. I'm 'bout that chedda, my dude, if I'm gonna be y'all's lil' muthafuckin' guinea pig, y'all crackas g'on have to come up off o' some mo' bread for my services, ya feel me?"

Valentino's bold demand for an increase in pay left the scientists dumbfounded. The sheer audacity, they thought, of making demands on the people who held his very existence in the palm of their hands was both extraordinarily impressive and more than a little foolhardy. However, the drug dealer's confidence alone brought him their respect and undivided attention.

"Of course, Mr. Valentino, you shall continue to be paid handsomely for your role in this all-important operation," Wilhelm said reassuringly. "I'm quite certain that our friends at the World Health Organization will have no problem adding a raise to your monthly stipend. You are a valuable asset to us, Mr. Valentino. Why would we dare treat you unfairly?"

Wilhelm smiled slightly before turning on the faucet, slowly lathering his hands to wash them before the procedure began.

"All right, I'll need for you to extend either your right or left arm so that I may swab a spot with alcohol. You know the routine. Make a fist for me so that I can choose a nice, prominent vein there, and we can get this party started. This serum will be slightly more acidic, which—I'm warning you—means that as the Biomax-O #2 reacts with your hemoglobin, it's going to be unpleasant. But don't worry, the resulting allergic reaction will pass quickly, more than likely after only a few seconds. And, on the bright side, you won't have to shoot up again until this time next April! Oh, also, one of the side effects of the Biomax-O #2 will be an increase in sex drive, firmer erections, and increase in seminal volume and more stamina. Just think of it as Viagra times five. Not that you need help in that area or anything."

"You're a real walking, talking Biomax infomercial, aren't you, Wil?" Meredith said while prepping Valentino for his shot.

"Both o' y'all shut the fuck up an' get this shit over with, aiight? I got shit to do today."

Both scientists strapped on green rubber gloves as Wilhelm raised a small vial of Biomax-O #2 gently from a tray of six.

"Your vitals are all strong and you are in perfect health, Mr. Valentino. Besides, you've got some guns on you. Do you work out often?" Wilhelm asked.

"Look here, white boy, is you gonna get this shit over with or talk me to death? Cause I got plenty hos back at the crib to do that. C'mon now, let's get this shit over with, dawg!"

"Very well, sir. Brace yourself," Wilhelm warned.

The drug dealer's arm stretched out, keenly muscular. As the thin, sharp metal point sunk into Valentino's raised vein, he gritted his teeth and struggled mightily against he leather straps which Meredith had applied while he'd lay, prostrate, on the bed. Bestial grunts and groans escaped his lips as he fought against the straps pinning him down. Heavy beads of sweat covered his entire face, neck and chest. Soon the shaking subsided, with each shudder becoming less and less violent, until he at last gave way to exhaustion and sleep.

Chapter 15

Eight hours later, Valentino leaned up against the wall in the smoke-filled, noisy interior of Fontaine's Pool Hall. He chalked the end of his favorite black and tan pool stick. A small pile of cash sat on an empty stool below the wall-length mirror behind the table. Of the eight games he'd played this far, he'd only won four—breaking even, which was piss-poor for a pro like himself, he thought. The music was lively, the liquor was strong, and the crowd was mostly female and fine. But Valentino had a million things on his mind, and pool just wasn't one of them. He had a plan for the Sentinels of the Illuminati, particularly for Dr. Wilhelm and his pretty coworker, Meredith Nader.

The racist Sentinels viewed him as just a pawn in their sick game to eliminate black and other minorities, and sure, he had agreed to play a part in their objectives, yet he planned, in turn, on using them as they'd used him. He knew that the tall, handsome German had no real appreciation for him and would more than likely seek to kill him after the "super AIDS" operation reached nation-wide pandemic status. Therefore, he'd have to beat the doctor to the punch. But for now, both parties needed each other and the street-wise drug dealer would milk it for all it was worth.

Valentino was intrigued by Dr. Nader in a different way. She too was in no way a minority-friendly individual, particularly hating black folks, he had deduced. She was nonetheless a woman, and it was his desire to break her down as he had done dozens of times before to innumerable females from all walks of life, including those who were considered out of his league. When it came to hustling and pimping, the man knew he had few equals.

A scuffle broke out near the bar, causing a crowd to gather there for several minutes before a surly bouncer tossed the inebriated combatants out into the back alley. Valentino lingered near the pool table, slowly gathering his money from off the top of the stool. While the crowd was dispersing, Valentino made his way toward the door. He'd had enough of the pool hall for the time being.

Driving along interstate 99 a few minutes later, Valentino dwelled on the two scientists, whom he planned to manipulate, especially Dr. Nader. The woman was clearly frustrated sexually and more than a little chummy with Wilhelm Von Strecker. He guessed Dr. Von Strecker had probably even hit it once or twice. It was written all over their faces, especially when they were together.

Valentino knew the dynamics of sex, and he set out a plan to get to Dr. Nader through her blond boyfriend. He obviously didn't pay her the attention she so desperately desired. All women, he thought, regardless of their ethnicity, social standing, or even age had basically the same vulnerabilities, and any man with the proper skills could exploit them. Meredith Nader was an attractive, but lonely chick who poured most of her energies into her work. Valentino realized that she had feelings for Wilhelm—feelings that hardly seemed mutual. She was also one hell of a flirt, which spoke volumes about her sexuality. She was no doubt a freak, a freak who would soon be another one of his conquests, regardless of the fact that he was black and infected with AIDS. He was a player pimp who considered this the challenge of a lifetime—one that would reap incredible dividends for him in the long run. He grinned to himself as he wheeled his big Saturn off the interstate ramp onto Rock Hudson Parkway, en route to Fujita City and his beachfront property.

***

Wilhelm ended a 15-minute call with his wife, and then flipped the top down on his cell phone, placing it down on the table beside his dinner tray. To the rear of him, near a row of vending machines, Meredith stood holding a Deer Park water bottle, silently fuming as she withdrew a container of yogurt from the nearest machine. She was so disgusted by the lovey-dovey chitchat between Wilhelm and his "loving" wife that she suddenly felt nauseous. Wilhelm looked up from his partially eaten meal and smiled weakly in her direction.

"Hey you," he said, "why don't you come on over and cop a squat? What do you say?"

Meredith felt the initial fury of hearing him speak to his wife subside somewhat, and she reluctantly joined him at the lonely table.

"C'mon, why the long face, Meredith?" Wilhelm asked.

"Wil," she answered, "do you really love her? Do you?"

"Meredith, please...don't do this. Not here, not now."

"Oh, gimme a break, Wil! You don't love her. I mean, my God, man, you hardly ever even touch her! Tell me, when was the last time you made love to the little wife? Yesterday? Last week? Three months ago, maybe? Pathetic, the both of you . . . fucking pathetic. You deserve each other."

"You're acting childish, Meredith," Wilhelm said quietly. "You're acting like an 8th grader with a schoolyard crush. I'm a married man. Can't you see that? Face it—there can be nothing between us romantically, Meredith. Okay? Let's just be friends—like we've been ever since we began working together."

The two scientists sat starting out into space, alone with their thoughts until Meredith said, "What about the night I gave myself to you, Wil? Do you remember? You said it was so perfect. What we had was special, Wil...incredibly special."

She had a twinkle in her eye as she lovingly gazed at Wilhelm. She got up out of her seat and draped her arms around the doctor's shoulders, caressing his cheek with her long, pale fingers and whispering into his ear.

"Meredith, for the love of God, woman, stop it! What we had was simply a one-night stand, all right? Nothing more!"

"Was that all that I was worth to you?" she asked. "A cheap lay? I see . . well, fuck you very much, doctor! And oh, by the way, Wil, I faked it—both times. And ya wanna know what I really think about Adolf Hitler? He sucks ass! Just like you and your shit-for-brains wife. And, please, lay off the booze, 'cause it seeps through your pores and give you body odor something terrible . . . just thought you ought to know that, asshole!"

She stormed away from the table with her snack, out of the cafeteria and back toward the lab.

"Meredith!" Wil called after her. "Meredith, can we talk about this? I'm sorry, okay? It's just that...Meredith! Damnit!"

With frustration, he shoved the dinner tray away from him and it fell to the floor with a loud racket. He wished that they'd never had sex. Things shouldn't be this complicated between them, but the reality of the situation was that they were, and with Meredith's feelings being a major issue, things weren't going to change anytime soon.

Meredith's anger was at a boiling point. Why couldn't she win Wilhelm's heart—or the heart of any man, for that matter? All of the good ones were either married, involved or gay. All that was left were the sexually deviant old geezers and punk kids. She was fairly young still at 32, and easy on the eyes, so she was baffled at her lifelong rotten luck with men.

A half-hour later, Meredith stood beside Wil's work desk, staring sheepishly at the floor.

"Wil, look," she said, "I . . I'm really sorry about what just happened. I don't know what got into my. Please accept my apology."

He looked up at her from his microscope smiling reassuringly, his intense blue eyes seemed to bore into her very soul, melting her already broken heart. He reached an outstretched hand toward her in a show of friendship. She hesitated, but eventually pressed her palm to his in a handshake. She hated herself for loving him still. What a fool she'd made of herself, she thought. All her life her mother had warned her against falling for married men. Even now she could hear her mother's chastisement echoing within the depths of her mind.

Wilhelm changed the subject, saying, "Well, I've completed the last of these clinical trials for the general members of the World Heath Organization, just as Dr. Harrington asked, so that no one will become suspicious about our true experiments. I'm heading on home. I . . . I've got my in-laws coming over for dinner later tonight, so I've got to get back to help Cindy with the meatloaf. Will you be so kind as to lock up the central lab for me?

Meredith nodded and Wilhelm stopped suddenly and added, "Oh, shit—I almost forgot, could you deliver this cash to Valentino for me? Don't worry, he actually lives in a decent neighborhood, unlike most of those people."

Meredith glared at him through narrowed eyes as Wilhelm gathered up his briefcase and car keys from his desk and exited through the glass doors beyond.

***

11:27 a.m.

Valentino sat on a plush leather and suede recliner in his spacious living room watching ESPN while drinking a cold bottle of Corona and eating nachos and salsa dip. He wore a gray, tight-fitting wife beater and knee-length basketball shorts. The surrounding living room floor was lined with fluffy, wall-to-all white sheep's wool carpet. Well over a dozen provocatively dressed women, a few barely legal, lounged around lazily, chitchatting and playing with on another's hair. The musical chime of the doorbell echoed throughout the spacious, beautifully furnished living room, bringing one of the live-in harlots to her feet and off to quickly answer the door.

"Well, well, look what the cat done dragged up in here," Valentino called from his huge recliner. "C'mon in here, white girl, an' sit down next to big daddy for a coupla minutes. Lemme holla atcha right quick."

"I don't think so, "Meredith answered. "You see, Valentino, unlike the rest of these airheaded white chicks you've got here, I'm not so into low-life nigger pimps. Sorry."

He smiled as he arose from his seat to make his way past the suddenly silent prostitutes toward the open doorway.

"You standin' in my door, holdin' my money and talkin' shit to me in my fuckin' place?" Valentino asked flatly.

The sharp-tongued scientist found herself in an unusually vulnerable position. She often ridiculed others without so much as a second thought of retaliation, but this was totally different. It was painfully obvious that she was out of her element here, and quite possibly in danger. Yet for some reason, the risk factor actually turned her on.

"Look if I offended you...good," she said, "because I don't particularly care for scumbags like you trying to hit on me. So why don't you take your money and we'll both call it a night, okay?" She reached down into her leather handbag and pulled out an envelope stuffed with cash. "Here you go. It's all there. I already counted it for you."

Valentino rudely snatched the envelope from Meredith's hand after stepping out and slamming the door shut behind them.

"I don't let bitches talk to me that way, ya understand?"

"Look, dipshit," Meredith replied, "I'm warning you, back the fuck away."

Valentino smirked, then reached out and roughly pulled her toward him.

"Shut the fuck up! What you g'on do now, huh?" he asked. "I ain't one of them science geeks you normally fucks with. I'm a real-ass nigga, bitch, and I can show you that betta than I can tell you!"

Meredith's blood pressure rose ridiculously high at that point, and her heart was pounding in sheer fright, but she tried to maintain some sort of composure in spite of herself.

"Get your fucking hands off me, you black bastard!" she yelled.

Valentino pressed his lips to those of the struggling scientist in a hard, but sensual kiss. She fought against him, but her struggles were for naught against her stronger adversary. His hands cupped her plump ass cheeks, groping her with the sexual aggression of an animal. Valentino's hand fondled the woman's hairy vagina beneath the sheer fabric of her satin panties, which yielded it's musky moisture once the pimp's thick index finger found its way into the slippery opening.

"Oh yeah," he said quietly, "you know you like it, don't ya? Uh huh, you like it."

Meredith finally managed to push away from the man who'd just violated her. She pulled her skirt down and adjusted herself with unsteady movements. She looked disheveled and shaken as she backed away from him.

"Bring yo'ass here, woman!"

Valentino's tone was threatening and full of street bravado. Reluctantly, a shell-shocked Meredith obeyed. Gently the pimp took hold of her chin, stroking it softly. He gazed into her fluid green eyes with a sense of accomplishment.

"It ain't hardly your fault baby...you act all hard an' shit 'cause you ain't got nobody to scratch that itch in a while, ain't that right?"

Tears welled up in Meredith's eyes and spilled down her reddened cheeks.

"You're a monster," she said.

Valentino feigned a look of startled surprise.

"Say what? Monster? Bitch, please, you not only needed that, you wanted it and from the way you was grindin' those hips when I was finger fuckin' you, you ain't been getting' no dick for a helluva long time. Now tell me I'm lyin'?"

"You just raped me."

Once again the pimp kissed her, only this time his tongue found its way into her mouth while he held her close.

The man had clearly overstepped his boundaries by miles, but what could she really do? Go to the cops? Tell them about their background? About the world's most sinister mass murder plot? But even more unsettling to Meredith was her unspoken enjoyment of the experience itself. She felt a satisfaction that she hadn't felt in months. Yet, she couldn't believe that it was a black pimp who'd given it to her. She had a ton of personal, as well as professional reasons not to enjoy what had just transpired on the front porch, overlooking the darkened beach. He was black. He was a criminal. Most importantly, he was a carrier of the most lethal STD on the planet—HIV10X. Doctor Meredith Nader backed away slowly from Valentino until she reached the steps, then she turned and raced toward her parked car. Driving away from Fujita City, Meredith sobbed all down the interstate highway. She was totally at a total loss as to what she was feeling.

***

By April 28, Dr. Nader had spent a significant amount of time out at Valentino's beachside bungalow, and seemingly for reasons other than the professional. The man really had no need to see any of the Sentinels of the Illuminati scientists until months later when he'd have to return for another shot of Biomax-O #2.

Other scientists in the Coventry Laboratory family noticed Meredith's distance, as well as her constant absences from work, but no seemed to know what was really happening. Everyone was in the dark except for Wilhelm. Having been intimately involved with Meredith, he better than anyone realized what the deal was. And he was disgusted by the very thought of his coworker doing the unspeakable. When they were alone together—which was often—he let her know how he felt.

"Meredith, I've got to tell you this. I think—in fact, I know—that it's a really bad idea to hang out with that scumbag nigger. My God, please tell me that you're not desperate or foolish enough to sleep with him!"

Meredith sighed loudly while folding her arms across her ample breasts. Wilhelm hated fighting with his acid-tongued lab partner, but this was one instance that he knew was important enough to suffer through the argument.

"All right, fine," he said. "If you want to jeopardize this program, your freedom, and not to mention mine, and even your life, then go ahead and be my guest. I just hope it's worth losing everything for."

Wilhelm slowly turned his back on her and strolled over to a row of cages filled with rats. He'd grown jealous because even though Valentino was a sexual death trap to any woman getting into bed with him, his way with the ladies was beyond anything that most guys—even handsome ones—could muster. Wilhelm realized that the chances that Meredith had fallen victim to the streetwise seduction of the player pimp were quite high, and that scared the hell out of him.

Meredith shook out a cigarette into her hand and wasted little time lighting up.

"Ya know what, Wilhelm? You are not the boss of me, so don't lose any sleep over what I do outside Coventry Laboratories, okay?"

Wilhelm felt himself getting angrier by the minute, nearly pushing a study cage to the floor as a result.

"I've had about all I can take of your snotty little attitude!" he said. "Right now you're being an irresponsible little shit and it's got to stop—here and now!"

Meredith tossed her long, dark hair back, all the while tapping her left foot as she bristled at her co-worker's harsh words.

"You've got some nerve," she said. "How dare you talk to me like that! Why, you didn't so much as hold my hand after we were together that time, not to mention making me feel like a common whore on top of it. And now the high and mighty Doctor Wilhelm Von Strecker wants to belittle moi? I wonder why? Are you afraid that maybe someone other than you seems to finally give a fuck about me and maybe even find me attractive? Or maybe you're afraid that his big black cock, tainted or not, will fill me up more than your little pale pecker did, huh? Is that it?"

The German's face flushed red with fury, and he felt the urge to slap Meredith as hard as he could.

"You are one sick puppy," he said. "You're fucking mental, that's what you are. You're going to regret what you're doing. Do you hear me?"

Wilhelm ran his fingers through his hair in utter frustration.

"Do you realize the seriousness of this?! You are dealing with a man who is a human biological weapon! Fucking him can and will kill you, and you know this! To make matters worse, your little 'jungle fever' fling could destroy this entire covert operation we're all working on! My God, think of all political fallout that would occur if our secret got out! This would become an international incident of colossal proportions, Meredith! Every one of us who is involved would face the wrath of the U.N., which would then surely result in prison time, or even worse! I'm not asking you to stay away from Valentino—I'm fucking tell you!"

Wilhelm turned away from her in anger. He hated talking to her in this manner and hated feeling like such an über prick even more.

"Look, Meredith, I . . . I'm really sorry to be bitching and moaning like this, but the guy is bad news—worse than bad news. He's just another stupid porch monkey like all the rest of them. A test dummy to help us to eliminate everyone who doesn't belong on this planet. You're Anglo and you're beautiful . . . way out of this loser's league. So, please leave that degenerate to be with his own kind."

Meredith seemed to be lost in deep thought. It was obvious to Wilhelm that his words of wisdom had gotten through to her—at least that's what it looked like. That was exactly what he'd been hoping for. If his hunches about his lab partner and Valentino were correct, disaster would sure befall everyone involved.

"You make it seem like I'm the one who's screwing everything up, Wil," Meredith said, "like I'd be the cause of the whole HIV/AIDS thing going belly up. Well, listen up, mister man, you started this ball rolling when you shared my goddamned bed! What would your precious little Cindy think about that, Doctor Von Strecker?!"

"You know what? This is getting ridiculous, Meredith—or, excuse me, Doctor Nader, since we're being formal here. Let's cut the crap, okay? Remember we're here at work and everyone needn't be aware of this discussion. Secondly, I'm warning you . . . Cindy has absolutely nothing to do with this, so leave her out of it. Do I make myself perfectly clear?"

Meredith shot him a dirty look while simultaneously flipping him her middle finger. He, in turn, simply stared with an iced-over coldness in his blue eyes in her direction.

"I so fucking hate you. I curse the very day that I met you," Meredith said just as coldly. "I hate you."

"Go see a shrink, Doctor Nader, because you need one bad," Wilhelm replied.

***

The huge plasma television screen illuminated the entirety of the living room with its pale glow. The majority of the prostitutes had retired to their respective rooms, leaving a lethargic, but still wide-awake Valentino leaning comfortably backwards in his plush leather armchair, watching back-to-back reruns of "The Twilight Zone" until he grew bleary eyed. He enjoyed the hauntingly real-life affirmations contained within the story lines of the classic Kennedy-era T.V. drama, particularly Rod Sterling's cool delivery at the beginning and conclusion of each episode.

Silence was always a welcome visitor in Valentino's world. Usually his days and nights were filled with activity of one kind or another. Between prostitutes and clients, not to mention the various dope fiends stopping by to seek a few dollars worth of joy, constant traffic circulated in and out of his doorway. He had a half-dozen stash and whorehouses to look after, and that in itself proved exhausting on most days, despite the good money they brought in. Then there was the ever-present danger of stick-up kids or undercover cops hoping to make a name for themselves.

Rest and relaxation were rare and welcomed luxuries for this busy man. He now had his best earner, Rosaria, back at home and she'd grown healthy and thick once more—a sure bet to keep the johns happy and paying well. Yet the closeness that had existed between them was gone now. The bitch could no longer be trusted because, unlike his other hookers, Rosaria had been more like an actual girlfriend to him than a mere sex worker. She was aware of pertinent information about his personal dealings that none of the other harlots were privy to. She'd been gone for a long time—long enough to have considered ratting him out to the boys in blue or hooking up with one of his many competitors from around the way, he was sure. Either way, if his hunches were right, she'd have to be put to sleep.

As he wrestled with those uncomfortable thoughts racing through his head, he continued to bask in the soft glow of the wide plasma screen, silently enjoying episode after episode of "The Twilight Zone." Other than the gentle hum of the refrigerator and the occasional snore coming from one of the snoozing girls in the back, he remained undisturbed.

Chapter 16

Gentle spring showers fell down for a week all across the greater southern California area, soaking Los Angeles, Orange, San Diego and Lariat with more than 9.5 inches of rain in some areas, and a whopping 12 inches in others. The threat of landslides from loose soil on the Whistler Hills prompted the city government to declare Mego Avenue and its surrounding streets a danger zone, at least temporarily until the rains subsided. Meanwhile, the prostitutes for a time had to find somewhere else to ply their illicit trade.

Rosaria sat alone sipping on a steaming cup of white chocolate mocha, while staring out of the window in the dimly lit back corner of the local Starbucks. She was in a mood of deep melancholy, as was evidenced by the tears streaming down her lovely face.

The pitter-patter of cascading raindrops against the window pane added to her feeling of sadness and introspection. She hated herself for ever having fallen in love with the likes of Lucien Valentino, a user and abuser of women and, for that matter, of men as well. He was a liar too. She used to believe every word he said. She'd have given anything to make him happy, and she did. She sold her precious young body for him, she peddled drugs for him, she even killed a man for him once. She should have listened to Mami and finished high school; then maybe she could have gone on to be a beautician or tried her hand at professional modeling like her friends had suggested.

But now everything was lost. She was a prisoner in a whorehouse and she'd be forever a slave to her pimp if she wanted to live. She was infected with some rare, aggressive and drug-resistant strain of HIV that mutated into full-blown AIDS within a matter of a few weeks. Without the special shots Lucien provided her with, she'd surely die. She nearly had a couple of months earlier, but for some reason he'd found her and nursed her back to health.

She was fortunate on one level, she knew—much more fortunate than some others. She knew of several girls who'd worked the streets for Lucien and eventually just disappeared. Each one turned up dead eventually. Their bodies were always emaciated to the point where they were literally walking skeletons shortly before their death, the skin lesions all over their corpses suggesting that they'd all succumbed to the AIDS virus.

She, too, had infected dozens of male customers with the virus Lucien called "HIV5X." For at least two months earlier in the year, the Lariat Health Department was bombarded with visitations and phone calls form terrified and ill citizen, both males and females, seeking help for their sudden health problems. As a result of her work, as well as that of her fellow streetwalkers and their pimp himself, the township of Cushing in South Lariat reported 26 people—10 women and 16 men—who tested positive for an unusually aggressive strain of HIV. Within a month's time, 15 of the infected people had died of AIDS. The remaining 11 were holding on by a thread as their bodies wasted away to mere skin and bones. The town officials declared the strange HIV/AIDS-related deaths a countywide health disaster, prompting Cushing-area health investigators to comb wide swaths of housing projects, searching for sick individuals from door to door. This large-scale operation forced Valentino to pack up and leave the immediate area, along with his prostitutes, in order to escape detection.

Rosaria's eyes, though wet and red from crying were constantly scanning the entrance of the coffee shop, shifting from one rain-soaked customer coming through the door to another. Valentino's drug and sex clients often served as his eyes and ears, informing him of anything of importance taking place in the 'hood. Therefore, she'd have to hurry up and return to the house to avoid detection. She occasionally stepped away from her beachfront prison by bribing the chief bodyguard of the pimp's security force, usually with a few hundred dollars. Even so, she was always threatened that she had better return within an hour's time. It was a risky way to seek a small piece of solitude, however, it was more than worth it to her.

She peeked at her wristwatch before downing the last sugary sweet drop of her mocha and headed out into the rain. Beneath the cover of her umbrella, she breezed past a group of prostitutes, several of whom looked ill and much thinner since she'd last seem them. One poor chick could barely stand as she coughed repeatedly and limped on spindly legs while the driving rain drenched her gaunt frame. She was no more than a day or two from death's door, and it looked like she was not alone.

Rosario knew that Valentino was no doubt the culprit. In order to both make good on his contract with the creators of the Operation Inner City Virus, and destroy the competition, he often masqueraded as a john himself, sleeping with many of the rival pimps' staple hookers. In this way he also took the pressure off of himself as far as the city's health department was concerned. By the time a major alarm was sounded, there would be far too many sick and dying individuals to trace ea single source of the virus.

Walking past the boardwalk of the neighboring shops, Rosaria thought about all of the people whose lives had been horribly altered by Valentino. She really couldn't have cared less about the women who sold themselves for a fistful of dollars, who just happened to be unfortunate enough to have crossed path with the AIDS-infected pimp, however she realized that no one was exempt from Valentino's seductive wiles. Even naïve high schoolers, star-struck by the man's criminally acquired bling were fair game.

After viewing a series of homemade videos on YouTube of a masked man going by the moniker "Trash Man" and claiming to have infected over 1,500 women with HIV, Valentino gleefully adopted the nickname for himself with pride.

"Man, I like that nigga! Shit, I like 'em a lot. As a matter o' fact, I like that cat so muthafuckin' much that I'm go'n use his shit...Trash Man...yeah, that's what I am. Greasy, grimy, trashy, 'cept I'm the *real* muthafuckin' Trash Man 'cause I got that killa shit in my nutsack, bitch! I got that 'fuck you up on site' type o' shit, plus a nigga gettin' paid to dead y'all sorry asses!"

He'd said it all with a sinister sense of pride.

"'Cept I'll let that nigga make all o' the lil' videos an' shit, 'cause that ain't my style, feel me? I'm go'n just keep 'em kill muthafuckas 'cause I agree wit the nigga, y'all bitches need to be taught a muthafuckin' lesson and I'm go'n use my bad dick to give 'em out!"

He laughed wickedly before his speechless streetwalkers, most of whom were already infected and actively taking Biomax-O shots.

Chapter 17

The golden glow of the California sun bathed the entire boardwalk as dozens of bikini-clad women mingled with the men proudly showing off their buff beach-worthy bodies below in the rolling white-capped surf of Winslow Bay. They engaged each other in a friendly game of volleyball upon the white sands, just beyond the busy foot traffic.

Meredith sat alone on a swivel chair at a bar under a thatched roof. To her, the Tiki Hut served the absolute best strawberry margaritas in town, and she awaited her date's arrival as she polished off a tall glass of the red-hued alcoholic beverage. She was already on her second drink. The laughter and cheers of the volleyball competition kept her attention focused outside of the Hawaiian-themed bar until a gentle hand resting upon her shoulder broke the monotony of the moment.

"S'up, Doctor Nader? You been waitin' 'round here long for me, beautiful?"

Meredith turned around on her stool, staring up into the smooth, handsome brown face smiling down at her. He reached out, taking the mixed drink from her hand and taking a quick sip for himself before placing it down on the bar and settling on a seat beside her. Then he took her hand into his, placing a soft kiss on the back of it. She felt herself melting inside. It had been quite some time since she'd been shown the kind of attention from a man that she was currently receiving.

"You really know how to woo a girl, don't you? Is this really real, or am I just another one of your skanks?" she asked. "Because I keep telling myself that for once maybe this is real . . . maybe I do matter to a man and, just maybe, he'll love me."

Meredith shed a single tear, which she wiped gently with a paper napkin lying beside her glass.

"Look, I...I'm sorry," she continued. "It's just that I've had a pretty lousy love life for the better half of a decade or so, so...yeah, I'm kind of desperate right now, you know? Especially with the whole biological clock thing...sucks, right? Maybe I should've become a lesbian. Then I wouldn't be such a psychological mess right now."

Valentino took hold of her soft, oval-shaped face and planted a kiss, long and warm, sensually upon her thin lips. The impulsiveness of it took her by surprise, yet she welcomed it by inviting his moist tongue into her mouth, fully enjoying a full thirty seconds of amorous self-indulgence before slowly pulling away.

"Girl, you gonna fuck around an' make me beat that pussy up for ya?"

Meredith grinned slightly as the giddiness of both the alcohol and her sudden sexual arousal took hold of her.

"Beat my pussy up? I'm sorry, but I'm probably the whitest woman you've ever met, so I'm clueless as to what that means, but it sure does sounds interesting. Painful, but interesting."

"Oh, don't worry about the slang, baby," Valentino said. "Once I get you in bed you gonna feel every inch o' what I'm talkin' bout."

Raising the glass back up to her pink painted lips, Meredith took down a long drink, emptying the contents until only the ice cubes remained.

"I'd love to, hon, I really would, but you know as well as I do that we can never take this relationship to that level of intimacy," Meredith said while placing a tip onto the counter for the cute, young bartender.

"You know that you have the know-how to make happen whatever you want," Valentino said. "Am I right? Tell me I'm lyin'."

She smiled at the pimp's witty, but truthful reply. As he sat beside her, she wondered how she'd fallen for a black man—and Valentino in particular. With Wilhelm already aware somewhat of her infatuation with Valentino, she couldn't afford for the others to find out about her extracurricular activities. Wilhelm still had a soft spot for her somewhere in that seemingly icy heart of his she felt, and wouldn't turn informant on her, even when it came to this delicate situation.

Meredith rose up slowly from her stool, taking Valentino's hand as she stood and walked arm in arm with him out into the sunshine and across the weather-beaten planks of the boardwalk toward his beach house in the distance. Once they arrived at the house, Meredith was ushered into a plush living room devoid of anyone else's presence. It was dimly lit and filled with the pleasant aromatic fragrance of Egyptian Musk incense, which wafted through the whole interior of the home.

"Welcome to my humble abode. Or, should I say, this right here is my crib, you dig?"

Meredith chuckled lightly at her host's humor while admitting the man's good taste in interior decoration. She'd expected to find a tacky-looking, loud-colored, cheap motel-like brothel, but instead she was standing in the middle of a plush, sweet smelling oasis of Zen-inspired serenity.

"You been workin' kinda hard here lately, on top o' all that research type shit you do for livin' so I want you to unwind, calm yo' nerves, baby girl, 'cause guess what? You 'bout to get the massage of yo' life."

She was led toward a mid-sized back room illuminated entirely by candlelight, previous lit by the now absent prostitutes. A leather massage table was a welcome sight to the slightly intoxicated biologist who, without being asked, began shedding her outer garments, en route to the table before her. She climbed onto it and stretched herself out, face down on the cool, comfortable leather. Valentino licked his lips lustfully as he gazed upon the surprisingly curvaceous physique possessed by Meredith.

Placing a touch of hot almond oil to the tender skin of her luscious ass cheeks, he worked his way slowly down her shapely legs, kneading them as he worked the oil onto her lower body before moving his hands back up across her buttocks. He moved onto her back, soon leaving her glistening within the warm glow of the flickering candles.

"My God, Lucien, you are good," Meredith murmured. "Really good. I want you inside me. I want to feel every inch of you . . . I don't care about your condition because I've already injected myself with Biomax-O. I knew that it was just a matter of time before I would give myself to you. Who am I kidding? I'm a lonely lady, Mr. Valentino, and I'm in need of a man . . . so what I need is for you to do what you do best. Take that schlong of yours out of those Bermuda shorts and fuck my brains out!"

Valentino slowly unbuckled his shorts, allowing them, along with his boxers, to drop down around his ankles.

"You ain't said nuttin' but a word, sweetheart," he said, stepping out from the crumpled clothing on the floor. Meredith's eyes went wide with astonishment at the very sight of the pimp's sizeable penis, remarkable in both its length and girth; the slightly curved, heavily veined member hung thick and menacing between his muscular thighs like an ebony python poised for attack.

Hopping off the massage table and onto the soft carpet below, Meredith received the black stud into her awaiting arms, wincing from painful bliss as she felt every inch of his huge dick filling the walls of her hot pussy. Her breathing came in hyperventilating spurts as Valentino thrusted himself into her with raw, unfettered passion. Orgasms unlike any she'd ever experienced caused her entire body to tremble with satisfaction.

During the course of their vigorous lovemaking, Valentino prompted Meredith to switch positions. She obeyed eagerly, adopting the classic doggy-style pose while reaching back and spreading her plump cheeks with both hands, fully exposing the moist pink opening of her yawning vagina. He mounted her, sweaty and still aroused, smacking the length of his thick man meat against her pale booty before easing the bulbous head into her slit.

Meredith squeezed, moaned and panted with zeal while Valentino aggressively rode her like a horse until he skeeted off a load of tainted semen deep within her vaginal walls.

Both of them spent from their lusty afternoon tryst, they fell fast asleep in each other's arms while the scented candles slowly burned down to a mass of waxy nothingness.

May 19, 2002
1661 Falcon Crest Way
3:56 p.m.

Meredith, upon hearing the incessant buzz beyond the living room with mild irritation, paused the DVD featuring "Billy Blank's Beginner's Tae-Bo" and made her way toward the front door. She peeked through the peephole to discover that it was none other than Wilhelm who stood upon her front porch. She greeted him with a weak handshake as she opened the door.

She looked fit and really hot in her workout leotard, Wilhelm thought as he stood gawking at her in the doorway. She noticed the gleam in his intense blue eyes and immediately knew that something negative would be forthcoming.

"Good afternoon, Doctor. How might I assist you today?" she asked with a hint of sarcasm, which instantly caused him to tighten his jaw.

"You haven't set foot in the lab for the past week and we haven't gotten so much as a phone call from you as to your condition, adverse or otherwise, or your whereabouts. Have you completely lost your mind, Meredith? Tell me!"

She smirked briefly, and then took his hand, leading him into the threshold of her home while closing the door behind them.

"Tell you what?" she asked. "Why don't you have a seat and let me get you something to drink. What would you like? Let's see . . . I've got Gatorade, lemonade, diet Coke, an unopened bottle of Sauvignon Blanc and . . . two bottles of Heineken. Or, if you're in the mood for something a little stiffer, I can fix you up a kickass martini."

He angrily shook his head as he stood in front of the fluffy green couch.

"I've been covering for you all this time and I'm going to level with you, Meredith. I just can't do it anymore. Suspicions are rising throughout Coventry Labs about you and I'm telling you, it's not good."

Meredith paced the floor, back and forth with her head hung down and her hands behind her back in contemplation. Finally, after a few seconds, she stopped in front of Wilhelm and faced him with a look of cool indifference.

"Is that why you came over here? To try and scare me, Wilhelm? Dude, I don't freakin' care about any one of those douchebags at Coventry or even the higher-ups in the Illuninati for that matter, okay?" She yelled angrily, her face now glowing red.

He shifted uncomfortably while the hot brunette stood before him.

"You're acting irrational, as always. I really do think you need to consider psychiatric help," he said.

"Really? Well then maybe I'll just go to the Center for Disease Control in Atlanta and bring along a neat little briefcase filled with research papers, payment records and HIV10X cultures. Now wouldn't that gain the attention of a whole lot of people? Then what will everyone do Wilhelm? Huh? Tell me...what would they—or you!—do in a situation like that?"

"That would be blackmail, Meredith," Wilhelm replied, "pretty damned evil, even for a cunt like you."

"Fuck you, asshole," she snarled, slapping his face angrily.

"You're making a huge mistake, Meredith. You're playing around with people and circumstances that are far beyond anything in your realm of reasoning. You'd be wise to return to work tomorrow morning, bright and early. And I'll come up with an excuse for your prolonged absence from the lab," he said, rubbing the left side of his reddening face. "I'm leaving now, but I must emphasize again—tomorrow at 9 a.m. sharp I expect to see you at your work station and ready for research."

She watched as her coworker walked through the door and descended the steps toward his white Jaguar. She slammed the door shut, leaning back against it while closing her eyes in contemplation of the enormity of her recent choices.

***

Pulsating reggaeton music filled the surrounding streets with energetic melodies. Ghetto youth danced about freely while onlookers leaned out of windows and sat along low-lying rooftops to catch a glimpse of the local reggaeton star. Daddy Yank, as he was known, rode within a tricked-out apple green Cadillac convertible, waving to the boisterously loud crowd while tossing long-stemmed roses toward the attractive young mamis screaming for him along the cobblestone curb.

While the reggaeton and salsa blared festively and powerfully from the street of Calle Norzaga Way, "Don" Lucien Valentino met with two of his former Puerto Rican bodyguards, who'd now gone on to become powerful drug traffickers in their own right. A small group of bandana-wearing hoodlums stood with arms crossed a short distance away, just beside the tall, cracked tombstones of the Santa Maria Magdalena de Pazzi Cemetery. Inside, they gathered.

Although they were now in business for themselves, neither they nor the rest of La Perla's dope boys were eating as well as they had during the Don's reign upon the island. Recently the Puerto Rican police as well as the National Guard had arrested many of the town's true ballers, therefore drying up over 78 percent of the illegal drug traffic flowing through the crime-ridden barrio. The young men reached out to their former boss as he did not let them down, immediately taking a private plane to the island nation in an attempt to offer whatever help he could. Meeting in the cemetery was the most logical thing to do at this point, due to the vigilant police presence on the streets, carefully monitoring the raucous reggaeton concert.

As he discussed business strategies with the Puerto Rican hustlers, Lucien noticed one of the youths acting strangely. Without hesitation, he called out in Spanish for the young man's homeboys to bring him over. The boy tried to run, but was tackled by three other boys, who roughed him up on the way over to their stern-faced elders.

Just as Valentino suspected, the boy was equipped with a wire. He looked at each of his cohorts, who nodded in silent agreement while the traitorous teen was stripped of the surveillance device and held tight by his captors. The boy's eyes grew wide as he saw the wicked blade of the knife emerge in the Don's grip.

In a swift blur, Valentino's right hand swung past the dope boy's throat, opening up a fatal gash across his Adam's apple. The boy cried out in pain for an earsplitting two seconds before gurgling on his own blood and crashing backward onto the muddied soil below. Three muffled shots from the man closest to Valentino put the dying youth out of his misery.

Smoke, thin and wispy, wafted from the end of the silencer held by Valentino's burly ex-bodyguard, who spat on the boy's twitching corpse for good measure.

Maybe this was the reason for their cop troubles, the men thought. Two of the other youths were then instructed to dump the teen's body into one of the many 19th-century tombs dotting the ages-old graveyard. Immediately afterwards, the remaining four teens were searched thoroughly by the ex-bodyguards while Valentino held them at gunpoint. Though shocked and angered by the sudden lack of trust and rough treatment from their superiors, the dope boys wisely remained humble and silent after their release.

With the drama now over, the seven criminals sloshed through the mud and tombstones toward the rear of a massive crypt, where they exchanged dope for money. Valentino accepts his friends' measly four Gs for well over $25,000 worth of crack cocaine in an effot to stimulate the La Perla drug trade. Both of the beefy Puerto Ricans embraced

Valentino gratefully, promising to put the addictive rocks to good use on the streets of the barrio.

"Mucho gracias, mi amigo!" they said simultaneously.

Valentino also handed over to them a black medical bag with two dozen vials of Biomax-O #2, for many of the residents of the barrio had contracted HIV5X from his days of running a brothel in La Perla.

Valentino stuffed the money down into a small duffle bag hanging from his shoulder. Together the group of seven made their way out of the aged cemetery and began the long trek back to the barrio.

When they arrived, the festivities were still going strong with a rousing salsa dance-off between neighborhood teenagers, much to the delight of the rapidly growing crowd along the busy street. From the rear of an old monastery emerged three policemen, who made a beeline for the iced-out group of thugs. The lawmen drew service revolvers as they approached, forcing the criminals back toward the monastery at gunpoint.

There, the seven men were all thrown into the back of a van and whisked away from the barrio. The men endured an uncomfortable, bumpy ride in the rear of the rattling van, all the while listening to the policemen up front discuss the murderous details of what was in store for them.

Valentino heard them talk about how, ever since the scientists left, more and more people had somehow contracted HIV. And it wasn't just any HIV, but some new version of the virus that seemed to kill folks in only a few weeks. Many Puerto Rican cities had reported cases of the deadly strain, particularly Old San Juan and its barrios, such as Ballajà, Mercado, San Cristo and Marina. Hit as hard as they'd been by the alarming rash of AIDS deaths, Puerto Rican authorities essentially quarantined Old San Juan and San Juan alike, in a desperate attempt to contain the virus' rapid spread. All the while, they had also been arresting and even murdering at times those who were thought to be the culprits in spreading it along to the island's impoverished masses. Many men patronized Valentino's brothel, which sat hidden from public view behind a lush tropical forest. And now those very same johns were either dead or dying with no more than a few weeks left in them, though still infecting others.

A panic had overtaken the community at large, creating both fear and hatred for those living with the disease. It had been really ugly on Puerto Rico, and the timing couldn't have been worse for Valentino to have come back. Even the citizens had recently adopted a violent stance against AIDS victims living among them. Over thirteen reports of various types of hate crimes ranging from simple assault to attempted murder began circulating weekly since early May.

Valentino knew that once the vehicle stopped and they were forced out by the cops there would be no guarantee that bribe money would spare them their lives. Thinking quickly, he spied the National Guard uniform of the officer sitting on the passenger's side of the vehicle. A member of the National Guard, a military outfit that had several key personnel secretly working along with the Sentinels of the Illuminati, the World Health Organization and the U.S. Army virologists in developing the Inner City Virus program. This would prove to be invaluable to him.

The vehicle came to a sudden stop, and after a brief moment of tense silence, the back doors were abruptly snatched open. Everyone was, as they'd expected, searched thoroughly by several uniformed officers, who then relieved the men of their money, crack cocaine, Biomax-O and handguns before leading them at gunpoint to the outside of the van. The wire worn by the now dead teenage boy had revealed everything to the captors, even the fact that they were all HIV positive. They were handcuffed and then blindfolded before being shot once in the back of the head one by one. Valentino steeled himself as well as he could while the younger drug traffickers were reduced to whimpering crybabies as one earsplitting shot after another reduced their numbers.

The air smelled of acrid gun smoke and blood. There was only one chance he had to save himself. The police, who numbered about ten or eleven, all after each handcuffed man succumbed to a fatal head shot. The breeze from the ocean was cool and crisp, an ironic contrast to the otherwise dark events unfolding atop the small hill overlooking Old San Juan. When

Valentino stood as the sole survivor of the group, he immediately began, in Spanish, informing the National Guardsman giving the execution orders about his affiliation with the Inner City Virus Operation and the Illuninati. The executioner to his rear ridiculed him and prepared to put a bullet in his brain, but the ringleader immediately commanded him to stand down while slowly approaching the Don himself.

The officer, a heavily bearded Fidel Castro-look alike, handed Valentino his cell phone and demanded that he prove his statements with a call to the mainland. Understanding his somewhat shaky status with the majority of scientists back home at Coventry Laboratories, he took the Nextel from the guardsman's heave hand and dialed Doctor Nader's cell phone number. He heard the phone ringing on and on before her voicemail picked up. Snatching the cell phone away from the pimp, the angered guardsman was clearly just seconds away from giving his gunman the okay to blast Lucien Valentino into oblivion.

Just at that moment, the phone rang and the guardsman answered to an American woman on the other end. The Puerto Rican, now more puzzled, angrily asked the caller in English about her association with Valentino and the Illuminati. She refused to answer until she his reassured by Valentino himself that she must.

After a brief conversation with Meredith, the National Guardsman was satisfied that Don Valentino was indeed telling the truth. He was uncuffed and allowed to freshen up, then given a small meal prior to being transported back down to the airport in Old San Juan. The authorities, however, did not return the cache of cash and drugs, and had they realized the value of the Biomax-O, they would have surely kept that as well.

Upon boarding the private jet awaiting him at the small Puerto Rican runway, Valentino was bombarded by a kaleidoscope of emotions. Comfort in the fact that he'd escaped death, coupled with the bitter anguish of losing his dear friends at the hands of a corrupt militia nearly brought tears to the eyes of the normally emotionless drug lord. Looking down at the lush greenery of the island's countryside,

Valentino came to the conclusion that he had probably visited his beloved Puerto Rico for the very last time.

Chapter 18

It was now June 27th and Valentino still had not returned from his Puerto Rico trip. However, he usually spent a few extra days out doing God-knows-what with God-knows-who after such long business trips. Rosaria didn't care; in fact, she relished in the peace and solitude brought about by Valentino's absence. The head bodyguard was used to her hanging out at the local coffee shop and because she stayed true to the strict curfew he'd placed on her the prior week, he allowed her a little more time away from the beach house brothel, ultimately allowing her time to plot a getaway, far from Valentino's clutches forever. However, she'd always need Biomax-O to survive, and she felt like she knew enough about the Sentinels of the Illuminati to acquire the drug directly from them.

She had saved up $18,000 since Valentino had brought her back during the winter of 2001. Her income had derived from freelance sex with guys as well as a few gals she'd met at Starbucks and the surrounding shops she frequented during her free time away from the house, in addition to the marijuana she sold in bulk in partnership with fellow prostitutes who cultivated cannabis plants in the basement of their suburban home.

It would be only a few more weeks before the first of her sex clients became ill. She'd have to then move on from Lariat completely, so as to not to be implicated as the carrier who'd made so many others sick. She knew that in order for Valentino to elude the cops and health officials for as long as he did, he'd screw the whores of rival pimps and even some of his own without informing them of his health issues. They then went on to spread the killer virus before dying themselves.

Rosaria had been the only one of the girls he saw worthy enough to provide with Biomax-O shots.

She walked into the house just after 6:00 p.m. and headed straight into her bedroom upstairs overlooking the cresting turquoise waves of the mighty Pacific. There she injected a quick shot of Biomax-O into a vein in her left thigh. She'd already prepared for the searing pain of the shot's aftermath by sniffing two long powdery lines of Peruvian flake up her nose to curb the typically unpleasant reaction to the Biomax-O.

This new and improved version of the drug was a particularly sinister lab creation because on top of being the source of the super AIDS virus known as HIV10X, it was also a powerful aphrodisiac, which forced her to seek sexual fulfillment. She tried to pleasure herself with a large battery-operated dildo, but it did little to calm the raging flames in between her deliciously thick thighs. She stuck both the index and middle fingers of her left hand deep into her pussyhole, feverishly fingering her clitoris with her other hand while moaning like a bitch in heat. The entrance of her vagina was soaking wet with her love fluids, and hearing the very sound of her digits working in and out of her sopping twat made her cum with raw intensity.

Nevertheless, her need for a man was insatiable enough to drive her back onto the ho'stroll. Mego Avenue had reopened after the threat of landslides disappeared, and was now busier than ever with late-night, illicit activities. Before heading out, Rosaria showered, dressed and placed a quick phone call to a marijuana customer of hers from Cushing who'd become somewhat of a confidant lately. The 27-year old Chicano, like herself from East Los Angeles, had been a gang member for the feared Mexican mafia. He grew to dislike the abuse Valentino seemed to relish in handing out to his girls, particularly Rosaria. He'd once told her that if she ever had any need to call on him for protection, he would be just a phone call away. For Rosaria, the time for that connection was now.

July 4 began and ended for Meredith Nader the same way—in bed. She had been up for most of the night in front of her computer, completing over nine hours worth of HIV10X research work for Coventry Laboratories. During this time, she'd managed to polish off an entire bottle of champagne. Alcohol helped her cope with the aftereffects of the Biomax-O shots she'd recently begun taking.

Wilhelm had tried to get in contact with her several times since he'd come by her house, but she'd refused to speak to him either by phone or email. After all, she thought, why was he so hard pressed now? He'd previously shown little interest in her; he had, in fact, seemed quite irritated by her constant attention. In an effort to avoid him but keep her job, she'd requested work-at-home detail, and the company had agreed. She knew that Wilhelm had been both jealous and worried sick about her dealings with Valentino, however she assured him that she'd never, ever sleep with a black man, much less one who carried a deadly virus within his bloodstream. That, of course, was a blatant lie, but she knew he'd believe it because he wanted to. He was awfully gullible for a man of his scientific brilliance.

Now she noticed through tired, red eyes that the German had emailed her a whopping 13 times since the day before, and was currently online. She then went into the virtual chat room to communicate.

eurotrash99: Finally! Why have you been avoiding me, Meredith? Is it because of the fight we had back in May?

Meredith read the text as it flashed across her computer screen.She answered:

biologyrocksMN: I've just been really busy as of late—that's all. Nothing personal, Wil

eurotrash99: Bullshit. Don't lie to me, Meredith. I know you too well and we both know you're pissed at me right now. Admit it...

Meredith grinned as she typed her answer.

biologyrocksMN: Okay, maybe I was a little upset but hey, shit happens...

eurotrash99: You're right. Shit does happen, but friends don't leave friends out of the loop about their plans to work exclusively from home, and friends don't treat each other like crap either.

biologyrocksMN: EXCUSE ME?! Wil, baby, if I recall the last time we met in person you weren't very nice to me. And remember when we shared the laboratory together? You acted as though I was a nuisance to you, so I saw no reason to inform you of anything I did.

eurotrash99: We were at work and we had to keep things as professional as possible. Meredith, you knew that. It was you who seemed to have forgotten those basic rules.

biologyrocksMN: Wil, listen up, I'm not really in the mood for another one of your whiney, egotistical, brain numbing rants, okay? I'm hung over, I've got PMS and I just missed all the fireworks on TV, so please just shut it, will you?

eurotrash99: You're such a cunt

biologyrocksMN: That may be, doctor, but you'd still love to fuck my brains out, wouldn't you?! ;)

eurotrash99: I bet you'd love to take it up the ass

biologyrocksMN: OMG, Dr. Strecker, what am I going to do with you? And I thought you didn't care...lol

Chapter 19

Lucien Valentino arrived back in Lariat on the 10th of July at 5:26 p.m. He'd spent a considerable amount of time up north in San Francisco establishing another small, but prime prostitution ring near Chinatown. Coming through the door, he was immediately greeted with the usual outpouring of affection and love by the dozens of half-nude hookers who fawned over him for what seemed like an hour as he doled out to each of them expensive, glittery pieces of bling or overpriced perfumes with fancy-sounding names—the spoils of his travels. Every one of the girls seemed to be happy to see him and thrilled with their gifts—every one except Rosaria. Sitting alone in the corner, seeming distant, she was clearly unimpressed by the whole shebang, the look in her eyes hostile.

Rosaria caught on that Valentino was curiously studying her as the other streetwalkers giggled and wiggled on and around him, so she got up from her spot in the corner and disappeared down the darkened hallway. Valentino was puzzled as to why she was acting so strangely, but he'd get down to the bottom of it at another time. Now he had to get with Shugawallz, his most senior trick at 51 years old. She served as the Madame, or "queen whore," of the house, controlling the money and delivering it to Valentino at the end of each day or, in certain cases each week.

While he sat on the couch counting his money at the coffee table, two of his older streetwalkers revealed that they'd seen Rosaria out and about with a young, tough-looking Mexican guy for the past few weeks, and that he seemed to be more than a mere sex client. Smiling, the gangsta pimp placed the large wad of cash upon the edge of the table in a neat stack.

He rarely, if ever trusted any one, least of all the whores. Rosaria had been the only one of his girls he'd allowed to have any level of access into his private world. She had, however, betrayed that ever-so-fragile trust, and was more than likely plotting to escape again—or maybe even, he thought, planning something more sinister. It was funny to him how dumb bitches occasionally slept on him as if he was one of the squares who paid for their worn-out coochies. Sometimes he actually found hitting on his women to be somewhat distasteful, necessary, but distasteful nonetheless.

Unfortunately, it occurred to him that Rosaria's recent behavior might warrant such a response. If his hunch was correct, she'd left him no choice. Once a whore began overstepping her boundaries, harsh and decisive actions had to be taken on the offending trick by her pimp, usually in front of all the others so as to both teach a much-needed lesson and send a larger message to her peers. Many an amateur pimp had ruined a potentially promising career as a boss playa by taking on too soft of a disciplinary role with his bitches.

He dismissed Shugawallz, who in turn directed the two other prostitutes to follow her back toward the sleeping quarters. Valentino took up the pile of money from off the tabletop and recounted it before placing it into a small safe deposit box. After locking the safe, he arose and ventured out onto the deck overlooking the ocean.

He wondered how much damage his AIDS-infected whores, particularly Rosaria herself, had done in the town of Lariat, California since he'd arrived there. Even the very doctor who'd produced the virulent disease itself had now become a carrier. He could still use Rosaria to his benefit. The blood money the Illuminati paid him handsomely to spread the virus throughout the ghettos of America. Yet, a weird twist of fate or karma, one of their own was now a living bioweapon, capable of infecting the members of society's upper crust— those who were never meant to be touched by the pain and suffering of the super AIDS experiment.

Valentino thought about how he had flipped the script, and how he would blackmail the Sentinels of the Illuminati once the virus began to spread amongst the rich and powerful.

No one would be the wiser, because by the time the HIV10X would be discovered within the wealthy, predominately white community, it would be far too late to quell it. Dr. Nader had been turned out just as easily as he'd turned out any of his prostitutes. She no doubt would be a willing participant in his own AIDS spreading agenda.

As the seagulls squawked and circled above the gently splashing surf, Valentino smiled devilishly at the thought of turning the tables on his equally evil employers, thus gaining almost dictator-like power. He left the warmth of the outside deck to return again to his cozy home.

A few of his prostitutes walked about the grand living room area cleaning and dusting the already pristine area. Rosaria, however, was not among them. Valentino walked into the kitchen and stood near the entrance, staring at three cute, girlish hookers who jabbered away with each other, while an older woman carried on a simultaneous conversation on the house phone. One of the girls caught an angry look from the Don and she quickly exited the kitchen, followed closely by her two galpals. As they walked sheepishly past their irritated pimp, he issued them a stern warning to them and they sprinted from the kitchen through the living room and down the hallway.

Slowly he made his way into the kitchen and picked up the receiver from its cradle on the wall. He dialed Dr. Nader's digits before placing the receiver to his ear and leaning back lazily against the countertop. Meredith answered in less than a few seconds. By the sound of her voice, he could tell that she was upset about something.

"Lucien," she said in a tone rife with annoyance, "I'm sorry that I sound this way, but I'm, like, totally ticked off right now."

Valentino's brow wrinkled in anticipation of what would be revealed.

"Talk to me, boo. S'up?" he asked, accepting a tall glass of cold lemonade from one of his prostitutes.

Meredith cleared her throat on the other end before speaking.

"Are you sitting down for this?" she said, still sounding emotional. "One of the guys down at the lab has tested positive for AIDS! And it's too late to treat him with Biomax-O."

Meredith went on to describe the victim, a white, male biochemist in his early fifties. He was married with two kids, and was now well into the final stages of the virus, full-blown AIDS. The man, who had once been an avid mountain climber and lacrosse player, now weighed less than 90 pounds. The skin cancer Kaposi's Sarcoma covered his brittle body in bright, swollen bluish purple blotches while ugly open lesions leaked putrid-smelling pus around his mouth and private areas. According to Meredith, the man was minded dying the most horrific of deaths.

"Aiight, and?" Valentino said. "Why the fuck you tellin' me this shit? If the muthafucka got AIDS then that's just too damn bad. Shit, say a prayer for the muthafucka for all I care, it ain't got shit to do wit me!"

Meredith chuckled sarcastically.

"Yeah, you're right, Lucien, this doesn't have anything to do with you. You just happen to work for us white folk who pay you to pass on HIV10X to as many people as possible, so no, you're not responsible...just as long as you only get the right kind of people sick, remember? Meaning, people of color, Jews, and the occasional poor white trash guy or gal...but someone must've forgotten that educated white scientists are off limits, hmm? Look, Lucien, I like you. I mean, hey, I like you a lot. I thought I'd never in a million years fall for a black guy, least of all you. You've got me hooked so much that I've even risked infection. No one's ever made me feel the way you do and—trust me—you make me feel like a queen. But you've got to think, sweetie, with this prick dying on us everyone at Coventry is going to want answers, which means the heat is going to come down not only on you but on me, too— especially if Doctor Wilhelm Von Strecker has anything to do with it."

"Fuck all them crackas," Valentino said. "I don't give a fuck 'bout them!"

Meredith sighed with a bit of frustration at her lover's words. He may have been a mover and shaker in his rough and tumble world of prostitutes, pimps and drugs, but on this stage he was far out of his league. She knew he shouldn't even be considering strong-arming anyone. This time around he was a small fish in a big and dangerous pond.

"Lucien, you and I—we both work for Coventry Laboratories, who in turn works for a select group of doctors in the World Health Organization, who then must answer to the Sentinels of the Illuminati. These people have access to unlimited financial resources and, politically, they're damned near untouchable. There's just too much riding on Operation Inner City Virus for them to allow an oversexed, psycho chick from Boise, Idaho and a black drug-dealing pimp in Lariat, California by way of Puerto Rico and D.C. to throw a monkey wrench in their plans for population control, so let's smarten up here."

"You think that I don't know who I'm fuckin' wit, Meredith?" Valentino snarled into the phone. "I fought in two wars overseas, so I know 'bout the powers that be and how they dog the lil' people out. That's why I said fuck 'em. Read between the lines, baby girl, aiight? Read between the lines on that one."

Meredith began to tire of Valentino's street-hewn machismo in light of the grave situation looming before them.

"I'm so happy that the Sentinels of the Illuminati or their affiliates resort to bugging phones or they'd be off us on your arrogance alone, ya' know that? You're really not taking this seriously, are you?"

Valentino's eyes narrowed with anger as he bristled over the cynical tone coming from Meredith. A boss playa like himself had made women pay for less before, and his hand clenched into a fist almost on queue in response to the scientist's disrespect.

"They know betta...besides, that cat coulda fucked around and got burnt fuckin' wit any number of triflin' ass hos—or, fa that matter, shit, he might take dicks. Ever thought 'bout that?" Valentino asked. "Ya see just 'cause y'all started out expectin' to wipe out all the niggas in the hood with this ole HIV5X or 10X or whatever the fuck ya wanna call it, you gotta recognize that once ya infect one muthafucka in the ghetto wit that shit don't think that one nigga gon' just pass that shit on to other niggas. Naw, baby, that ain't thinkin' outside the box, now is it? You know how many fiends I got huntin' me down for coke and crystal meth a week? Shit, I can't even count 'em no mo' and they're all rich white folks from Fujita City, not to mention the number o' clients from the F.C. that actively solicit prostitution on Mego Avenue's ho stroll. Bottom line is...you can't contain this shit once you turn it loose on society. The world ain't ya goddamned laboratory and the hood ain't hardly no controlled environment for y'all's lil' fucked up experiements and shit. So don't go blamin' a muthafucka when the shit gets outta hand."

"You're probably right, Lucien," Meredith said, "but these guys don't give a rat's ass about anything you just said. For starters, Wilhelm already has a hunch that we've been seeing each other—a hunch that I've been able to successfully disclaim because of your 'positive' status as an AIDS carrier as well as my 'racial intolerance.'"

There was a pause, and both Valentino and Meredith seemed to calm down somewhat.

"Don Lucien Valentino ain't never feared no man, and I ain't 'bout to start now," he said, breaking the silence. "See, I know the game they're playin' and trust me, it's gonna work in my favor, Meredith. You see all them so-called big-time politicians an' shit ain't got nothin' on us niggas in the 'hood, real talk. All they got on us is book smarts and a whole bunch o' big words an' shit, but cats out here on the pound...shit, them niggas got the real sense...'cause they gots street smarts. I make damn near eight-hundred grand a year, give or take a few dollars here and there, and my black ass ain't never seen the inside of a fuckin' college or university."

"Wow."

"You damn right, girl...wow," Valentino said with arrogance. "Not only will I bless you with this big-ass rod I'm tot'n between my legs, but I'm gon' bless you wit the type a lifestyle you ain't never had befo', Meredith. Think about it— them dudes ain't never paid a fly ass broad like yourself no mind. As a matter o' fact, that bitch ass Wilhelm pretty much used you. And once he taxed that ass he dropped you like a fuckin' bad habit, didn't he? Them muthafuckas don't give a fuck 'bout neither one of us. Shit, I think them peoples gon' use us until they get what they want from us and then they gon' try to set us up to be killed, 'cause we know too much. C'mon now. That's why *we* gotta get these punk bitches before they get us, ya feel me?"

After a brief moment of silence, Meredith spoke softly.

"I...I don't know why I feel about you the way that I do, but I'm crazy for you, and every inch of that ginormous cock of yours," she said. "You're right—I've never had anyone love me ever—not like you do, and I get it when you trash those dweebs I work with. They're the absolute worst. I'm ready...so ready to stick it to their asses just as I'm sure you are. Let's do it. Together, my love, let's show those white racist bastards who's boss, shall we?!"

Chapter 20

Rosaria licked around a freshly rolled blunt with her sensual tongue before placing the end of the weed-stuffed stogie to the awaiting flame of a cigarette lighter. She relaxed and savored the taste of the marijuana's aromatic flavor throughout her mouth.

She hated the taste of semen in general, but this last guy's spunk was the absolute worst she'd ever had. To her it tasted like fish oil, onions and egg yolk. She charged him a hundred dollars extra right after he'd skeeted in her mouth just because of it. Kush always took away the stinky cum taste, especially that good Cali kine bud she'd just sparked.

This john, a long, lanky giraffe of a man, shared the blunt with her as they both sat back upon the warm leather seats of his mammoth '76 Buick 225. The man sat beside her the whole time talking about a whole lot of nothing in between trying to copy a quick feel of her naked breasts. Angrily, Rosaria slapped the customer's hand away roughly, declaring herself off limits to groping unless she was once again hired. The man agreed eagerly, plunking down three crumpled Benjamins next to her leg on the broad car seat. She scooped up the three large bills and placed them into her purse, which was swell stuffed from an evening of good business out on the ho' stroll.

Luckily for her, the gangly old lecher simply requested a hand job to top off the night. She quickly fellated him to erection before masturbating his vein-filled cock with slow, deliberate strokes, using her own saliva as a lubricant. Within three minutes of tugging on his tool, the man shot his load in strong, creamy spurts onto the dashboard and seat. The driver then collapsed in a sweaty heap behind the steering wheel while Rosaria cleaned the remaining sperm from in between her fingers and prepared to step out of the vehicle.

The cool, gentle breeze coming off of the nearby Pacific Ocean was a welcome refreshment after spending so much time in the stuffy confines of the deuce and quarter she'd just left. She decided that she'd earned enough money and waved goodnight to a few of the other ladies of the evening who continued to flaunt themselves for the cars cruising along the avenue. Then, suddenly, a pair of automobile headlights illuminated the quiet side street she'd taken as a shortcut toward the beachfront home of Valentino the car raced along the street like a bat out of hell, startling the Latina prostitute as she braced herself against a graffiti-covered wall. The white Volkswagon Passat came to an abrupt and screeching halt directly beside the curb where Rosaria stood.

"Get in the car!" Wilhelm Von Strecker barked from the open window. He glanced outside nervously at the unfamiliar landscape surrounding him, then again at the startled young woman standing near the darkened wall of the street corner.

"Now!" he yelled, pointing a .38 caliber revolver in her direction for good measure.

Though Rosaria was hesitant to enter the stranger's vehicle, she had little choice staring down the barrel of a snub nose. She walked over toward the idling vehicle and stepped into the passenger's seat, closing the door gently behind her. After driving along Rock Hudson Parkway for a considerable time without speaking, the doctor broke the uneasy silence.

"I know that you work for Lucien Valentino and that you want out from under him, as well this God-awful lifestyle you've been forced into. I can make that happen for you if you, in turn, help me. One of your clients told me everything about your situation. And I'm willing to help you get out o f here if you help me find someone. Her name is Meredith . . . Meredith Nader. She's my coworker and I need to know where she is. It's a matter of life and death!" As requested, the shaken prostitute directed the German scientist toward Valentino's beachfront dwelling.

They arrived in front of the gangsta pimp's home around 1:17 a.m. The house was dark, but for a side window, illuminated by the glow of television light coming from within. Upon seeing Meredith's pewter-colored Hyundai Elantra parked beside several of Valentino's high-end whips in the parking lot, Wilhelm raced out from the car in a jealous fit of rage. He banged on the front door furiously for several seconds before it was snatched open by an angry Valentino.

"Have you lost yo' muthafuckin' mind, bitch!"

Wilhelm narrowed his eyes, gritted his teeth and clenching his fists together, bracing for a fight. Then thoughts of the virulent HIV10X came to mind, causing him to rethink the idea of striking the pimp for fear of bringing the blood-borne pathogen into play. Instead he quick reached down into his trouser pocket to withdraw the .38 revolver. He noticed Meredith standing in wide-eyed horror directly behind Valentino as he drew the handgun from his right pocket.

Wilhelm was acting off of pure emotion now, like a lovesick teen. The sight of his ex-lover standing behind the black pimp dressed in little more than a sheer teddy distracted him just long enough for Valentino to pounce.

Strong fingers grasped the doctor's wrist, causing him to relax his grip on the weapon, which fell upon the wooden floor of the front porch. Wilhelm swung at his assailant with his free hand, but his punch breezed harmlessly past Valentino's head.

"You nigger bastard!"

Valentino landed a crushing blow to the German's slender jaw as he yelled out racial slurs. The punch felled Wilhelm, who tumbled backwards onto the steps and into the loose gravel of the walkway. He struggled to his feet only to be kicked back into the sand again by the pimp, who yelled out in a torrent of profanities at him as he stood above him. His ribs burned with searing pain with each breath he drew, causing him to fear that few were badly cracked.

Two burly bodyguards came barreling out of the doorway over to the place where Wilhelm lay upon the ground. He was hoisted up onto his feet by one of the hulking guards, who dragged him across the white sand toward his vehicle. For several seconds, he endured a brief but brutal beating at the hands of Valentino's goons, leaving him battered and bloodied beside his car.

"F- Fuck you!" he called after them.

Wilhelm slowly, painfully climbed up onto his feet, which wobbled unsteadily beneath him. His entire body was racked with pain, causing him to wince with each step. His rib cage burned from where he had been kicked, and he fumbled with the keys in his pocket, opening the door to his car with much effort.

The streetwalker was gone, likely scared shitless, he thought. He wanted to go back onto Valentino's porch and confront him again, but the idea was foolhardy at best, with his gun now missing and the bodyguards prepared fro anything else stupid he might try. He peered at his bruised face in the overhead mirror on the visor flap, doing his best to clean himself up.

He took out his cell phone and dialed Meredith's number. After a series of rings he listened to her message, with its perky, upbeat greeting, awaiting the beep.

"Meredith, what have you done?!" he yelled into the phone. "You're mad! You're going to not only ruin the cause of this program, but you're going to get both of us killed messing around with that bastard Valentino! If you don't cut this bullshit out, so help me I'll...goddamnit, Meredith!"

The bodyguards who'd trashed him just minutes earlier opened the front door of the house and stepped out onto the porch. They were joined by Valentino, who stood between them, chatting and pointing to Wilhelm's Passat with malice in their eyes. Wilhelm's hands fumbled around with the car keys for a few seconds before finally placing the proper key into the ignition and pulling out of the parking lot and on the busy street.

He wondered if he had finally gone bonkers, stalking a woman who was clearly emotionally over him now and risking his life by confronting perhaps Lariat's most violent criminal. However, he had to make contact with his coworker for more reasons than one. He doubled back across town toward the red light district where he'd picked up Rosaria earlier in the evening.

"Excuse me, can you help me find a particular girl tonight?" he asked through the open window, speaking to a small group of scantily clad hookers huddled together near an old flickering gas lamp.

The streetwalkers seemed reluctant to answer, even after he flashed a wad of cash in their direction. One of the older women walked away from the lamp and out of the streetlight's illumination, and the others followed suit.

Wilhelm drove away in frustration, knowing that Valentino must have alerted his whores to the situation at hand. Four prostitutes passed his vehicle within a matter of minutes. They were all young—far too young, in fact, to be selling their bodies to strangers for profit. He attempted to solicit information from the girls with the promise of a cash reward, but they, like the others before them, would have nothing to do with him. With mounting frustration, he sped away, out of the red light district and back onto the freeway, where he once again tried calling his coworker's phone.

"C'mon, c'mon, pick up the goddamned phone, Meredith," he said under his breath.

So immersed was he in his phone line pursuit that he swerved in and out of his traffic lane a few times, drawing the ire of this fellow drivers, who he was sure took him for someone who'd had one cocktail too many. He left three new messages for Meredith has he navigated the busy Rock Hudson Parkway. He couldn't allow Meredith's behavior to jeopardize the success of Operation Inner City Virus.

He turned off the parkway onto an adjoining ramp heading west toward Coventry Laboratories. He pressed hard on the gas pedal, breezing past an elongated 18-wheeler and cutting off a Mazda Miata in his haste to get to his office. Once he'd pulled up into the parking lot, he knew that few, if any of his coworkers would be present at this hour. He dabbed at the blood that oozed from his facial wounds before entering the facility.

As he swiped his building pass against the card reader, the glass doors slid apart, granting him entry. There, a drowsy security officer perked up from his catnap as the scientist approached.

"Just checking on some lab results, officer. I won't be long, I promise," he said, flashing his I.D. as he quickly walked past.

"Of course, Doctor Von Strecker, take your time," the guard answered.

In his locker room attached to his office, he took time to shower and tend to his bruises and cuts properly, with ointment, gaze and bandages. As the scientist stood before the mirror dressing his wounds, he thought about who he could trust to right all of Valentino and Meredith's wrongs.

Suddenly, he had an idea. He emailed Doctor Dennis Brooks, who had been away on special assignment in Atlanta for the Center for Disease Control. Wilhelm looked at the clock, realizing that Doctor Brooks, an early riser, might be awake already, as it was close to 7 a.m. on the East Coast. And, in fact, Doctor Brooks had been in front of his computer for nearly a half hour.

Eurotrash99: Dennis, are you there?

Dennistheman_515: Yeah, what the hell are you doing up so early?

Eurotrash99: Dude, we've got a problem.

Dennistheman_515: What kind of a problem?

Eurotrash99: It's Meredith—she's gone off the deep end. It's serious.

Dennistheman_515: Meredith has always been a little quirky—you know that. We all do. It can't be that bad.

Eurotrash99: You don't understand—I think she's sleeping with Patient Zero!

Dennistheman_515: Say what?! Wil, are you drinking again? That's hard to believe—even for her. Are you sure?

Eurotrash99: I'm sure. Since you've been down south she's been acting weirder and weirder. She hasn't been in the lab in over a month. She's working from home—somehow she got Doctor Harrington's approval to do that.

Dennistheman_515: Wow—that's some deep shit. Well, what are you doing to do about it?

Eurotrash99: I was thinking that you're down there in Atlanta—maybe you could get in contact with your cousin?

Dennistheman_515: Which one are you talking about?

Eurotrash99: C'mon—you know the guy I'm referring to—the ganster guy.

Dennistheman_515: Wil, I haven't got a clue who you're talking about.

Eurotrash99: Okay—remember you said you were distant cousins to some guy in Peola, GA that just happened to be a professional hitman or something. Does that job your memory?

Dennistheman_515: Oh, yeah—you're talking about Whiskey—Whiskey Battle. Yep. He's yeah my third cousin on my mother's side. I haven't seen him in a while though. I was out west for over a decade, and I never come down to visit Peola. Anyway, why do you need me to get in touch with him?

Eurotrash99: Well, he's in the business of making people's troubles disappear. I want you to tell him about a certain low life pimp I'd like to see disappear. And no price is too high!

Dennistheman_515: Are you serious?

Eurotrash99: I'm up emailing you at four in the morning—what do you think?

Dennistheman_515: Do you know what you're asking me to do? First of all, Valentino's a major player in the Illuminati's population control plan. Secondly, if Meredith is stupid enough to expose herself to the HIV10X virus by messing around with the guy, then so be it. It's her funeral—not ours. Sorry, dude, but I'm not getting myself involved in your little weirdo love triangle. You need Dr. Phil, not Whiskey.

Eurotrash99: Look, Dennis, I've helped you out a lot since you've been with Coventry Labs. I took you under my wing when others in the agency would never have done it. And now you can't help me out here? Maybe I was wrong about you, Dennis. I thought maybe you were one of the good ones.

Dennistheman_515: Fuck you for saying that, Wil. Fucking Nazi bastard! Why don't you grow a pair and fight your own battles, asshole!

Eurotrash99: I strike a nerve there, Dennis? The last time I checked you were working with us Nazi bastards, developing a virus that will eventually eliminate your entire primitive race. What would Al Sharpton or Farrakhan think about that, Dennis? Or your own mother, or should I say Mammy?

Dennistheman_515: Eat shit and die Von Strecker!

Wilhelm's computer flashed: *Dennistheman has singed out.*

Wilhelm smirked uneasily as he too signed off of his email account, turned off the computer and then the lights within the laboratory. He exited the darkened room slowly, closing the heavy door behind him as he went.

***

The next day, July 19, Meredith checked her phone messages as she sat at the kitchen table, eating a cup of frozen yogurt. She listened to Wilhelm's desperation from the previous night coming through the speaker. He sounded completely taken with grief, so much so that for a split second she started to cry. He would always be a part of her, no matter what. In a way he had been her first love, the one man to have taken her virginity on that lone night of passion they had shared.

Suddenly Valentino's husky voice shattered her fleeting trip down memory lane as he whispered into her ear while draping his strong arms around her shoulders.

"I know how you musta felt 'bout ole boy, but he can't give you what the Don can give you, baby girl. Believe that," the pimp said boastfully. "C'mon now, dry those eyes and fix big daddy something ta eat with ya phine self."

"Umm, sure," Meredith said. "I'll take out the ground beef. You're going to love my meatloaf."

She pressed the power button on her cell phone, turning it off.

"I really thought that Wil could be someone I could've married. What waste."

She took out a frozen pack of meat from the freezer, placing it down into the kitchen sink while she went through the overhead cabinets in search of seasonings. As she stood up on her tiptoes to reach upwards, Valentino took in the svelte, hourglass figure displayed before him. He eased up behind her and taking hold of her narrow waist, he pulled her gently toward him, turning her around to face him. Without hesitation, their lips met in a torrid kiss that lasted a tantalizing seven seconds.

Breathing heavily with sexual arousal, Meredith threw her head back as her handsome lover caressed her pale neck with kisses and gentle love bites. She again placed her hungry lips upon his as he lifted her up into his strong arms, taking her into the living room and laying her down on the couch, where he undressed her, slowly removing her garments one layer at a time. By the time her head had cleared from the stupor of sensual arousal, Lucien had already inserted his thick, curved rod inside of her dripping punani. She winced and sighed with breathy delight as her ebony lover hoisted her shapely legs above his shoulders and pumped her vigorously on the couch. Meredith's eyes rolled upwards and her mouth fell agape, allowing an elongated groan of ecstasy to creep out as she reached orgasm. Her orgasm multiplied by four, bringing her to the brink of unconsciousness.

After this last intimate encounter, Meredith was certain that she'd officially "gone black." Valentino had fully conquered her now, mind, body and soul—and he knew it. So did she, and there was absolutely nothing that she could do to change it, nor did she want to. She was sprung. The gangsta mack gave her a kiss on the forehead and strolled upstairs to take a hot shower. While his lady love slowly gathered herself up, she recovered from the delightfully wicked romp. Just thinking about it as she pulled herself together caused her to become wet with arousal all over again—a condition that caused her to finger herself in an attempt to satisfy her lust until her lover returned.

Valentino, however, had had his fill of sex play for the moment. His thoughts were now focused once more on Rosaria, whom he was certain had become a liability. Her latest betrayal had caused him to order his security to snatch her up off the streets and make her disappear for good. However, he'd just received a phone call informing him that no one had seen hide nor hair of the lovely Latina anywhere. Even after three hours of combing the entire area for her, focusing primarily on the prostitute's favorite hangouts.

He cussed under his breath as he hung up the line, tossing the cell phone onto the bed adjacent to the bathroom's entrance, and stepping under the steaming water cascading down from the overhead spigot. He stayed locked in deep thought as he slid the Irish Spring bar across his trim body, working up a sudsy lather in the process.

Rosaria had tried to set him up for failure and had almost succeeded. And now she was a ghost. With her street smarts and a little bit of cash, there would be no telling where she could be at this point. As expected, she walked with enough vials of Biomax-O to last for at least two years, and he hadn't received a dime from her in over a month, even though he knew she had been turning tricks. And the audacity of Wilhelm Von Strecker to have approached him as though he wanted to bring it had earned him a death sentence as well. All over a bitch. It amazed him how pussy caused cats to act out of character. Too bad they both had to get their wigs pushed back to prove a point.

He turned the shower off and stepped out of the tub after pulling the bamboo print shower curtain aside. Dwelling on Rosaria made him think back on a few of the other women whom he'd infected with the deadly virus. Susan Norris came to mind as he dried himself. A sexy middle school math teacher with a bubble butt and impressive oral skills had fallen for him during one of his brief trips out of the country. He'd met her in Barbados and spent over a month with her on a cruise ship before flying back stateside with her to Chicago. She had died quickly—within a two-month period after their whirlwind romance. He finally remembered looking down on her in her hospital bed. She must have dropped at least 85 pounds before the AIDS-related lymphoma put her out of her misery.

She had been a wonderful fuck for him at least, he thought to himself. There had been at least five others who had crossed his mind on this day. They had all met the same terrible fate as had the cute teacher after sleeping with him.

Then there were those whom he had spared, for one reason or another, such as Lydia Maddox, a 35-year old dentist whom he had preyed upon financially in return for ran occasional booty call. He was very careful with this one and never went up in her without a quality condom strapped on, which was rare for him. He usually broke her off orally and that was enough to satisfy most times. She was too important for him to take out at least for another month or so, which would be just enough time to drain her bank account. Then he'd give her the dick raw next time around, skeeting off his death-dealing cum into her.

He dialed her up as he dressed, speaking to her in a rich, deep tone that he knew had once brought shudders to her.

"How are you, beautiful? You miss me?"

"I'm doin' fine," the female voice replied, "and yes I do miss you, baby. When am I going to see you again. I'm hot and bothered if you know what I mean."

"Ha ha!" Valentino laughed. "Yeah, I know exactly what that means, ma...I'm comin' over there in a little bit to beat that thing fa ya, aiight?"

"Boy, you so crazy! Well, c'mon now, I've been waitin' too long for that good dick."

"I'm gonna give it to ya too, just like you like it—rough and rugged! Now, don't forget to hook a nigga up wit that ?, aiight? 'Cause I gotta pay some bills and I'm a bit short so I'm gon' need fa you to do that fa me, aiight?"

"I got you, baby," the woman purred. "You just bring your phine ass on over here."

He whispered a seductive goodbye before placing it down upon a mahogany nightstand. Turning toward the bed he picked up his car keys, wallet and phone and made his way down the winding staircase.

***

Wilhelm Von Strecker sat slack jawed at the end of a dimly lit Cobblestone District bar downing one whiskey sour after another. However, even in his besotted condition, he still could not shake the thoughts of vengeance for what Valentino and his thugs had done to him on that fateful night. He felt both betrayed and sickened by Meredith's sudden desire for the gangster pimp and swallowed down an entire glass of the booze in anger, disgusted by the image of the two of them together. This was an undesirable, one of the lower races, as well as human lab rat who carried the lethal HIV10X virus within his blood stream, yet still Meredith seemed to throw all caution to the wind, as well as the commitment of the Sentinels of the Illuminati for the sake of jungle fever. He grimaced with revulsion after dwelling on the matter for a few seconds.

Finishing off his sixth whiskey sour, he glanced up at the clock over the bar and realized that he'd spent the better part of three and a half hours drinking alone. It was now 12:47 a.m. and he was truly trashed. There was no way that he'd risk an accident driving home, so he decided to crash at a nearby motel for the night. Not long after, bar soon began filling up with college kids and yuppies seeking cheap booze and a good party spot. Listening to a beer-guzzling throng singing along to Journey's "Don't Stop Believing," an inebriated Wilhelm slunk through the crowd and out the door past a growing line of lively twenty-somethings, waiting impatiently to gain entrance. He walked hastily, if not a bit unsteadily, and paid a local parking garage attendant to babysit his vehicle while he slept off the alcohol.

After paying the attendant, Wilhelm made his way back out onto the familiar cobblestone streets of the upscale neighborhood. Once he'd selected a room for the night, he quickly showered and logged onto his laptop just before turning in. Though he was quite drunk, he always checked his email messages just before bed, and tonight was no different. However, he was unprepared for the photos he saw upon opening his email account—photo after gruesome photo of the dying and dead victims of the HIV10X-fueled AIDS terror. However, few if any of the emaciated corpses portrayed in the ghoulish pictures were of African Americans, nor were the victims from the targeted areas in which the Illuminati had mapped out for population control. Instead, each and every one was a rich person—those from Lariat's upper crust areas. An uneasy feeling immediately crept over Doctor Von Strecker, bringing a nasty queasiness to his stomach as he clicked the mouse. Overcome with nausea, he rushed toward the bathroom, vomiting up a night's worth of drinks into the toilet.

He awakened an hour later collapsed beside the commode and forced himself up from the cold, file-covered floor, washing his face and mouth clean. He brushed his teeth and showered before dressing to leave. By the time he checked out of the room, his cell phone was ringing upon his side with a steady stream of calls.

As he waited for the clerk to return his credit card to him, he finally took the phone into his hand and scrolled through his incoming call log and saw it was fellow Coventry Labs coworker Reuben Mintz. He'd sent a text message stating that everyone at Coventry Laboratories believed that somehow Patient Zero, Lucien Valentino, had gone rogue, infecting not only other blacks, but white citizens as well with the AIDS virus—and that it was believed that Meredith was his accomplice in these murderous endeavors.

***

Valentino sat behind the wheel of a fresh looking Cadillac XLR, silently gazing at Rosaria through a pair of dark sunglasses. It was a humid July day, typical of a mid-summer afternoon in southern California. He'd followed Rosaria all the way to L.A. after a cocaine client had contacted him with her whereabouts a week earlier. She was wearing a bright green floral print sundress, which hugged and complimented her wickedly delectable curves perfectly. Her glossy, raven black hair flowed down her back and out from a matching green sunhat. Her smooth skin was a gorgeous golden bronze.

Since he'd last seen her, Los Angeles had been very good to her. He almost fell a little bit in love with her a second time, sitting there watching her. In actuality, he still adored the lovely, young Hispanic hottie, however it was simply in the rules of the game that she be taught a lesson. Switching was a sacrilege within the 'hood and those found guilty of it were hated, shunned and many times come up missing. Rosaria would be no different.

Valentino lit up a cigarette as he lounged lazily in the plush leather bucket seat of the Caddy. He thumbed through his phone's digital menu looking for a number belonging to a group of stick-up kids, crackheads, ex-cons and gangbangers who'd jump at the chance to peel Wilhelm Von Strecker's wig back for a nice piece of change. As he pondered the matter further, he realized that Meredith herself could be used for the job.

Quickly, Valentino caught the attention of a Chicano street peddler who worked traffic hawking bouquets of fresh-cut roses in between the vehicles whenever they stopped at the light. He purchased a dozen long-stemmed roses and went back to spying on his former prostitute. She'd been shopping for over an hour along one of east L.A.'s busiest streets buying a combination of clothes, CDs, shoes and other items from the numerous street vendors haggling with customers over their prices.

The sexy Latin diva turned to cross the busy street bearing the spoils of a successful shopping spree in one hand and a ring of car keys in the other. Coming across the street, Rosaria pointed the keys toward a red Toyota Prius, deactivating its alarm and unlocking it.

Valentino waited anxiously until she pulled out of the parking lot and into traffic. For fifteen minutes, he trailed her by no more than two cars to the rear of the freeway toward Watts. Once she pulled into the parking lot of her modest new apartment in the 'hood, Valentino slid his Cadillac into the empty space to the left of her car. He emerged from his vehicle at the same time as she got out of hers.

Rosaria's eyes went wild with shock at the sight of her erstwhile pimp and a sharp shriek left her open mouth while the shopping bags fell from her trembling fingers to the ground below. Fear's icy fingers crept up and down her spine as she stood face-to-face with the devious Lucien Valentino.

"Calm yo' nerves, Rosy," he said, displaying the flowers. "I brought you roses—see? Aren't they lovely? Just like you, sweetheart."

"What the hell are you doing here, Lucien? What do you want from me?"

Valentino gently placed the bouquet in her hands and draped his arm around her shoulder, drawing close to the shaken young woman. Rosaria was in a complete state of disbelief as Valentino kissed upon her slender neck and fondled her ample behind as they leaned against her Toyota. She wanted to reach down into her purse and slice his face with the switchblade she kept for protection, but the inherent fear that a prostitute holds for her pimp caused her to think better of that idea. She knew the man who stood beside her better than most others. She'd seen firsthand what he was capable of doing when angered. She thought about the time he'd beaten a john to death with a crowbar for spitting on his car. She'd cried out for him to stop, but her pleas had fallen on deaf ears as Valentino continued to beat the poor bastard. By the time the bodyguards wrestled their boss off the sex customer, he was already dead, his face reduced to a bloody mess.

Rosaria's voice trembled with trepidation as the pimp's hand settled gently around her throat.

A tear fell down her beautiful face and she swallowed hard as she attempted to speak, "Papi...it...it wasn't me—it was that man, that white man...he had a gun and he forced me—"

"Baby, don't worry 'bout that cracka. I got that covered already. He's a dead man walkin' and don't even know it," Valentino said.

"Papi, please believe me when I tell you that I had nothing to do with him coming over to the house, with all that drama."

She fidgeted with nervous energy and mumbled, stuttering, becoming more anxious by the minute. Valentino seemed pleased by the girl's discomfort and stammering speech.

"Damn right, you nervous as a muthafucka, ain't you?" he said. "I tell ya what, how 'bout we step into yo' little whip here an' I'll let you treat ya nose with a little bit o' this good coke I brought fa ya?"

Rosaria's eyes went wide as she zeroed in on the $100 mini Ziploc bag of powder dangling from Valentino's fingers before her.

"Aiight, aiight," he continued, "calm down, go ahead. Ladies first."

Rosaria wasted little time unlocking the door and entering the vehicle. Instinctively she went into her handbag, taking out a small vanity case that flipped out into a vanity mirror. She watched as her ex-boyfriend shook out a hefty clump of cocaine onto the armrest sitting between them. Rosaria carefully lifted the vanity onto her lap, where she took a razor blade from Valentino and began rapidly chopping and spacing the coke before separating two thin lines of powder from the rest of the pile. She rolled up a crisp five dollar bill from her handbag and used it to greedily snort up the two lines of powder.

With her pretty brown eyes glazed over in a cocaine-induced daze, Rosaria prepared yet another line upon the mirror to snort, and then another after that, and another still. The little mound of cocaine slowly dwindled down to nothing, save for a small bit of white residue scattered on top of the glass.

"Don't worry, I brought along an ounce o' 'girl' just for you," Valentino said while running his diamond ring-covered fingers through her silky, rich, ebony mane. "You betrayed me, Rosy, but it's all good...I forgive you."

Rosaria shot him a mean look before lowering her head down to snort the last bit of coke from the small bag lying on top of the dashboard. She took a bit of the powder on her index finger and smeared it across her gums, savoring the stringently bitter taste.

"You ran away not once, but twice, then you fucked around and snitched on me to that Nazi muthafucka...that's not a very nice thing to do to ya man, now is it?"

"Fuck you, Lucien! I told you that the man had heat, didn't I?! He put a goddamn gun to my head after he kidnapped me off the street! What was I s'posed to do?"

Rosaria was shaking from both anger and the cocaine. She ducked her head down toward the mirror, sniffing the remaining line of cocaine deeply up her nostril.

"You can have this ounce I got here, but to get it you gonna have ta break me off," Valentino said casually. "I'm in need of some head, so getcha lips ready to polish this knob."

"Sure, Papi...you know I love sucking that big dick of yours."

"Cool," he said, "well, what the fuck is you waiting for—Cinco de Mayo? Get on yo muthafuckin' job, trick."

Valentino leaned back comfortably against the cool, velvety fabric of the seat while Rosario worked to remove the pimp's massive, curved cock from out of his trousers with careful consideration of the sheer size of the man's member. Her full lips felt heavenly wrapped around the bulbous mushroom-like head of his dick. He felt himself throb with carnal bliss as his Latin lover orally worshipped his rigid, saliva-covered erection with skillful attention.

Grasping her dark, flowing hair in his clenched fist, he forced her down as he pumped himself vigorously into her warm, wet mouth until he felt that familiar feeling down deep in his nutsack, which came surging upward in a stream of the toe-curling satisfaction. Rosaria gulped a huge quantity of Valentino's heavy ejaculate.

Licking the remaining cum from her luscious lips, the prostitute smiled devilishly as she placed her ex-pimp's now flaccid meat back into his boxers before zipping up his designer slacks, knowing she'd earned the once of cocaine in grand whorish fashion.

Grinning like a Cheshire cat, Rosaria gladly took the hefty bag of powder from Valentino, stuffing it down into her oversized handbag as they exited the car and she stepped out into the cool air of the relatively silent parking lot. She threw her arms around him affectionately, while planting a long, sensual kiss on his lips. She then drew back a step or two, sheepishly hanging her head.

"Papi, I owe a lot to you for everything you've done for me so far, but..."

"Ssshh...ain't no need for all that, baby," Valentino said. "I know that you're happy to be back here in East L.A. Shit, this here's ya home, ain't it? Aiight, then, hasta la vista, baby! I'll be seein' ya around from time to time."

Valentino smacked Rosaria playfully on her ass before walking over toward his parked Cadillac. He had scarcely gotten into his ride before the young Latina disappeared from view into her apartment building where she no doubt immediately set the scene for a long night of boozing, coke snorting and *Hell Date* reruns on BET with her girlfriends. Valentino drove away from the parking lot knowing that he'd no longer see the gorgeous Rosaria alive again.

The cocaine in which she'd been inhaling had been purposely mixed with the deadly mescaline containing the ultra-poisonous alkaloid cystine, purchased from an old Mexican herbal doctor. Valentino had the lethal beans ground into a fine powder to be added to the coke.

Late on the evening of July 23, 2002, the dead bodies of 23-year old Rosaria Gonzalez and two other unidentified Hispanic females would be discovered by the L.A.P.D at Gonzalez's East Los Angeles apartment unit.

At first the deaths were attributed to drug overdoes, but later that week the city's medical examiner concluded that the three women succumbed to an acute case of cystine poisoning. An investigation was launched in the case, but like so many inner-city murders, the search came up fruitless and was eventually placed on the back burner.

By that time Lucien Valentino was back in Lariat handling business as usual. He had said his goodbyes to Rosaria and he now thought of her very little, going so far as to forbid any of the other hookers to mention her name in his presence.

Wilhelm Von Strecker had few, if any confidants to turn to and as a result he found himself frequenting local taverns and pubs, drinking himself into an alcoholic stupor most evenings. It was the only way he could cope. His drinking problems grew worse as the summer came to a close, affecting both his job and his marriage adversely. At times, his drunken ramblings exposed the truths he knew about Meredith and Patient Zero, as well as his love for the attention-starved biologist. Eventually, these remarks forced his wife to file for a motion of legal separation on the grounds of adultery on September 17.

Rueben Mintz, unlike the others at Coventry Laboratories, realized that if Wilhelm's accusations about Dr. Nader were indeed correct, it could have devastating consequences for them all. He'd worked with both scientists for years, and knew the chances of Wilhelm fabricating such a story was highly unlikely, especially with Nader's history of man problems. Reuben knew that something had to be done rather quickly, before word of the suspected affair reached Doctor Harrington and the other head honchos of the Illuminati—that scenario would certainly be disastrous for everyone involved.

It was around 10:55 p.m. when Reuben walked into the Tiki Hut. As expected, Wilhelm sat at the edge of the bar near a flickering tiki lamp downing a shot glass filled with gin. As his fellow lab worker approached, Wilhelm didn't even look his way. He simply slid the empty shot glass aside while grasping a newly filled one from the lei-wearing bartender who rotated between serving drinks and watching the Chargers vs. Chiefs game on the overhead plasma screen.

Rueben took a seat beside his inebriated, brooding pal. He took a swig from the small container of gin back in one gulp, grimacing from the bitterness of it. Wilhelm looked a mess, with his usually well-kept blonde hair disheveled and dirty, along with a wrinkled suit that seemed both soiled and slept in.

Right away he noticed the rank odor of alcohol exuding from Wilhelm's pores.

"Wil!" Rueben said loudly, raising his voice an octave or two above the din of the overhead television and the blaring Elvis tunes coming from the nearby jukebox. "What's goin' on, bud? Thought I'd stop by and have a drink or two with you if you don't mind!"

"Cut the shit, Rueben. That's not why you're here," Wilhelm said, turning to glance briefly at him with bloodshot eyes before downing another shot of gin.

The German was gruff and standoffish; clearly this was not going to be a smooth conversation, Rueben thought.

"Well, let's just say 'yes and no,'" Rueben said, plunking down a down $10 bill on top of the bar as a bartender brought him a pitcher of dark ale. "We need to talk...I need to know what's been going on lately between you, Meredith and the patient."

He stared at the drunken doctor intensely while pouring himself a glass of the seasonal brew. Wilhelm hung his head for several minutes before swiping a lock of his golden hair away from his forehead, sighing deeply as he straightened himself up upon his stool to face Reuben.

"We made love...in the office a while back. Did you know that?"

"Wil, please don't do this to yourself," Rueben said.

Wilhelm fought to stop the tears, but they fell anyway as he continued on.

"I should've treated her better. I should've given her the love that she needed . . . but now she's with that fucking monkey! I hate him, Rueben, I fucking despise that nigger," he growled with an alcohol-fueled rage.

"I know how you must feel, Wil, but this entire affair should never have happened. Lucien Valentino, known to all of us as Patient Zero, is part of a covert government operation and you know this—his safety, comfort and cooperation in this population control agenda is paramount and none of us has the right to interfere with the greater goal at hand."

"Fuck off, Mintz," Wil said. "At this point I couldn't care less about the goddamned agenda. Just look at me! Does it look like I give a rat's ass about this psycho operation we're into? I've lost my family, I've lost Meredith, I've lost everything! Now if you'll excuse me, I'm going to finish drinking myself to death."

"Okay, okay...you got it, bud," Mintz said uneasily. "Just try to keep it down a tad, all right? The kid behind the bar is getting a little shifty eyed . . . Let me at least polish off my Sam Adams before we both get our butts booted outta here, okay? And look, I know how much you love Meredith, okay? And let me say that we all know she's always had the hots for you too. Everybody at Coventry Labs can see that."

Rueben poured himself another foamy mug of lager. He needed to reassure and calm his friend down before continuing on with his plan.

"Yeah, she was always flirting with me and begging me to bang her. You're right—she so wanted me," Wilhelm said with fond nostalgia. "Rueben, all I want is to just hold her close one more time—can you help me with that? Huh? C'mon, man, you just have to help me get to her."

Rueben smiled. This was the exact reaction he'd been banking on. He called the young bartender over from the rear of the bar where he looked upward, cheering fervently as the San Diego Chargers took a 21-10 lead in the waning minutes of the game. Rueben peeled off a twenty-dollar bill, handing it over and asking for four extra shots of gin for Wilhelm. The young man took the bill and returned within a few minutes, pouring a hearty dose of Beefeaters into four empty shot glasses before the already plastered German.

"To you and Dr. Meredith Nader! Cheers!" Rueben said with a broad smile.

Wilhelm wolfed down two of the four shots of gin in rapidly.

"You know what, Rueben? She still has the hots for me. I know she does."

Wilhelm was a hearty drinker who could hold his liquor well, but after this tenth shot he was slurring and staggering, which gave his beer drinking buddy all the more reason to smile.

"If I were you, I'd go let Meredith know just how much you loved her and wanted her. She's probably waiting up for you right this moment, ready to wrap her loving arms around you."

"You're right for once, Rueben, and you know what? I'm going to go over to her place and I'm going to make love to her tonight!" Wilhelm proclaimed confidently before finishing off the remaining shot glasses of gin.

He stood up to leave, teetering to and fro before Rueben quickly took him by the hand to help stead him.

"Easy does it, bud," he said. "I've got you. I'll drive you over to Meredith's, okay?"

"Thanks," Wilhelm replied. "I can walk out of here by myself, you know? I've been drinking since the age of 16, Rueben, so you don't have to hold me by the hand. I'm fine—really. Oh, by the way, Meredith's address is 1661 Falcon Crest Way. She lives in Beach Lake."

"I know exactly where that is," Rueben said while dialing a quick series of digits on his cell phone. "Go on to the car at the end of the lot—it's unlocked. I'll be there in a minute."

Rueben awaited an answer at the other end as the number rang monotonously. The scientist watched closely as his associate entered the moss green Toyota Tercel after urinating against a street lamp. A familiar voice answered on the other end, husky and threatening.

"Yeah, wassup, my nigga? Talk to da Don."

Glancing around cautiously as he stood in the cool, crisp seaside air, Rueben spoke quickly, spinning his car keys around on his right index finger to calm his frazzled nerves.

"Valentino, he's in the car and I'm about to hop on the freeway en route to Dr. Nader's. Is everything set up on your end?"

"Man, didn't I tell yo' monkey ass, everything's good to go? I got this!" Valentino replied.

"Look, we need this to go perfectly—no fuck ups. I'm serious. There's a lot at stake here."

"First off," Valentino said, "get that muthafuckin' bass out your mouth, white boy, you ain't talkin' to one o' yo' lil' nerd-ass doctors, ya understand? You'll fuck around and come up missin' fuckin' wit me. Now let's try this again, aiight? I don't do disposals fa free, so you best be havin' my twenty grand in my bank account by tomorrow evenin'. Do you? 'Cause I got my end on lock, holla!"

Nervously, the scientist ended the call and proceeded across the parking lot to enter his vehicle, where he discovered the German involved in a lively phone conversation of his own—with Dr. Meredith Nader. Rueben smiled wickedly and pulled out of the parking lot with his unsuspecting victim in tow.

"Tell Meredith I said 'hi,' Wil," he said. "Let her know that I got her latest lab results from last Friday and everything's perfect. Tell her to keep up the good work."

"Sure, Rueben, I'll let her know, dude...in time, though. Right now we're busy discussing something else."

"Got it, big guy," Reuben said. "Sorry, didn't mean to interrupt."

A few minutes later, the two arrived at the home of Doctor Meredith Nader. Just as Rueben had expected, the intoxicated scientist wasted little time seeking out his lady love as he burst from the passenger seat, partially running and partially staggering toward her front door. Once there, he pounded with his clenched fist for several seconds before an irate Meredith snatched it open to confront him.

"Wilhelm! What do you think you're doing, banging on my door at this time of night? Are you nuts?!" She reached out and caught him by the arm, pulling him into the threshold. "For Christ's sakes, man, what is it with you lately?"

"I should be asking you that same question, Meredith...what is it with you?" Wilhelm said coolly, slamming the door behind them. "I know that you want me, Meredith. Hell, I want you too. I know that now. And my wife and I have separated, so you don't have to worry about her anymore."

He reached out and took hold of her, bringing her close to him. He kissed her lips passionately, but she was repulsed by the stench of alcohol on his breathe. She pushed him away abruptly.

"You're a stinking drunk!" she said with anger and disgust. "Look at yourself, Wil. You're a wreck!"

The German's eyes narrowed with instant fury. His hands clenched once again into fists.

"I used to be in love with you, Wil," Meredith said. "So very much in love, but you took that love for granted and paid me very little attention. You said that you loved your wife and you stuck to that. Well, good for you. Now I've met the man of my dreams—a real man who knows how to make me feel like a woman, and frankly, Wil, Lucien would not take kindly to your being here right now."

She backed away from him as though he were a dangerous animal. Valentino had ordered her to have sex with Von Strecker before dispatching him, but she couldn't lower herself to fucking this alcoholic shell of a man. He no longer attracted her. Now, he was a pitiful, revolting sight to behold, with his ragged beard, unkempt clothing and that God-awful smell, hovering around him like some malodorous halo. She'd have to bypass. The sooner she got it over with, the better. Valentino had given her a small .22 caliber revolver, or "deuce-deuce" as he called it, to complete her murderous task. He'd shown her how to comfortably hold the weapon in her palm and how to breath comfortably while squeezing the trigger to prevent jerking.

She reached down, finding the nickel-plated pistol lying upon the small coffee table in the living room. Wilhelm, driven by rage and liquor, spewed profanity in both English and his native German as he rushed toward her. Meredith stood her ground as the drunken Wilhelm staggered forward, voicing threats as he approached.

"I'm sorry, Wil, but you brought this upon yourself."

"You nigger-loving bitch, I'll teach you a thing or two!"

He reached out for her throat, stumbling again. The awful muzzle of the gun was now level with his upper chest. Meredith's finger tensed on the trigger. He was nearly on top of her now, so close that she could smell the stink of gin coming from his breath. His blue eyes glazed over with a reddish film of toxicity, and onward he came, bellowing like a charging bull. She braced herself for the impending impact.

"Die, you Nazi bastard! Die!" she yelled.

The handgun kicked forcefully in her grasp as she unleaded several rounds of hollow point shells into the upper body of her former love. He let out a shrieking cry before collapsing onto her, as the both of them crashed up against the couch and then onto the floor below.

He bled heavily from the gunshot wounds in his torso, but still managed to reach out and grasp her by the ankle as she attempted to run. She aimed the weapon at him and fired off three more shots, muffled by the attached silencer. The first two bullets pierced his larynx and shattered his right collarbone, while yet another smashed it way through the left side of his face, ripping his eye from its socket and carrying it fourteen feet away, where it slid off of the colorful kitchen wallpaper and onto the neatly tiled floor, leaving a bloody trail where it made its way down.

Wilhelm Von Strecker was dead now for sure. Meredith Nader breathed heavily as she slowly lowered the handgun to view the bloodied corpse, which had once been Coventry's leading scientist, lying dead on the floor below. Flecks of red were sprinkled all across her face and blouse. The living room smelled of gun powder and gore. Yet she felt proud that she had done something that would please Lucien Valentino, her beloved. Whomever he hated, she would in turn hate also. She was his totally through and through, for what he had given her was what she had so desperately needed her entire life. And for that, she was forever grateful—grateful enough to do anything he might have asked of her, even to take a life.

Rueben Mintz, behind the steering wheel of his car listening to talk radio, observed a dark van parking beside Meredith's Hyundai Elantra. A band of Valentino's henchmen emerged and headed toward the house, where they were talked with evidence removal. By 12:57 a.m., they'd removed the scientist's body, cleaned the townhouse and disappeared without a trace. Dr. Rueben Mintz could now breath easier with Wilhelm Von Strecker dead and Meredith Nader prepared to leave the country at the request of Lucien Valentino himself.

***

November 19, 2002
11:11 a.m.
Bogotá, Columbia

Lucien Valentino breathed in the refreshing cleanliness of the brisk breeze coming down from off of the mountaintop above the lush Columbian countryside. He enjoyed this South American country for many reasons. Today's perfect weather reminded him just how much more he appreciated it with each visit.

Meredith had lived here now for a total of two whole months, since the shooting of her former colleague and lover, Wilhelm Von Strecker. Valentino smiled as she came running into his arms from the porch of the lovely sky blue, stucco-lined apartment where she resided since leaving the states. Unspeakable joy showed in Meredith's beaming smile and giddy laughter as she covered her man's handsomely chiseled face with kisses. Her initial infatuation with the pimp had grown into what she could only describe as true love.

Valentino took her delicate left hand in his, slipping a two-carat, princess-cut diamond ring on her finger, grinning with satisfaction while an overjoyed Meredith Nader hugged him warmly. Tears of happiness streamed down her face as she remained snuggled close to Valentino. He raised her chin upwards with his thick, diamond-cluttered index finger to meet her lips with his, his own in a long, breathy and passion-filled kiss, which brought her nearly to the brink of orgasm. He pulled her even closer to him while withdrawing his rock hard erection out of its enclosure. She gasped with wanton expectation as he shoved the length of his trouser snake deep into her pink, wet crevice. The fully clothed lovers immediately enjoyed themselves there on the porch as tropical birds flew overhead singing melodiously throughout the rainforest as the grunts and groans of the copulating couple echoed along the lonely countryside.

Meredith drew fine beads of blood along Valentino's broad back as she dug her long nails into his skin as his frenzied stroking forced three consecutive orgasms from her. She shuddered with post-orgasmic bliss as her lover released a warm torrent of semen that swirled into her cervix.

Valentino pulled himself out of Meredith's dripping snatch using a small cloth from his pocket to wipe down his greasy, swinging penis as the exhausted scientist pulled her sheer skirt back down around her shapely legs before slumping onto a white wicker recliner just beside the entrance. She was completely spent.

Meredith was so deeply consumed by her undying love for the man known to her medical peers as "Patient Zero" that it was as if she needed him to even survive from day to day. It was a far cry from the fierce racial hatred she'd once harbored for African Americans.

"You just can't get enough of this good dick, can you, white girl?" Valentino asked.

"You bet your sexy ass I can't, studmuffin!"

"Shit, I don't give a fuck what they say, flattery will get you everywhere, even though a bitch talkin' 'bout this muthafucka, she ain't lyin'."

"Lucien, I want us to be together forever. I've never felt this way about anyone. Please say you'll marry me . . . please?"

"Marry?" Lucien said. "C'mon, woman, you know better than that. We s'pose ta be part o' this secret operation, remember?"

Meredith folded her arms across her bountiful breasts, turning her face away from his as it turned crimson with anger. She tapped her bare foot with disappointment, while biting down on her lower lip in order to keep her tongue in check.

"I'm a playa pimp, mama, ya understand? You know this. I ain't got time fa no marriage an' shit, not ta you or nobody else, baby, but that don't mean that I ain't ya man, 'cause I'm already that."

"But, Lucien," Meredith said, "I don't wan tot be just another one of your hos! I want—hell, I deserve—more from you! I want to share your last name. I want to bear your children. I want to belong to you and you alone, goddamn it!

I'm crazy for you—can't you see that? Or does it not even matter?"

"Look here, bitch, we both got that shit, ya know what I'm sayin'? We gon' have ta shoot up that Biomax-O just ta live from one year to another...that ain't no kinda ordinary, everyday-type shit...how in the fuck we s'pose ta bring young'uns into this world with that HIV5X or 10X or whatever the fuck you wanna call it and subject them to the same type o' bullshit we goin' through? Huh? Plus, you gotta know that on some real gutter-type shit them futhafuckas, that's usin' us ta wipe out niggas in the hood is gonna turn right around and rock us to sleep an' that's no bullshit. We aint' got no time for lovey-dovey-type shit. We got ta keep it tight and watch each other's back, aiight?"

A tear welled up in Meredith's eye and inched its way down her rosy cheek. Valentino pulled her close to him, kissing her lovingly and long.

"You're an addiction—no better than cocaine or heroin," she said. "An addiction I wish I could break."

"Yeah, right, you don't believe that ya damn self, girl," Valentino said. "I own you now and you know that. Ya see that bitch-ass Nazi Wilhelm couldn't move you 'cause he wasn't man enough fa the job. He was a soft-ass square like all the rest o' them punks. It took a real man like the Don to beat that pussy up proper-like and spit game atcha like a boss playa s'pose ta, in order to make ya feel like a woman should, which is why yo' monkey ass ain't goin' nowhere."

Bitterness from her past heartbreaks shrouded her very being like a wet blanket. She was tired of being hurt and it showed.

"You know what? Maybe this is a mistake, Lucien," Meredith said, sighing dejectedly. "You're right—our relationship would never work. How totally stupid of me."

Valentino saw his lady's despair and took her by the hand, kissing it gently.

"Meredith, you're talkin' crazy, girl, 'cause bein' my lady is an honor for bitches, you ain' no different. This is the way playas play, baby. You either givin' orders or you takin' 'em, feel me? Now the Sentinels of the Illuminati, them muthafuckas think they pimpin' me, but check it—I'm pimpin' them for real, and if you stick around with the Don, you're gonna go on this magic carpet ride wit a nigga."

"I don't know if I can do it, Lucien—I just can't be hurt anymore."

Valentino cupped Meredith's plump ass with his huge hands as he moved in close to her. He'd had this type of thing happen to him on numerous other occasions before; few women were immune to the psychological head games of a well-seasoned mack like himself. He caressed her pale neck sensually, bringing forth a soft moan of pleasure from the sexy scientist.

"Let's get this money together, ma. Those punk bitches don't give a fuck 'bout us, baby. All they wanna do is spread AIDS everywhere. I'll help 'em out just as long as they pay me, but I'm gon' spread the shit to mo' than just po' black folks."

When Meredith smiled and rested her head against his chest, it brought supreme satisfaction to the boss player. A smile slowly found its way on this ruggedly handsome face in reverence to the art of macking, which had served him well on so many occasions. Dr. Meredith Nader however might have been his greatest conquest, considering her past. He would indeed use her until he saw it necessary to move on. There should've been absolutely no way, he thought to himself, that the Stanford University-educated biologist would be subjected to the streetwise, slick talk of a common crook like Lucien Valentino, but she was. Even though she knew beyond a shadow of a doubt that she was more than a little bit foolish for risking her entire career—as well as her life—for the affection of a man who could never truly return her love, she couldn't help it. She was in too deep now to turn back.

***

Bogotá, Columbia
April 17, 2003
7:16 p.m.

Trussel's Villa

Meredith felt like shit as she walked away from the death bed of her latest Latino lover. He'd become the latest victim to fall prey to the horrific HIV10X. The skeletal form of Manual Gomez trembled slightly, then shuddered before death overtook him.

Gomez was the seventh man who had contracted the aggressive AIDS virus from the beautiful brunette vixen who hung out at the various local drinking spots in search of intoxicated flirts desiring one-night stands. For two months she went on an AIDS-spreading tear throughout the province of Chia. Her grasp of the Spanish language strengthened due to her conversations with Don Valentino, and it was this same master of Espanòl that sealed the fate of so many Columbian men. By early June she had infected over two dozen men, with thirteen of them succumbing to the painful symptoms of full-blown AIDS. She was indeed a terror to an unsuspecting community until the virus began to attack her own immune system.

***

Bogotá, Columbia
June 22, 2003
8:33 a.m.
Trussel's Villa

Two months later, Doctor Meredith Nader gasped with shallow, strained breaths. Her once beautiful green eyes stared out, bloodshot and glassy. She was in the throes of dreaded Phase 5 level, known to most laymen as full-blown AIDS. The heartbroken doctor had realized that she would more than likely never experience true love, and had completely abandoned the all-important Biomax-O injections which had allowed a plethora of viruses, bacteria, fungi and cancers to dismantle her body's immunity. Tuberculosis and lymphoma had rendered her so weak that she remained bed-ridden and unable to eat. Rapid weight loss had reduced her hourglass figure to mere bones. It was clear that death was imminent for Meredith Nader.

Valentino shook his head with disappointment as he stared down at the pitifully emaciated woman dying on the bed before him.

"You've really disappointed me, ya know that?" he said, tipping his Armani sunglasses to peer at her. "You didn't have to resort to this, Meredith. You had me. I was yo' man for as long as you wanted. You could've had anything you wanted—money, jewels, mansions, fly-as rides, whatever. Plus you one o' those doctors who made the Biomax-O, so you would've been straight just as long as you kept ya shots up."

"Lucien," Meredith said weakly, "please...let me die in peace."

Don Valentino placed a single long-stemmed rose upon her brittle chest.

"You coulda lived a helluva long time, girl, a hulluva long time," he said sadly. "Why would you go and do something like this, baby, why?"

He leaned down and kissed her blotched forehead.

"I love you, white girl," he said, "I truly do. I know I'm gon' ta hell when my time comes, but I pray that God has mercy on your soul, 'cause you're an all right broad for real...you ain't never meant nobody no harm. You just needed a lil' bit o' love, that's all."

He waved over an old, gray-haired housekeeper to fetch Meredith a glass of cool water to ease her parched throat.

"May the good lawd bless and keep you," Valentino said.

The pain of various AIDS-driven infections tore through her frail body like wildfire, causing her to groan in agony with each and every excruciating spasm, which shot to and fro within her. Meredith felt her chest tighten, as well as her windpipe. Her breathing became forced and labored, rattling with thick phlegm and stopping within her throat. Her eyes went wide as the slow sensation of unconsciousness threatened to envelop her in its heavy, unrelenting grasp.

This was it...Meredith was experiencing that which all flesh must.

"Don't fight it, baby," Valentino said. "Just relax and let go...It's gonna be all right...just close your eyes and sleep."

"I love you, Lucien."

She gasped deeply and gurgled slightly before her chest heaved one last time. She relaxed completely, her head falling limp to one side as her tongue lolled out. Her eyes stared ahead with stationary focus.

Valentino lowered his lime green derby against his heart in a brief show of silent reverence for Meredith's passing. He closed her eyes with his hand and stepped away.

Afterward

The Don was once again a man on the move. The deaths of the Coventry Laboratory scientists had been too close for comfort for the likes of the Illuminati, and as a result they had terminated their contract with the Lariat-California based group.

Meredith Nader had proven her worth as a valuable member of Valentino's stable, even though she hadn't been a prostitute in the same way many of his others had been. He'd lost many a ho in his day, and rarely did he feel anything about it. However, he would indeed miss Meredith. Yet, the game allowed no time for mourning, and it took little time for Valentino to adjust favorably to his new surroundings.

"Baby, I just wanna show you a good time and that's all, sexy lady," he said.

The atmosphere of the cozy courtyard at the Grand Café Key West was exquisitely modern. The crowd was a pleasant blend of tourist and locals, mingling together along the wraparound wooden porch of the outside dining area. The hazy, humid night brought out fireflies and fat, fuzzy moths that fluttered about around the tall lamps which dotted the courtyard.

The famous Key West sunset was as beautiful as Hemingway had described in his memoirs, and the player pimp already seemed to be drawn in to the exotic night life of the famous vacation spot.

"Cheers to us. You are something else, you know that, Lucien? I really feel comfortable with you. You're not like all the others. I think...I think I'm falling in love with you, mister."

Valentino smiled wide as their oversized martini glasses clanked together.

"Hey, baby, it is what it is. Don't fight the feeling."

The Don's sexy, honey-voiced love interest beamed with girlish infatuation at the dapperly dressed gent sitting across the table from her.

"I've got somethin' here just for you, Ms. Lady...This right here is a genuine emerald surrounded by twelve half-carat diamonds...This is to represent our love, baby girl. I know ya lovin' this, ain't ya?" Valentino said, taking a swig of his martini.

The two locked lips just as a blushing waitress arrived with their meal. She carefully placed the scrumptious-smelling plates of seafood down onto the gold satin-covered table while the amorous couple continued to swap spit.

This woman, a 33-year old hotelier who managed the three largest hotels in the Florida Keys, was an almond-hued beauty with flowing, silky brown hair, a Coca-Cola bottle figure an a stunning pair of legs that would have rivaled Tina Turner's. Valentino had put his mack down upon first meeting her at a local fundraising event. She shot him down at first, playing hard to get for over a month before getting turned out by the masterful Valentino.

He took her dainty hand into his own, slipping the emerald ring onto her slender finger while simultaneously planting a kiss on top of the same bling-adorned hand. Unlike Meredith, this woman was neither insecure or in need of male companionship, yet still she—like all the women whom he'd encountered before her—was vulnerable to the flattery and smooth talk of a skilled man. She had youth, good looks and, most importantly, a bank account that would serve Valentino well during his sojourn down in the keys.

He would still have to answer to the Sentinels of the Illuminati as they carried out their population control plan in exchange for the Biomax-O serum and he'd still receive a monthly stipend for his part in this 21st century Tuskegee experiment. Eventually this beauty too would sicken and die from the AIDS virus and he would be relocated to yet another town where he would continue to spread the terminal STD just as he was instructed. Many would fall victim to the charm and good looks of the man known as Don Lucien Valentino. And in wooing these women, Valentino vowed to remain the ice-cold pimp that he'd created—a legend now for so many years ago. With such a man at large, the nation—indeed, the world—would be a little less safe and a lot more frightening. There would always be a possibility of encountering a Lucien Valentino . . . he could be in any city, any country, in any bed on any given night.

CPSIA information can be obtained at www.ICGtesting.com
Printed in the USA
LVOW120224030912

297096LV00001B/49/P